This edition limited to fifteen numbered and signed copies.

No. 11 of 15

For Susan —
Hope you enjoy it!

Nick DiMartino

Love
in the
American Empire

by
Nick DiMartino

University Book Store Press
Seattle, Washington

LOVE IN THE AMERICAN EMPIRE
© 2012 by Nick DiMartino
Anna Micklin, publishing coordinator
Jake Monderen, photography and cover design
Brad Herst, technical consultant

UNIVERSITY BOOK STORE PRESS
Espresso Book Machine
First Printing: November 2012

All rights reserved.
This is entirely a work of fiction. The characters are invented, and should not be confused with real people.

4 December 04 – 2 January 05
15 January – 15 February 05
19 March – 1 May 2005
16-23 August, 2-10 October 2012

for
IRIS MURDOCH
"Love must never supersede the truth."

With special thanks to Aaron Rabin, Brad Craft, Paula Bennett, Joline Karwoski, Alexandra Chordas, Siobhan Wallace, Mary Morgan, and Master Sergeant Dalea Bitzas

ISBN: 978-1-937358-20-4

UNIVERSITY BOOK STORE
4326 University Way NE
Seattle, Washington 98105
www.ubookstore.com
206-634-3400

For autographed copies with free shipping, call:
206-543-5896

1
Electric Toothbrush

That sounds like my wife.

She's just getting home from work on this chilly November afternoon. She's probably hanging up her coat in the front closet right now, thinking she's all alone. Ordinarily she would be. I'm home a little earlier than usual, so she doesn't expect me to be here. I'm standing in front of the bathroom sink, my hands wet from washing the electric toothbrush. I'm very confused. I put it back in its plastic stand on the blue tile shelf, where it belongs. I dry my hands on the towel. Rachel hasn't said a word. In a moment, she'll be heading this way. I don't want to scare her. So I make an odd decision. Instead of calling out "Hello!" and possibly startling her, I decide to simply warn her of my presence.

I flush the toilet.

"Is that you?" she calls. Rachel appears in the bathroom doorway, a smile of welcome on her face. The smile changes and she looks surprised. "Colin, you're home early."

Love in the American Empire

It's no big deal, it's just a look, but the expression on her face is the wrong one.

"Expecting someone else?"

"Of course not." She's used to my sarcasm so she ignores me, and instead gives me a kiss.

I think my wife just lied to me.

She's a sight, my wife. I never get tired of looking at her. Her face belongs on an ancient Roman coin. She wears her hair short, in a thick helmet of black curls, and her eyes are almost as black. Right now her cheeks are still flushed from her walk home and she's got that Mediterranean skin. I'm proud to be her husband, and a little defensive. People expect a woman like Rachel to be married to someone more sexy and exciting than a pale, skinny English professor.

"Decided to call it a day," I say, explaining my presence. "Thought I'd better stop seeing students before I committed homicide." I try to sound light, and fail. "Student intelligence seems to be declining." I'm watching her face. I just saw her glance at the electric toothbrush on the shelf. Now she knows that I know, so it's probably as good a time as any to bring it up.

"What made you throw it away?" I ask, in a voice that's quiet and calm and neutral.

"Throw it away?" She laughs awkwardly. "What are you talking about?"

"I found the electric toothbrush in the trash can."

"You *what?*"

Love in the American Empire

I point down into the plastic-lined container. "That's where I found it." We've only had the electric toothbrush for three weeks, an anniversary gift from her parents. Ten minutes ago I discovered it in the trash can under the sink, the brush heads dislocated from the sausage-shaped body, amid stray bits of hair from trimming my goatee, moist wadded tissues, and little dust bunnies of cat hair.

She laughs again in confusion. "And you thought I threw it away?"

"You're the only possible suspect."

She regards me with an odd smile. "Why would I do something like that? Am I the kind of wife who throws away appliances?"

"Of course not." After seven years together, you'd think I would know my own wife. She's Italian, yes, so she's prone to a dramatic moment or two, maybe she raises her voice now and then for emphasis, she certainly knows how to use her hands to make a point, but nothing like this. For one thing, she's not destructive. She's sensible and centered, a woman with inner peace who knows what's important. Moreover, she very rarely loses her temper, a distinction that sets her apart from most of her Italian relatives. When she does get angry, it's a flare of hot words and it's finished. There's no temper tantrum. She's not a ripper and breaker. The wife I know does not throw away electric toothbrushes.

"Is it still working?"

"Yes, I just tried it."

"Good." She puts her hands on her hips and scowls at the blue tile shelf and the trash can. She does not look me in the eye. "It must have fallen somehow."

"If it fell off the shelf, it would have landed in the sink."

"Could it have bounced?"

"Physically impossible."

Boo pokes his nose into the bathroom at this point to see what's so interesting. He's a black-and-white shorthair cat who moved into the house the same time we did seven years ago. Apparently he comes with this wooded hillside in the University District as part of the package. He's never worn a collar. He's independent and sure of himself. He's shared the house with us ever since, allowing us to feed him and open doors for him and provide our laps for his comfort. He's handsome, smart, and energetic. He prefers my wife.

"Is this your doing, Boo? Did you get up here and knock this off?"

Boo stops in his tracks and regards me with lofty contempt, insulted. Then he turns around and strolls out, tail righteously in the air.

He's the only possible suspect. I'm not convinced of his innocence. "He'd have to jump up on the sink. Can he really jump that far? That's the only way he could get to the bathroom shelf, unless…"

"Don't blame the cat."

"What makes you so sure?"

"He's never gone up there before," she explains patiently, logically. "Why would he start now?"

In emphatic confirmation, ripping and tearing sounds come from the living room, where we can hear Boo taking out his frustration with the thick-headed human race on his catnip clawing-post, rending the fabric with his claws in the hopes of dislodging a few provocative fumes of his favorite drug.

"Well, if it wasn't Boo, then who was it? It didn't just leap off the shelf."

"Could you have banged it without noticing?"

"Hardly, dear. I'm not numb."

"Well, it wasn't me." She laughs. It's not her one-hundred-percent laugh. "Maybe there was an earth tremor in our neck of the woods."

"Either that, or poltergeist activity." I can see from her look that she is not in the mood for my sarcasm. I try to lighten the tone. "Or possibly a heavy passing truck. Guess we'll never know. At least it's still working. We should probably sterilize it before we use it."

To my surprise, she laughs at me. "I hardly think we need to sterilize it. You washed it, didn't you? A little hot water is all it needs."

"Hot water? Well, you can clean your brush attachment with hot water, if you want. I'm going sterilize mine, thank you, since I like to think that what I put in my mouth is clean. God knows what gunk is in that trash."

She smiles. She's not listening. She's thinking about something else. "I mean, really, it's silly, don't you think?"

"What's silly?"

"The whole idea of an electric toothbrush! Why should I need electricity to brush my teeth?" She gives another one of those half-laughs, as though it's such a ridiculous idea it really doesn't deserve a full laugh. Suddenly she's revealing her real feelings about the electric toothbrush. I'm shocked. "The rest of the world seems to manage to do it by hand. Feeble Americans need a little help, those brushing muscles get weary. I mean, the very idea that I would need a timer on the brush to tell me how long I've been brushing." She laughs again, and this time the laugh is just about genuine, but she's looking at my face and she can see I'm not laughing.

We're far from done with this conversation when there's a soft popping sound, like a chewing-gum bubble exploding in your face.

Wham. We're in darkness.

With an overhead crackle, I'm abruptly facing a shadow instead of my wife.

"Now what?" groans Rachel.

"No big deal," I say. "Looks like a light bulb went out and broke the circuit." I talk with all the authority of a man who doesn't know a thing about electricity. "I'll go flip the circuit breaker." This act is at the limits of my technical know-how, but for that reason I'm all the more eager to do my part for home maintenance.

Love in the American Empire

In the kitchen I reach into the tools drawer and feel around in the dark until my fingers close around the flashlight. I'm glad to see the batteries aren't dead. Then I open the side door in our kitchen that leads into the cement-walled laundry room, and pull the light cord.

Click-click. Nothing happens.

I don't need the overhead light to know my way. I aim the flashlight beam into the dark, dingy little cement tomb. The room is an afterthought wedged in between the upstairs kitchen and our unit. The new Russian landlords no sooner moved in than our shared laundry room became a depository of half-used things, shelves full of cans of hardening paint, rolls of extra carpet, broken bicycles, yard tools, and several old pairs of skis. It's difficult enough to get to the light switch when the room is fully lit. In the dark, it's an obstacle course. Using the flashlight beam to feel my way, I bump into a stool, nearly knock over a suitcase, and send a cherry-colored child's wagon rolling to the wall. Then I open the circuit box and shine the flashlight beam inside.

There's the culprit, the one red circuit in the box. I reach inside, dodging a thread of spiderweb. In one corner of the box, minding its own business, is the maker of the web, hard at work. Without disturbing the spider, I flip the circuit-breaker switch.

Light blazes down from the laundry room bulb.

I'm just smiling to myself at my own technical brilliance when I notice something dark at my feet. Is that oil?

No, that's the shape of a shoe. It's footprints. I hope that isn't me. I'll have to clean it up before Rachel notices. Have I stepped in something? I squat down and look closer. It's mud. It's not me. Someone has been trekking mud onto the laundry room floor.

There's another one, smudged, over by the door. That one gives me a bit of a shiver, because it looks like someone came in from the yard without wiping his feet.

If I step back out from under the light bulb, I can see a faint Rorschach blot of crisscrossing patterns of ridged rubber soles. My landlords are sometimes messy but always clean, so I'm surprised. I check to make sure the bolt is in place on the door. It's not. The door is unlocked.

Now, that bugs me. I slide the bolt across. My landlords are far too careless about keeping this door locked. They occasionally hire Russian immigrants to do repairs or take care of the yard who have access to the basement. These part-time workers understand only Russian. They do not understand, "Lock the door when you leave."

I consider grabbing the broom. I resist. It's their house now. If the Volkonskys want to leave muddy footprints on the floor, they can clean them up.

It's not like them, though. I glance around myself. Nothing much here to steal. Even with the light working, it's chilly and bleak in this old half-finished room, just shadows full of nothing beneath the staircase and behind the boiler, piles and shelves of boxes of unnecessary items, left unmoved for so long they've become like furniture. Still, it's a way into the house.

I call through the wall to the bathroom on the other side. "How's that? Everything working now?"

Rachel calls back. "The light over the medicine cabinet is fine. But not the overhead light. Just a second, let me try another bulb."

I wait, staring down at the muddy prints.

"Okay, try it now," she says.

I flip the switch several more times. The laundry room light goes off and on. "Anything?"

"Nope."

This is bad news. It's not the first time we've had trouble with our overhead bathroom light, but I get the funny feeling this may be the end of the line. We dare not bring the trouble to the attention of the Russians, for fear they will either tear apart our bathroom to find the electrical problem or else decide to start renovating the entire apartment, which would necessitate our moving out.

"Damn," I say, returning to the half-lit bathroom and the half-lit figure of my wife, "looks like it finally gave up the ghost."

"There's a spare lamp in the kitchen cupboard," says Rachel, brushing past me, out of the darkness and into the light of the living room. "It's got one of those attachable clamps on the end of it." A moment later she's back in the bathroom with me, the electric toothbrush momentarily forgotten as together we attach the lamp to the shelf beside the toilet and plug it in.

Click, and a beam of light blinds us both.

"Really, it's time to move out of this place," I mutter. "We can afford it. We've got two incomes. We could live in a house with enough electrical outlets and a bathroom light that worked."

"We can't leave this house and you know it," says my wife. "Boo would be devastated. This is his territory. He'd be lost without it."

"I think our comfort is just a tad more important than the cat's," I say a trifle too smugly, because I can see I'm really irritating her.

"Our comfort, oh, it's so important," she says, an unusual sarcasm in her voice. "We're so, so inconvenienced by our bathroom light. Really, this hardly qualifies as a problem. Compared to most people on this planet, we're living in the lap of luxury. We've got electricity all day long. We've got clean water. We can manage to survive without an overhead bathroom light."

Our voices are getting a little loud. We're both tense with each other, and neither one of us knows exactly why.

Boo is watching us from the bathroom doorway. He's waiting for one of us to come to our senses, sit down in the armchair, and read. Boo's desires are simple ones. Right now all he wants is a lap, and there are no laps available. Once again the feline world expresses its continuing disappointment with blundering, insensitive human beings.

Rachel turns on and off the improvised makeshift light.

"Good," I say, to break the tension. "That should give us enough light to do what we need to do in here."

"Yes," she says, "that should do for now."

As we leave the bathroom and I turn out the light, my glance falls on the electric toothbrush, gleaming on its shelf where it belongs, as though it's always been there.

2
Political Depression

Something is bothering her.

Maybe it's me. I'm a little stressed out lately. I could be over-reacting. Maybe Rachel hasn't been remote and secretive the last few days, a little jumpier than usual, preoccupied.

When you've lived for seven years with someone you love, you learn how to read between the lines. But then maybe we read too much?

For all I know, it's simply the general gloom gripping the city. A week has passed since the catastrophic presidential elections. The sane world is still reeling from the result.

"I'll fix dinner," she says, and turns her back on me.

"Hon, you're not upset about anything, are you?" I say to her as she heads for the kitchen.

"Nothing you can do anything about, sweetheart."

She passes by today's newspaper on the coffee table. It's hard to miss, with the smiling face of the victorious President in glaring color. She grabs it in contempt, folds it in half, and slaps it back down on the coffee table.

"How depressing to think that that half the people in this country actually believe that illiterate comedian!" I deeply regret leaving the newspaper there for her to see. "Him and his war for freedom in Iraq." The very sight of the President's

Love in the American Empire

face enrages her. "He's changed the very meaning of being an American. We've become a moral black hole."

I can hear the wet catching of her voice.

"Don't get yourself all worked up, hon," I offer lamely. "The elections are over. You've got to let go of all that anger. It's not good for you."

"Sorry," she says, sniffling. "Enough. That's all the political spouting I'm going to do. What's the use? It's over."

She's so idealistic. The American war machine leaves her feeling ashamed and helpless. Me, I don't let myself feel anything. Politics aren't my thing. I'm the neutral one in the family. You want politics, you talk to Rachel. Of course, like any informed person I'm grieving over the potential damage our misguided country can now do to the rest of the world. I intellectualize and complain, but don't act. I've given up on political action, I keep my opinions to myself. I no longer believe I can change anything.

The newspaper flops back open, unable to stay folded over the President's irrepressible smile. "Greed and ignorance have triumphed," she says bleakly. "We've become the world's greatest fear."

I kiss her. She hardly notices.

People in Seattle still stubbornly display their blue buttons and blue bumper stickers. For a city that could talk about nothing but politics for months, suddenly no one in Seattle wants to even read the front page.

Love in the American Empire

My wife took it especially hard. She's such an idealist. Sometimes she breaks down crying. Me, I say let it go, but she can't. She's ready to fight like a pit-bull for every single freedom she has left. The radio evening news is turned off now. The newspaper goes unread. The magazine subscriptions are cancelled. She can't bear to see the President's face. Maybe all that anger is making her behave so oddly.

It has to be political depression. What else could it be? Something has gone wrong deep inside, and she won't share it with me. Is she just politically grieving, or is it something more personal? All I know is that a curtain has been drawn that wasn't there before, and after seven years of marriage my wife has started hiding things from me.

"Go get some work done," she says, dismissing me from the kitchen. "I'll get dinner ready."

It will feel good to change into something comfortable. I've just come home from my Wednesday afternoon office hours, my weekly endurance test, one hundred and eighty minutes of voluntarily remaining accessible to students, confined to my little sandwich of a book-stuffed office on the third floor of Padelford Hall. After an exhausting hour wrestling with spoiled, lazy, illiterate students who were willing to do just about anything except actually read the material, I took out my frustration by slashing my way through a dozen dull, uninspired midterm essays. Faced with half an hour left to endure, I couldn't take any more and locked up

Love in the American Empire

early. I fled, depleted, with the few wits I had left. I had nothing more to give.

Now I stare at my computer screen in the comfort of my own home. I read a sentence three times that doesn't sound right, and shift some words around. Then I put them back the way they were.

I can't quite forget finding the electric toothbrush in the trash can. And what about those muddy footprints? They gnaw at the back of my mind as I try to get my work done, as I focus on my new book, attempting to bring the fifth chapter to some kind of intelligent resolution.

For the last three years, my field has been the contemporary novel. I'm interested in the living practitioners of the first-person narrative and what they're doing with it. Fortunately this quarter I'm just teaching one class, so I can focus my time and energy in class on the book at the same time. It's already five chapters into reality. When it's completed and published, it will represent the best scholarly work I've ever done, the most compelling and pertinent textual analysis I've ever attempted.

My only publication so far has been *Feminism in the Classic Victorian Ghost Story*, not exactly a bestseller. My new book is called *First Person American*. It deals with the single-perspective narrative in American fiction, from *Huckleberry Finn* to *Catcher in the Rye*. It goes right to the heart of literature and tackles the primary problem of recorded transmission: capturing the truth from a limited point of view.

Love in the American Empire

That's my topic. I study how people who tell stories distort reality by their limited point of view, how life and literature are always distorted by a single perspective, how we spend most of our time guessing at motives and misunderstanding everyone in our lives, often ourselves included.

We know so little for sure. That's reality. I can watch other people for hours, guessing at what they're thinking, guessing at what they're experiencing, but that's me, the watcher, the thinker, Colin Wetmore, never the life of the party, never the star of the team, preferably with my nose in a book – which is exactly where my nose is happiest, buried in a story full of emotional misunderstandings and moral conundrums and thoughtful language.

That's one thing my wife and I agree on, books. We've been trying to pay off our bookstore account as long as we've been married. Rachel reads like some people breathe. Tonight, after dinner, we'll do what we do after dinner every night. I'll retreat to the computer room at one end of our home, and she'll settle into the reading armchair at the other end, in the half of the living room she's transformed into her library. Two happy people, with a date to meet in bed in just a few hours.

Her reading addiction is fueled by her job. Rachel manages the campus bookstore, where I met her shortly after joining the faculty. Not only was she an eyeful, she could talk books with me, Chekhov and Proust, Conrad and Austen. Though I'd experienced puppy love before, she clobbered me with the real thing. I was a goner from the start.

Love in the American Empire

Her little bookstore is in the student union. She supervises a staff of four. She's been working there for fourteen years, shelving pens and notebooks, selling computer supplies and candy, folding University of Washington T-shirts, ordering magazines and receiving deliveries. She's a workaholic and loves her job. The long, stressful lines of impatient students waiting to buy their exam books just fire her adrenalin and make her feel useful. Most of the time.

"You'd think by now I'd be sick of it," she says, as I walk into the kitchen, lured by the inviting smells. I get two plates down from the cupboard.

"Sick of what?"

"The bookstore, what else? I need to find another job."

"You love that bookstore too much to ever leave it," I say. "You're wasting your time there, but you love it."

"I should be grant-writing."

"Or editing. Or writing hot-blooded romances. But you're not. Because you love books."

"Sit down," she says, getting ready to bring a bubbling pot from the stove. "This is hot. Stay out of my way."

"Is that what I *think* it is?"

"Do I treat you right, or do I treat you right?"

I can't help it. Something is wrong with this picture. There's something she's not telling me.

3
Problem Student

Eating in silence is not our usual way. I listen to the tinkle and scratch of silverware on plates, the gurgle of the old refrigerator, the drip of the kitchen faucet, the whoosh and whine of passing cars below. When the phone rings, it's a relief. Rachel is far too eager to answer it, rushing from the table as though released. Her cell is on the coffee table. It's her mother. From the next room, I can hear every word her mother shouts.

That's just normal. Rita Vespucci wants to be heard.

"He's so stubborn," she shouts, "he doesn't listen to me, now he's paying the price. You should see him. He can hardly get out of his chair. What's an old man like your father doing lifting all those heavy boxes, can you tell me? He's trying to give himself a heart attack, that's what."

"How is she?" I venture, observing a discreet silence after the conversation.

"Fine. Still beating up on Dad."

The marriage of Nick and Rita Vespucci, both in their seventies and almost inseparable since they married fifty years ago, has evolved into a sadomasochistic co-dependency. This much is beyond dispute, because it's always on display. Mrs Vespucci constantly scolds Mr Vespucci about the thousand-and-one things he perpetually does wrong, including driving, gardening, housekeeping, golfing, dusting, vacuuming, and washing the dishes. It's harmless, it's their love-song, and it's probably an Italian thing, but it can be pretty hard to watch.

The phone rings again, and this time she's not as quick to pick up her twitching little cell. It's her best friend, Gloria. I help myself to seconds.

"Hi, sweetie. Hope you've been able to hold something down." She listens, nodding sympathetically. "It's the election results. It's making everyone sick. Yes, I saw the Falluja pictures. Heartbreaking."

"How's Gloria?" I ask, when she's had a chance to take a bite or two.

"Fine," she says sharply, axing that topic in a blow.

My wife's best friend is Gloria Goldberg, a 98-pound, frizzy-haired intellectual from New Jersey with a gloomy sense of humor who appreciates everything of value and outspokenly scorns the rest. I can only take so much of Gloria. My wife adores her.

Don't get me wrong, Gloria has all the right values, is politically up to date, and is always ready to pick up a sign and march. She feels guilty over just about everything and has stopped eating to prove it. She consumes nothing that has ever experienced consciousness. She's just exhausting and opinionated as hell, a self-appointed critic of the world, and particularly of me. Gloria isn't exactly a Colin Wetmore enthusiast.

Love in the American Empire

Rachel can deny it up and down, but as far as I'm concerned, Gloria has a bit of a crush on Rachel, and wouldn't mind terribly if I fell in front of a bus. My wife laughs this off and thinks I'm imagining things. Rachel also thinks men don't notice her body.

Her book lies next to the fruit bowl, pushed to the far side of the table. "What are you reading now?"

"*War Trash* by Ha Jin." She raises the thick tome. There's always a book somewhere near Rachel. "Dario loves it. It's about an American POW camp in Korea, incredible writing and insight, but oh, my God, some of the violence is hair-raising. Dario says it's worth it."

Well, if Dario says so, it must be so.

Dario Focaccia knows everything, and his literary taste is beyond question. Besides, he's Italian, which in my wife's eyes gives him extra depths of instant understanding.

This is another one of my wife's friends who makes me summon up reserves of patience. Rachel is fascinated by colorful, larger-than-life types, and her workmate is certainly one of them. He's the bookbuyer for the little student union bookstore, a dead-end job he's been in for over thirty years, and he's got a literary opinion on just about everything, Greek classics, Victorian novels, bestsellers, you name it. He reads as much as my wife, so he and Rachel get really chummy. Fortunately he's gay, so I don't have to worry.

Of course, one of the reasons both Gloria and Dario torment me is that they make me wonder why Rachel married

Love in the American Empire

someone like me. If you like vivid, exciting, flamboyant types, why would you marry a man so colorless and undramatic, so ordinary and reserved?

Sometimes I don't know why Rachel loves me.

She's a million miles away from me now, sitting beside me at the table. The conversation has exhausted itself. Time has slowed to a halt. The only sign of life is the sound of our chewing. I put down my fork, take off my wire-rimmed glasses, massage that sensitive little spot at the top of my nose where the glasses clamp hold of the bone.

There's a topic I've avoided, the one knotting in my chest. I decide to vent my frustration and tell her what happened today.

I can't quite get that Wheeler kid out of my mind.

On principle I try to leave my campus work behind me. I've been teaching for nine years, so I've had time to learn a few techniques for mental health. When I close the office door in Padelford Hall, I shut off my whole sense of responsibility to the English Department, to the University of Washington, and to my students. I'd rather spend dinner talking with my wife about our life together, our mutual friends, movies we want to see, the situation in Iraq, some matter of consequence to our personal lives.

I'm so frustrated with this particular student, and the silence at the dinner table is getting to me, so I decide to tell her about him, to bring my professional life to my private table and see if talking about it helps. It's bad enough to feel frustrated at work without feeling frustrated at home. Maybe it will help Rachel and me connect again. I hate this feeling of separation between us, when issues go unresolved and emotions get bruised.

"I've been fighting with myself all afternoon," I say. "I think I may have to flunk the only genius I've ever taught."

Rachel doesn't look up. She wipes her lips on her napkin. "What on earth for?" she asks in a neutral voice. She wants a common ground, too. She wants to forget about the electric toothbrush and whatever happened between us in the bathroom when the light went out.

"I've told you about him – that kid from eastern Washington."

"The one who was home-schooled?"

"That's the one. This is the first time he's ever been in a classroom with other students."

"Hard to believe." She yawns. "Weird thing to do to a kid. Is public education really that dreadful?"

"You get a little more critical when you're talking about your own kid," I say without thinking.

She quietly freezes.

I realize my mistake immediately. We promptly drop the subject. Rachel can't have children. We keep trying, but we've always known. I want a child very much, and we're thinking about adopting. The question is when. It's a delicate topic between us, packed with pain and shame and disappointment. We don't go near it.

Love in the American Empire

"His father made an appointment to come see me in my office. He's a small town minister, some little crossroads in Eastern Washington."

"Oh-oh. Redneck country."

"He's a fine man, actually. Lucas Wheeler. Caught me by surprise. He's too good to be true, really, lean and liberal and friendly. He talked to me openly about home schooling. He told me how smart the kid was, no hang-ups, no peer group experimentation, no weird competitive streaks, just a healthy body and a healthy mind and a healthy attitude. He's proud of his son, obviously. No public school teacher has ever messed with his kid's mind. Lucas doesn't trust teachers. At the beginning of the quarter he paid a visit to each of his kid's three profs."

"How's the boy in class?"

"Ideal. Almost too good to be true. He knows exactly what to do in a classroom, because he learned it by watching television and movies."

"Does he have friends?" she asks, without sounding completely interested.

"I don't think so," I have to admit. "Probably just a matter of time."

"I think I remember you mentioning him," says Rachel. I get the feeling she doesn't remember anything about him, that she's not even listening, lost in thought about something else. She's been like that for the last couple days, not really hearing what I say. I've lost her interest, but I go on anyway.

Love in the American Empire

"Dillon is a joy to have in the classroom. Reads the assignments, does the homework, asks thoughtful questions, you name it, a completely courteous and civilized kid."

"So, what's the problem?" asks Rachel. She's losing my train of thought. I'm going on too long about this kid.

"The problem is he doesn't finish his papers," I blurt out, as though it's right up there next to matricide. "He struggles and struggles with the ideas, writes about the book copiously, organizes his notes and comes up with a dozen insightful paragraphs that don't add up to anything. He won't come to conclusions. When term papers are due he has nothing to turn in, and papers are most of his grade. His observations are brilliant, inspired – they just don't go anywhere. He not only reads the books I assign, he reads other books by the same authors, he does research, he knows his stuff. In a room full of sorority girls with cell-phones and fratboys with hangovers, there's this kid who wants to study and learn and think and read great literature."

"So, give him an A."

"How can I judge him by different standards than I judge everyone else? Papers are required. Papers have arguments and conclusions. Papers have beginnings, middles, and ends. His don't. His are bits and pieces, late and unfinished. He hasn't fulfilled the requirements and the other kids do. That's patently not right."

Love in the American Empire

She pushes back her chair from the table, rises, and brings her plate to the sink. "Flunking him is not right, either," she says, her back to me, turning on the faucet.

"I know that!" I yelp back at her. "That's the problem. Passing him is unfair, but so is flunking him."

And that's it. The conversation ends. Neither of us has anything left to say. I wish I'd never brought it up. I don't feel better in the slightest, the problem is unresolved, and the awkward silence has us in its grips. We do the dishes together, like we do every night, bumping into each other in our tight little kitchen, clearing the table, sponging down the stove and drainboard. She washes, I dry, but we've run out of things to talk about, she just passes me one dripping dish after another.

As soon as we're done we escape to opposite ends of the house. While she reads her Dario-endorsed literary masterpiece, I work on the fifth chapter of my book, confidently pounding out the conclusion in appropriately stuffy language. Literary criticism is so much more manageable than life. If you sound profound, you are. This is where I belong, in a dark room staring into a bright monitor screen, generating language.

We cross paths in the bathroom a couple hours later, as she's taking out her contact lenses and I'm brushing my teeth. We're both tired and in our underwear. She says quietly, "Guess I'll call it a night," and I mumble something similar back to her. I can't really talk too well, because my mouth is full of suds. I become painfully aware of the electric

Love in the American Empire

toothbrush buzzing in my mouth, as though I'm guilty of collaboration with the enemy. I've already taken the time to immerse the brush heads in boiling water while she was reading, hers included. I spit, quickly bring my little hygienic ritual to a conclusion, and close the bathroom door behind me, not wanting to know if she uses the electric toothbrush or not. Hopefully she won't throw it in the trash can.

I head straight down the hall into the living room to go to bed.

I should explain that. Our living room defies the American standard, which is television-centered. Neither of us watches television. We don't even own one. Instead, half the living room has become my wife's reading room and been overtaken by her outrageous library, shelf after shelf piled two deep right up to the ceiling, and the other half of the living room – not that it's free of books, by any means, because books are everywhere – is centered around our king-size bed. Long ago my need for a private place to write my scholarly exegesis outweighed our need for privacy in the bedroom. My home office took over where our bed used to be, bumping the king-size mattresses into the front room. Admittedly a bed in the living room drew a few wry comments. It inhibited faculty cocktail parties. It crowded Vespucci family dinners. But in a house where every room was clogged with books, the biggest piece of furniture belonged in the biggest room.

It's a spacious house with high ceilings. In November it can get pretty cold, but the electric heaters have been clicking and pulsing for an hour and the house is starting to get cozy. I turn out all but the reading light, shed my clothes and slip under the blankets. I hide my face behind my open paperback, peeking over the top to see when my wife is coming.

I'm re-reading *The Postman Always Rings Twice* – a classic example of first person American. They're just getting ready to murder the husband when I hear Rachel enter the bedroom. I don't look up, so I don't realize she's naked until she slides up against me and wraps me in her arms.

"I hate when we fight," she says into my chest.

"We're not fighting," I mumble, kissing her forehead.

She looks up at me, her eyes so close to mine there's nowhere to hide. "Then what do you call it?"

"We're misunderstanding each other," I say feebly. We're too close to each other to lie very well. "But we love each other so much, we always get over the rough spots."

She suddenly squirms up and kisses me, grabbing my head in her hands like a coconut that she's going to drill with her tongue. That's all it takes and boing, I'm rock hard, and we're all over each other. Not even seven years of marriage can ease the sheer lust I sometimes feel for her. We mash each other's mouths like we've only got thirty seconds left before the world ends, our bodies pumping and banging and agitating.

This is when Boo chooses to meow.

Amid all the huffing and puffing, the sound is unnaturally loud. He's standing at the front door, tail straight up in the air, facing the chilly crack between the door and the frame where a little draft of November air squeezes through. He's giving an unmistakable signal that cats have been giving human beings for thousands of years.

We both silently agree to ignore him. We're rolling over and over on the bed, out of our minds with pleasure, our arms and legs tangled together, her tongue in my mouth, my tongue in her mouth.

A claw nicks my foot.

"Ouch!" I kick out angrily, but by then there's no one there. And suddenly we're both laughing in each other's arms. "Okay, okay, Boo, you can go out. Just a second."

I somehow pull away from Rachel, throw on my bathrobe, and I'm tying the cord as I obediently follow Boo to the front door. A low, waist-high bookshelf separates the front door from the bed, and it's much chillier on the other side, out of my wife's arms, away from the electric blanket.

I flip the lock, but the door sticks. I have to tug it open. A gust of cold air blows in. My bathrobe flaps open. Boo launches himself through the door. I'm shivering and closing the door, wrapping my bathrobe around me, trying to keep out the cold air as I wait for Boo to rush across the porch to the railing and stare out into the night.

Except this time he doesn't.

He comes to a halt midway across the porch and freezes, crouching, on the alert. He seems to be backing away from something. I quickly peer out the window, protective as a parent, to make sure a neighbor's cat or a wandering raccoon isn't about to threaten my little pal.

That's when I see something move, back in the maple and laurel branches along the edge of the property.

I can hardly believe my eyes. Living near Ravenna Park, the occasional raccoon isn't too surprising, but they're the size of dogs, not people. When I peer out again into the darkness, there's nothing there. I keep staring, my heart suddenly pounding in my ears.

Is that someone behind those branches?

A shadow steps back.

Someone's out there. One more move, and I'm going to phone 9-1-1. It's not a drunk student, we've had those before and this is nothing like that. They make plenty of noise. They trip and break things and throw up. Whoever is out there now isn't making a sound and doesn't want to be seen.

"What is it, honey?" asks Rachel from the bed on the other side of the bookshelf.

I watch as Boo slowly relaxes. Whoever it was is gone. Boo approaches the edge of the porch, sniffs, and then plops off into the darkness.

"Nothing," I say, and lock the door.

4
Jake in the Rain

At first I don't recognize the sound. I open my eyes and listen without budging. The refrigerator hums. The boiler drones. The faucet drips. Then I hear it again. The sound is coming from my wife.

It's like a soft whimpering, but I can't be sure until she turns toward me and I can see, from the light of the streetlamp through the window, that her cheeks have glistening wet streaks. She's sound asleep. I wrap my arms around her, but the tears just keep coming so I nudge her awake.

"What is it, hon?" I whisper in her ear.

She rubs a hand across her face, smearing the tears. "Sorry. It was a bad one." She turns away from me in embarrassment. "Sometimes it just gets to me."

I saw the pictures, too. It's the war. The news today was especially upsetting. An all-out assault, massive destruction and death. Bodies in the streets. No water, no electricity, children dying. It drives her crazy. It obsesses her. She's always thinking about it, and all the feelings she buries inside come out in her sleep.

That's the kind of person Rachel is. That's why I love her. She can't turn off her heart. She can't stop thinking about what we're doing in Iraq, the bombing and the shooting, the house searches, the torture in the prisons. She can't get it out of her mind. Funny, some Americans find it perfectly easy to never think about it at all, but Rachel can't seem to forget it. She's always brooding over it in the back of her mind, pissed over the body count, pissed over the righteous doublespeak about democracy and freedom, snapping off the television news or throwing down the newspaper saying, "Dead people don't vote."

Personally I think she's getting more worked up about it than usual from hanging around Gloria too much. Gloria rubs her face in it. Gloria thinks you can't know enough about the misery of the world. Well, wherever it's coming from, the sadness and hatred and pain of Iraq really upsets her. She starts imagining the old people and sick people, the sewage, the wounds, the hunger. And the children! She can't let it go. I watch her helplessly. What can I do?

If she's in public, it's worse. God forbid she overhears someone in a movie theater or bus or supermarket repeat some thoughtless media-endorsed praise of the President. "What? That scheming liar? Are you talking about the man who dragged America into this senseless war over weapons of mass destruction – is that who you're talking about?" I never know when I'm going to suddenly turn around in a department store or gas station and find my wife in some stranger's face, letting him know what's what.

She tries to vent her frustration in anger, but I can see how much it hurts her. She doesn't have to tell me. I feel that hopeless sadness gripping her now, as the tears line her face.

Love in the American Empire

"Come on, hon. Let it go. You can only do what you can do. Get some rest, baby. Take it easy on yourself."

Soon she's sound asleep, her face so beautiful when she finally relaxes that I let my eyes just stare, drinking their fill. I brush back a wisp of hair, kiss her hot, troubled forehead. Too bad I'm not asleep, too, but at least I'm looking at someone as lovely as my wife. I lie here in the darkness, my arms around her, knowing how lucky I am to be loved by a woman so beautiful inside and out, treasuring every night with her.

Maybe because of Rachel crying tonight over Iraq, when I finally fall asleep I dream about my old college friend, the most intense friend of my life, Jake Bagley. A year ago I heard from a mutual friend that Jake was stationed in Iraq. Finding that out upset me more than I expected. It gave the war a way-too-human face.

Back in college I'd started noticing that every time I zoned out in the campus bookstore, I'd see another student there in the science fiction aisle. One by one, he was reading all the novels of Philip K. Dick. He was in ROTC, not at all my kind of guy, but somehow we got to know each other and grew to be friends. We ended up in a class together, then took one together on purpose, then started jogging out to Gas Works Park on weekends, until for his last six months on campus he rented a room right above mine.

If Jake Bagley could have majored in thinking, he would have been a happy man. He came from south Seattle, from an industrial neighborhood and lower middle class

Love in the American Empire

parents. His blue-collar practicality fell head-over-heels for the soaring idealism of philosophy. When I met him, Jake had just fallen in love with Sartre and Camus.

As a philosophy major, his choice of profession was literally insane, but he came from a military family so it made sense to him. He was a natural jock, with a classic all-American mug straight out of a Norman Rockwell painting, even a few nose freckles, big white chopper teeth constantly on display in his good-natured grin. He didn't enlist casually. He put his heart into ROTC. He really believed he could make a difference. He was the kind of guy who would die for his country. Maybe that's why I've been having these dreams about him and the war. Like the dream I have tonight.

Bombs are whistling and exploding outside in the dark. I dream that I get up from my bed and walk to the window. They're streaking down from the sky, blowing up houses and buildings. It's like I'm in Iraq, but I'm here in my house in the University District at the same time, and there are rain and thunder and bombs, it's pouring, like the end of the world, a turbulent and angry night in the middle of a war.

Rachel is still sleeping in the bed behind me. She doesn't hear a thing. I can hear people shouting and screaming in the street down below, people crying, gunshots. I've got to protect her. Where will we be safe?

Suddenly there's a pounding at the door.

That wakes her up. She stares at me, wide-eyed, scared. I'm afraid to open the door. I'm shaking. The pounding gets louder. Then the lock on the door breaks. The door swings open and bangs against the wall.

Jake Bagley stands outside in the pouring rain, drenched to the skin.

Close the door. Close the door. Close the door.

That's the way Jake stood there in real life that terrible night near the end of my college days, the night our friendship ended. That's where the dream ends, because the sight of him there always wakes me up. It's a night I don't like to remember. I'm sorry it's come to mind.

Rain was pounding the windows that night. I was studying for a final. There was a knock at the door. I opened it. Jake was just wearing a T-shirt and he was sopping wet. His face was red, and even though he was drenched I could smell liquor.

"Hey, Colin," he said, holding the door open.

I stared at him, bewildered. I got the feeling he'd been out drinking with his ROTC friends. "Jake, what's up?"

There was something in his eyes that spooked me. Just to look at him made me almost sick with fear. "Man, I think tonight's the night," he said. I just stared at him. His words didn't make any sense to me.

"The night for what?"

"It's on your mind, too. I know it is."

He couldn't have meant what I thought he meant. "I don't know what you're talking about," I lied.

Love in the American Empire

"You're not fooling anybody, Colin," he said. "I can see right through you. I know you love me as much as I love you." Those were his words. Probably the most shocking words any man has ever said to me in my life. "Come on, let's just admit it and get on with it."

The memory haunts me because I'm so ashamed of my behavior. I couldn't speak. I was so terrified that the only idiot thing I could do was to slowly close the door in his face. Maybe I did love him a little back then, the way college kids sometimes do, maybe he was right, but I just stood there stupefied, with him on one side of the door and me on the other, shaking. He knocked, and he knocked again, and he twisted the doorknob, but by the time I realized what I'd done and flung the door open, he was gone.

Now I'm lying here in bed, wide-eyed and trembling and aching with regret. I'm wet with sweat, my heart pounding. Seems like so long ago. I was just a stupid kid. I didn't know how to react to someone loving me. I didn't even know how to love myself.

Rachel is so deeply asleep she just groans and snuggles deeper into her pillow. I gently ease out of bed and towel myself down in the bathroom. I haven't thought about Jake Bagley for a long time, not since I found out he'd been shipped to Iraq.

I slip back under the covers without shaking the mattress too much, angling my legs around the warm lump of cat sleeping at the foot of the bed, and find a new position, snuggling up against my wife, my arms around her. She's my lifebuoy on a big, big sea. I close my eyes and try to relax, try to slip back into that numbing blissful darkness, but there'll be no more sleep for me. All I can do is pretend to sleep.

I'm still pretending several hours later when my wife carefully extricates herself from my arms to go on her morning run.

Love in the American Empire

5
Al-Jazeera

By the time Rachel strides back into the house, flushed and sweaty and vibrantly alive, I've finished reading the newspaper. Besides running two miles every morning, she also stretches, takes vitamins, does aerobics twice a week and swims a quartermile as often as she can, while constantly watching what she eats. She's in superb shape – she may have just hit forty, but when she runs around Green Lake, guys turn to look at her.

Both my wife and my cat are more athletic than I am. Me, I'm more of a watcher and thinker. Give me a book, or a monitor and a keyboard, and I'm happy.

Keeping the pages of the newspaper all in reasonable order, just the way she likes them, I fold it up again and set it on her chair.

Not that she'll read it. She hasn't read the newspaper since the elections. She turns off the radio. She doesn't want to know. That kind of extreme behavior worries me. I keep thinking any day now she's going to start up an interest in the news again. Denying reality isn't healthy.

I watch her stride into the kitchen, moving briskly in tune to some inner clock, brushing back her wet hair. She picks up the newspaper and sits down, but she doesn't really look at it. She just sets it beside her plate, and reaches for her glass of orange juice.

Since I'm the morning person in this marriage, I'm usually the one to make breakfast, though technically we're supposed to take turns. The meal was effortless but it's one of her favorites, oatmeal with brown sugar and plenty of chopped walnuts. It's warm comfort food, just what both of us crave. She pours milk into her oatmeal while taking another glance at the headlines. She gives the front page approximately four seconds of her attention, and then sets the newspaper on the other side of the fruit bowl. "You'd think the war would be important enough to be somewhere on the front page."

"Maybe it's a good day, and nothing happened," I say with ridiculous optimism.

"Not very likely," she says. "Three more American soldiers refused to fight in the war today. It made news everywhere else in the world, just not in the country that's court-martialing them."

I blink at her. "And it's not there on the front page?"

"Of course not."

The radio is on all day at the bookstore, so often Rachel hears news before it appears in print. "Good for them, the poor wretches," I say, taking the information for what it is and not worrying about the source. "Pass the milk, would you?"

She's tucking into that oatmeal like she hasn't eaten for days, hardly taking time to blow on it before sucking it down. "Some gung-ho Israeli soldier shot three Palestinian kids."

Love in the American Empire

"I'm afraid to ask why."

"They crossed a line in the ground that you're not allowed to cross."

"Lord," I say, dumping too much brown sugar into my oatmeal. Something is odd here. "How do you know all this?"

I've asked the right question. She pauses for a moment, and this time she blows on her spoonful of oats and nuts. "I've been getting my news online," she says, and then her lips close over the spoon. She swallows and says, "Our newspapers in Seattle are useless as far as the war is concerned."

"And what do you use instead?"

"Al-Jazeera," she says, without batting an eye. "If I want to know what's really happening in Iraq or Israel, I certainly won't look in an American newspaper, will I?"

She's startled me, and she knows it. She concentrates on her oatmeal. For some reason, just knowing that my wife has taken to consulting the Arab news agency about the war rattles me.

"You should try it sometime," she says over her spoon. "Get a different slant on what's happening. See us the way the rest of the world sees us. It's easy to bring up on the Internet. I've marked it as a favorite."

She's done *what?* This is just great. I'm as liberal as any sane human being, but I do not want to be on any government list, categorized as a terrorist sympathizer. Must Rachel always be so extreme? These are conservative times. A little prudence is called for. I decide it's not worth bringing up.

Love in the American Empire

The topic drops into silence. I can hear the kitchen clock ticking.

She folds up the newspaper and sets it aside. "You were restless in bed this morning," she says, sipping at her mug of coffee.

"Terrible dream," I tell her, and crunch into my slice of toast. "A nightmare, actually, about an old college friend. Did I ever tell you about Jake Bagley?"

Rachel spills coffee down the front of her blouse. She jumps to her feet with a shout.

"Oh, look what I've done!" she wails, and immediately begins unbuttoning. Pulling off her stained blouse, she flings open the door into the laundry room wearing only her bra, and in a moment she's crossed to the shelf above the washer and dryer, seized the plastic squirt container, and doused her blouse with Spray 'n Wash. I wait until she closes the laundry room door behind her and plops down her blouse in a damp, frustrated wad on the drainboard.

I'm not worried about the blouse. "Did you burn yourself, hon?"

She strides out of the kitchen to get another blouse. "No, no, I'm fine. I'm just pissed, that's all. I'm so damned clumsy this morning."

"I'll clean up in here, don't worry about it," I say loud enough for her to hear in the bathroom.

I quickly wipe up the coffee on the leg of the kitchen table, and the splatter across the green-and-white linoleum

Love in the American Empire

floor. I hardly notice what I'm doing, however, since I'm replaying the scene over and over in my mind. I know it's just my sick imagination, but it seems to me that Rachel flinched when I mentioned my old college friend's name, that the flinch was what made her spill her coffee. Though she's never met Jake Bagley, maybe she remembers me talking about him. Of course, maybe it was just an accident. "I should call his mother, and find out if she's heard from him."

Tucking in a fresh new blouse, Rachel emerges from the bathroom. We do our usual dash-around during the last few minutes before we leave for our walk up to campus. We live only three blocks away, although those three blocks are long and winding ones, tree-lined and parking-restricted, far enough away from the fraternities and sororities that we're not subjected to earth-shaking stereo speakers and late night drunken cries.

Well, not too often.

We rent the bottom floor of an old three-storey house which, when we moved in, was surrounded by maple and laurel trees, with wild thickets and ferns on all sides. Since the family that built it almost a century ago did all the work themselves, the house possesses a host of illegalities and code infractions, but the inconveniences are compensated by so much Old World charm that the little minuses don't matter.

Five years ago the benign academic couple who owned the house sold it to Omar and Odette Volkonsky, an immigrant Russian couple who gutted most of the interior and now live in the completely rebuilt, modernized upstairs with their two little boys.

Suddenly the house shakes. Slam-slam-slam. The ceiling overhead rattles. Ilya, the oldest boy, is running across the living room floor. A piercing shriek. Two-year-old Vanya is testing his vocal cords.

Gone is the former tree-sheltered solitude. The pastoral wilderness of the backyard has been bricked over to become a patio, basketball court and outdoor ping-pong room. Only our first-floor home has been left untouched by the Russian renovation. As long as nothing goes terribly wrong, the Volkonskys are letting us stay.

We're just getting into our coats for the walk up to campus when the phone rings. This early in the day it can only be one person, which for me only compounds the sense of oppression. Rachel is too good a daughter not to answer the phone. Rita Vespucci is the matriarch of my wife's family. She talks loud enough for me to hear every word. Rita Vespucci feels the world would be a better place if everyone could hear her.

"I just wanted you to know that I'll be having Thanksgiving here at my house. Dinner will be at four o'clock."

This is not to be confused with an invitation. This is an order. It's a commandment with the status of dogma. Rita Vespucci cooks the family feast on Thanksgiving. Dinner is at four o'clock. Any other arrangement is unthinkable.

Love in the American Empire

Attendance is mandatory. This is a warning, for non-Italians like me who don't know any better, that the stakes for violating this law are psychological abuse beyond my wildest dreams.

"Thanks, Mama," says Rachel. "How's your foot?"

Mrs Vespucci has launched into a detailed description of seventeen different kinds of pain when she gives a yelp. "Nick, what are you doing?" she barks. "No, no, no!"

"What is it, Mama?" asks Rachel in concern.

"Your father appears to have forgotten how to dry the dishes. No, no, no, Nick, you know it doesn't go there."

"Now, Mama, don't bully poor Daddy, he's doing his best," says Rachel.

"Well, he doesn't hear a thing you say to him. You know how he turns down that hearing aid."

Now there's an ingenious remedy devised by a loving husband, a solution my mother-in-law will never appreciate. "We've got to leave for work, or we'll be late, Mama. Love you, bye."

An awkward silence grips us as I zip up my briefcase.

"Don't ever treat me that way," I have to tell her. "I know she loves him but really, no matter how old and senile I get, don't ever order me around like that. I'd rather you shot me in the head."

I probably shouldn't have said it, and under normal circumstances it probably would have led to an argument and tears. I'll never know, because a sudden burst of shouting upstairs cuts through the stillness of the house.

Omar Volkonsky is unleashing a massive dose of outraged patriarchal fury on some hapless member of his family. There's no telling what's being said, since it's all in Russian, but the words are hitting like bullets and bombs. His silent wife or poor terrified children are getting a verbal flogging. I wince to think physical abuse may be accompanying this tirade, and listen for cries, whimpers, slapping, human bodies falling to the floor. I wonder if there's a special phone number to report domestic violence.

Rachel hears it, too. "That poor woman. Those poor kids." She turns away from it, as though her hunched shoulders can muffle the sound. "Come on, we'll be late for work."

She opens the front door and Omar's voice is just as loud outside. Then I hear their front door upstairs bang open. I look up, half-expecting his poor wife or bruised children to come tumbling over the banister. Instead, Odette Volkonsky, poised and lovely Russian beauty, descends the staircase at a stately, regal pace, completely unfazed, in her elegant winter coat. She smiles graciously in our direction and passes on. So it's the kids he's yelling at? Is she heartless, to stand by and let her husband browbeat her children into submission?

But next comes heavy-footed Ilya, followed by little Vanya in the arms of the live-in nurse, all bundled up in brightly-colored ski parkas. No sign of tears or terror. Neither child has so much as a frown. They squeal and wave and continue down the stairs. Even the nanny smiles.

Last comes Omar Volkonsky himself, ruggedly handsome in his trimmed black beard. Omar does not acknowledge us. He continues down the stairs red-faced with rage, shouting furious Russian curses at the top of his lungs into his cell-phone.

Apparently that was just a Russian phone call.

Rachel and I walk to campus in thoughtful silence.

6
Dario and Gloria

I'm finishing a Cobb salad at the Faculty Club, sitting over by the windows at a small table by myself. I'm turned away from the other tables so that no long-winded colleague of mine will think I'm lonely for company. Watching the leafless branches sway and rattle in the wind, it occurs to me that what Rachel and I really need is a night out for dinner and a movie. That new one, *Kinsey*, about the sex researcher looks intelligent, and it's playing at the Egyptian Theater up on Broadway. We could stop in at that new Thai restaurant, the one that makes such good peanut sauce. We need a treat in our lives, a little positive energy, a little indulgence.

It's such a good idea that I can't wait to ask her. I finish up the rest of the goodies in my salad, the chicken and olives and bacon bits, and leave a little lettuce behind. I navigate through the dining faculty members without getting too close to anyone who might try to persuade me to stay. Pushing open the doors, I hit the chilly wind head-on, and wait for a pause in between cars to dart across the winding campus drive to the student union building.

As I'm passing by the big showcase window just outside the bookstore, glancing inside at the bright new covers on display, I can't help noticing once again how blatantly liberal they all are. Dario the bookseller is so outspokenly anti-

Love in the American Empire

war and anti-Bush, as well as pro-women, pro-choice, pro-minorities, pro-environment, pro-Arab.

I stop in my tracks. Pro-Arab, of course. That's where she got this Al-Jazeera thing. It's that pain-in-the-neck, loud-mouthed, opinionated bookseller, Dario Focaccia. I step inside the double-door entrance, hoping to spot her from a distance and avoid getting verbally tangled up with her co-worker. Rachel is nowhere in sight. Dario spots me immediately.

"Colin!"

Shouting my name across the little bookstore, causing every customer to turn and look at me, he eagerly makes his way straight toward me through the book display tables.

Dario looks like he's in his forties, though Rachel says he's actually in his late fifties, a bald, intellectual primadonna who enjoys being eccentric. From Rachel I know that he's a miserably lonely gay man, a playwright who hasn't had a play produced for the last five years, or a date, for that matter. He always dresses boringly the same, in a white polo shirt and blue jeans. What little hair he's got is buzzcut, and he's got a goatee like I do, so that sometimes I see myself in ten years when I look at him, an appalling thought.

He's like my wife. He goes too far. Maybe it's an Italian thing. Before the election he featured every anti-Bush title in print. Dozens of them. Tables of them. He took the re-election of the President as a personal defeat. Rachel says he didn't come to work for three days. I mean, I was miserable, too, we all were, but Dario made a melodrama out of it.

Love in the American Empire

As usual, his greeting is effusive, like we're lifelong friends, far too loud, with an unnecessary hug. As usual, he looks at me a little too long, like he can see through my clothes and is taking pictures. When I ask him how his day's going, he gives a dramatic sigh.

"Notice, no more political books. No one wants to read about it anymore. None of it did any good. We're a ruthless empire, like it or not."

This is just what I was afraid of. I don't want political slogans, I want my wife. "I don't see Rachel around."

"Rachel? But she's at home today," says Dario, amused by my blunder. "Remember?"

"Oh, uh, right." Damn, another one of my wife's little surprises. That gets my attention. I'm on guard now. "She's feeling okay, isn't she?"

"Of course!" says Dario. "Why wouldn't she be? A little spaced out, maybe an early case of holiday blues. She went home at lunchtime to feed Boo, and then she phoned and said something came up. Say, have you seen *Kinsey* yet?"

"Not yet, actually, but..."

"Fine little movie, very nicely done," says the know-it-all film critic. "Excellent acting, even down to the minor roles, and instead of climaxing the movie with something cheap, like a car chase, you know, he ends it with Lynn Redgrave doing such a brilliant star turn that it's a total showstopper," and blah blah blah blah, on and on, a fountain of opinions, the gay intellectual cliché come to life. He'd like to launch into a detailed review. He'd probably like his own television show.

I cut him off.

"Maybe I'll just head home then. Nice to see you, Dario." That's my exit line, and I intend to use it. I circle a table of overpriced chocolates, cut behind a display of imported French journals, and would be out the door of the bookstore and halfway down the hall if I didn't look up in time to see Gloria Goldberg standing in my way.

She isn't blocking my path, since she hardly takes up any room at all. She's about as formidable as a broomstick. Gloria gets skinnier every time I look at her. She's bundled up to the chin in furry collars and a heavy-duty, cold-weather coat, in gloves and cap and fur-lined boots, but not even her multiple layers can disguise her fragile frame. She carries herself with dignity, like the empress of a starving nation.

"Hi, Gloria."

"Hi, sweetie," she says. "So, what were you doing downtown yesterday?"

That certainly stops me in my tracks. "I don't know what you're talking about. I wasn't downtown yesterday."

"You weren't?" Now she's as surprised as I am. "But I saw you. At least, I thought I saw you. I saw Rachel for sure, there's no doubt about that, and there was a guy beside her in the car. I thought it was you."

A chill shivers down my spine. "Nope, it wasn't me."

"Oh, well then." She may be brassy and defensive and from New Jersey, but she's sensitive enough to see she's just slid a dagger into my heart. "Maybe I'm wrong. It probably wasn't her, after all. Is she here?"

"No." I'm mustering all the calm I still possess, trying not to jump to conclusions. "She's gone home early. Something came up."

"Oh, sure," says Gloria. "Well, listen, she and I made plans to go out to dinner tonight and a movie. We're going to go see that new one, *Kinsey*. Want to come with us?"

I feel like a plastic, blow-up man who's just been jabbed with a pin. "No, thanks," I say, deflating rapidly into a miserable puddle of disappointment. "I've got too much work to do tonight. You girls go ahead."

"Let us know if you change your mind."

Gloria strides away down the hall, stiffly upright, caught up in the flow of student traffic.

I slip out of the bookstore, out of the student union, and am soon hurrying across campus. It's a disturbed hive of activity in between classes, lemmings rushing in all directions, sheep being herded into corrals, half of them talking into cellphones, half-there and half-somewhere else, oblivious to the hatred swelling and festering in the world these privileged sleepwalkers are about to inherit.

7
Dillon and Gloria

By the time I reach home this afternoon, it's lightly raining. The skies are getting darker by the minute with more and more heavy, swollen clouds. I'm inside and shaking out of my wet overcoat, scolding myself for forgetting my umbrella at home again this morning, when I notice that it's unnaturally quiet and Rachel hasn't come out from wherever she is and given me a welcoming kiss. Not in the kitchen. Not sitting at my computer. Not in the bathroom.

"Rachel?"

No answer. I've concluded that she's not home when I notice, from under the mound of blankets and bedspread on the unmade bed, a bare arm and shoulder. I approach the bed. She appears to be sound asleep.

"Honey?" I jiggle her shoulder. "Are you okay?"

She moans softly and her head emerges from a place I thought was a pillow. "Why is it so dark? What time is it?"

"Almost five o'clock. What happened? Did you take a nap?"

She props herself up on her elbow, scratching her curly hair. "Something like that. I came home for lunch today, and I was just exhausted."

"I know. I went over to the bookstore to find you."

Love in the American Empire

"Did you really, sweetheart?" She kisses me. "I'd better get ready. Gloria will be here any minute. Is it cold out?"

"It's raining."

"Raincoat, then. Sure you won't come with us?"

For a moment it's almost tempting. Sitting shoulder-to-shoulder with Rachel in a dark movie theater is exactly what I'm in the mood for – but I don't want to share her with anyone else, not tonight. "No, thanks. I'm going to be a good boy and get the rest of these papers graded."

"Sometimes, dear, I think you're a little too good."

I'm caught off-guard, laughing nervously but weighing her words, trying to decipher if she's telling me something, when she startles me by grabbing my crotch. I gasp, and instinctively try to pull away, but she's not letting go. She's got hold of me right through my pants, giving me a boner on the spot, and tugs me down on top of her. Suddenly we're both hot and bothered and helplessly laughing. She pulls me all the way over onto the bed, wraps her warm, bare arms around my neck, and kisses me. Not until she pulls away for breath does she say, "You had a visitor this afternoon."

Not where I thought the conversation was leading. The oddness of her timing immediately eases the wooden eagerness between my legs. "I did?"

"Guess who?"

Personally I hate guessing games. They make your imagination run riot with sickening possibilities. I shudder to think of every horny old coot on the faculty who's ever looked at my wife with a flicker of lust in his eyes, every randy grad student who ever offered to help her clean up after the faculty party, every gas station attendant, supermarket clerk, and take-out delivery boy I've caught in the act of checking her out. Fortunately she doesn't keep me in suspense long. "It was that student, the brilliant one who's giving you trouble. The one who can't come to conclusions."

Now that shocks me. "Dillon Wheeler?" I squeak.

Mentioning him at dinner last night was bad enough. Now that frustrating student has actually invaded my private sanctuary. To just show up at a professor's home uninvited violates every sense of protocol. But then Dillon isn't exactly just any student.

"You never mentioned how attractive that boy is," says Rachel with a coy smile. "He's drop-dead gorgeous. Funny detail to leave out, Colin. I suppose you men never notice things like that."

"Spare me." Sometimes I think she enjoys making me jealous. I'm perfectly aware what Dillon Wheeler looks like. So is everyone else in that class, thank you. When you're lecturing, you always notice when someone else in the room is getting more attention than you are.

"I'll tell you someone who really reacted to Dillon big time." She rolled her eyes toward the armchair. A peaceful mound of fur was spread over the cushion. Its tail occasionally lashed.

"Really?" Boo usually avoids or ignores our guests.

Love in the American Empire

"That cat couldn't leave him alone. He was all over Dillon from the minute he set foot in this house. Like he was made out of catnip! Marking Dillon's forehead, bumping him nose to nose, rubbing back and forth against Dillon's ankles, insisting on sleeping in his lap. The cat was obsessed."

Boo's fondness for Dillon really isn't the issue here. "Did he leave a message? Did he say what he wanted?"

Before she can begin explaining to me why this student would seek me out at home, we hear someone knocking at our front door.

"Get that, would you?" says Rachel, flinging off the covers. "It's probably Gloria."

To my surprise, she's completely naked. As welcome as the sight is, it rattles me. Why would she take off all her clothes in the middle of the afternoon? Our bed is, after all, in the living room. She hurries away from me down the hall. I admire her every step of the way.

As soon as she's out of sight, however, the agony begins.

The pieces seem to be forming a picture. She's strangely exhausted. She stays home from work. She's completely naked. I find myself very much hoping that she undressed *after* the visit from Dillon. I'm desperately hoping that my gorgeous wife did not answer the door in her bathrobe. What if she invited him inside? What if they talked together, and that was all she was wearing? I can't stop thinking about the two of them in this house, and what must have been going through his horny young male's mind.

"Colin, please, don't zone out on me, hon." She's quickly dressing. "Tell her I'll just be a minute, would you, sweetie?"

I can hear the door into the bathroom slam as I make myself presentable and open the front door. Gloria is all dolled up, which means she looks like a skinny, effeminate boy. "She's getting ready, I suppose," she says. "It's a universal female thing. You wouldn't understand." Having successfully marginalized me within the first thirty seconds as a mere man, she strolls inside, hands in her pockets, and does everything but whistle nervously while she paces back and forth in the living room, waiting for my wife.

"Care for a drink, Gloria?"

"No, thanks. Not now." Then she is compelled to add viciously, "Maybe we'll stop somewhere for one after the movie."

Fine. So she'll be keeping my wife out late. I try to keep my face blank, to not show that I'm bothered. Go ahead, have a drink with my wife. Ladies' night out. I'm not bugged at all. If Gloria knows that she's bugging me, she'll start smirking. That I couldn't take.

When Rachel steps out of the bathroom, she's wearing lipstick and a slinky blue shift that radiates sex appeal and shows far too much of all my favorite places.

Love in the American Empire

"You look good enough to eat," I say enviously. "Dang!" I'm really starting to feel left out, and somehow it's all my own doing. "I thought you were just going to a movie?"

"I want to look my best, don't I?" says Rachel, giving me a kiss on the cheek and a whiff of her perfume before Gloria escorts her out the door. "There's some meatloaf in the refrigerator. You can warm it up for dinner. And some apple crisp, but remember your diet. Don't stay up late waiting for me."

Gloria closes the door, giving me a last smile of triumph before cutting them both off from view.

Disappointed and sulky, determined to go off my diet in sheer defiance, I microwave the meatloaf and a major serving of apple crisp. I carry the plate into my home office, determined to flagrantly ignore grading papers because I'm not such a good boy, after all. Instead I'm going to eat dinner at my computer while working on *First Person American*.

But my thoughts are elsewhere.

I'm leaning back in my office chair, my hands behind my head, staring at the cobwebs on the ceiling and trying to formulate a literary theory: *first person narrative is the genre of misunderstanding*.

I notice a folded note bumped to one side of my desk, and my thoughts come roaring back to that Wheeler boy's unexpected visit. I sit up abruptly in my chair, and my feet come down heavily on the floor as I snatch up the note, and

Love in the American Empire

read it again. It's been lying there on my desk for over a month, never quite forgotten.

Out of the blue, on the first day of Autumn Quarter, this oddly friendly, clean-cut young man comes strolling up the classroom aisle after class and presents me with this note:

> *Dear Professor Colin Wetmore. Thank you for taking the time to meet with me. You've put my worries at rest. You strike me as a good man, and I'm almost never wrong about goodness. This is my son, Dillon. Seattle may be a bit much for him at first. If he needs someone, I told him to seek you out. May I ask this of you? Lucas Wheeler.*

Teachers get many notes from parents. I've been praised, I've been damned. Most I throw away. Why have I kept this one? The audacity of the note is balanced by its overwhelming sincerity. I never showed it to Rachel. She wouldn't have understood. She would have said that it wasn't my job to be the boy's counselor. When someone calls upon your goodness to do something, it's hard to refuse. Besides, what was the likelihood of the boy trying to contact me?

Apparently now the boy has done just that.

What could be troubling him? I toss the note back onto my desk and do my best to ignore it, as I have been doing week after week.

I've laid out Chapter Six and have finally managed to wring one paragraph out of myself that doesn't read like pretentious hot air when I hear a dragging and scraping that sounds like the laundry room door being opened. The door swells in the rain, and has to be tugged or shoved over the uneven cement floor. Someone must be downstairs, on the other side of the wall. I wonder who it is. I assume it's either Omar or Odette, or maybe the woman who takes care of their kids, and I wait to hear footsteps going up into their home above me.

No footsteps.

The sound is not repeated. Whoever came into the laundry room has stayed there.

Finally my curiosity becomes unbearable. What could anyone be doing so quietly for so long down there? I click on Save and push back my chair, leaving the computer to go check out the laundry room.

Opening the kitchen door, I peer into the darkness. If one of the Volkonskys had come down the laundry room stairs, they would have turned on the lights. Beyond the glowing white edges of the washer and dryer, I can see no shadows that look unfamiliar.

I snap on the overhead bulb.

Of course, no one is there. Some nagging doubt makes me walk all the way inside, past the staircase, beyond the big boiler, through the storage area on the other side.

I stop and stare. Someone has swept away the muddy footprints. Not a speck of mud is left. The back door is closed, nothing looks amiss, and I'm about to go back to my work, but I give a cursory glance at the lock to make sure it's bolted.

It's not.

I come to a dead stop, thoroughly puzzled.

Is it possible that someone wasn't coming into the laundry room at all? Is it possible someone had been there all along, and was going *out?*

8
After Class

I go to bed early, bored and alone, and wake up in the middle of the night in an empty bed.

The sight of her untouched pillow causes me a moment of panic. Something's happened. I snap on the light and look at the clock. It's only ten thirty. They've seen their movie and they're having a drink. It's early yet. There's absolutely no reason to worry. Stop acting like a suspicious husband. I turn off the light and try to relax back into sleep.

Gloria is in love with my wife.

Stop. Don't go there. You have absolutely no evidence that Gloria is a lesbian. Besides, Rachel has no sexual interest in women.

I listen for any sounds in the laundry room. I know the door is bolted now, because I slid across the bolt myself. Maybe it's the nanny who forgets to lock it. She only speaks Russian and does most of the cooking and cleaning. Omar and Odette are both professors on campus, with little time left over for children and household chores and silly things like locking basement doors.

Right now the house is silent, except for a nervous rustling of wind chimes on the upstairs porch.

I make myself comfortable in bed again, pull up the electric blanket. I try to peacefully slow down the thudding of my heart. Rachel is fine. Rachel is safe. Rachel will soon be home in bed with me. Rachel has no lesbian inclinations. I'm about to give up on falling back asleep when I wake up this morning to find Rachel in my arms.

I must have slept right through her arrival. I'll never know how long she's been here. But she feels so warm and wonderful, I don't care. I snuggle up against her. The next moment she's sliding away from me, out of reach, out of bed. How can it be that time already?

"Have a good run," I say to her mournfully.

"Whose turn is it to fix breakfast?" she calls from the hallway, as she pulls on her running trunks. "Oh no, it's not mine, is it?" She comes over to the bed and leans over me, kisses my neck, nibbles my ear. "I'm such a bad girl. What would I have to do to convince you to take my turn?"

I bury my face in her breasts, which smell like heaven. "Oatmeal and walnuts, coming up," I murmur into her chest.

It's all hot and ready for her when she gets out of the shower.

"So, how was the movie?" I ask her, sitting across from her at the breakfast table.

"You would have loved it," she says, blowing on a hot spoonful of oatmeal. "Is there any more orange juice?"

"I'll get it," I say, quickly rising from the table. I've finished my breakfast. I scarfed it down. It wasn't exactly that I was so hungry, I just needed something to do with my hands and my mouth.

Love in the American Empire

"The movie gave you something to think about," she says, as I reach over and pour her another glassful. "Talk about timely. That Kinsey, I didn't know much about him. You have to admire the guy. He was brave enough to ask questions and really listen to the answers."

A rumbling sound begins circling the ceiling. It sounds like divine judgment but it's only little Vanya on his new rubber tricycle, riding it around on the wooden floor upstairs while Mommy and Daddy are getting dressed. Rachel and I both ignore it.

It stops suddenly, with a sharp parental command in Russian. Into the breakfast silence, I quietly insert my long-meditated statement. "I noticed last night that the laundry room door was unlocked."

Silence grips the breakfast table.

"Oh, really," says Rachel at last, wiping her mouth on her napkin. "Don't look at me, officer."

"And the day before that, I found muddy footprints."

She looks at me quizzically. "I would laugh, but I can see you don't think you're being funny. Why would that bother you, Colin?"

"Why?" I find her reaction dumbfounding. "Because we have no lock on the kitchen door. If someone can come into the laundry room from outside, they can come directly into our apartment. Whoever leaves that door unlocked is unlocking our house." I can't read her expression. "Do you think I'm being unreasonable?"

Love in the American Empire

She doesn't have to say a word. She kisses me on the cheek, treating me like a child. "I'll mention it to Odette if I see her. She and Omar were putting their stroller downstairs yesterday. Now that little Vanya walks everywhere, they don't need it anymore."

The stroller!

My mind clutches at the idea eagerly. Yes, of course! Omar probably wheeled it in from outside, and forgot to lock the door. Maybe it was too cumbersome for Omar to get it through the door easily. Maybe he had to carry it, and didn't have room or time to wipe his feet. My anxieties are immediately appeased.

Of course, it must have been the landlords.

Rachel's rational voice as she lays this out before me, her logical explanation, completely satisfies my curiosity and drives away that nasty swarm of doubts. There are no dangerous strangers creeping into the laundry room uninvited, lusting after my wife. The only intruder has been Dillon, and he came straight to the front door and asked for me by name.

He's in class this morning, long legs in the aisle, big grin, like a gawking, good-natured country boy. Dillon Wheeler seems so much more intelligent and alive than the other students all around him, he's like a different species. Outside the sky is thick with clouds, so that the sunlight reaching the tall gothic windows here on the third floor of Miller Hall seems to be gray, a light that's not quite clean,

Love in the American Empire

turning the whole room into a black-and-white movie, with one character alone in Technicolor.

First you notice his blue eyes and the bright red blush of his cheeks. Then you notice his gangly body, which is flat and lean and slightly awkward, his immaculate white T-shirt, and then you might notice that his arms and legs are a little long, and his head a bit oversize, and his feet too big.

Dillon listens to every word of the lecture, smiling at my little asides that no one else understands. For a home-schooled kid, this guy has read more classics than any other student in the room. I find myself talking directly to him, knowing he'll understand the difference between Fitzgerald's narrator and Hemingway's, confident that he wants to know the difference between Melville's narrator and Hawthorne's, that he cares about what I'm teaching, that he's read the assignment, that he's taking down my nuggets of wisdom, that he's catching my lame professorial jokes.

This time in class, however, is different than all the others. One thing has changed. Dillon is now a young man who has been alone with my wife, possibly when she was wearing only a bathrobe.

I study his face for a knowing smirk. I evaluate his smile. It seems effortless. I don't doubt it's genuine. Does it still seem quite as refreshing and candid as before? Or has it become a smile of intimate familiarity, of having enjoyed secret pleasures, of having seen what no one else has ever seen but me.

Love in the American Empire

He doesn't leave the room when the bell rings at the end of class, so I don't have to ask him to remain behind. The clattering herd evacuate, a noisy student congestion of mumbling and laughter, merging with other currents of students outside from adjacent classrooms in the hall into a bumping and jabbing mess at the staircase. We're the only two left in the room.

"My wife says you paid us a visit yesterday."

"Dad said you wouldn't mind."

I should just let him ask what he wants to ask, but instead I find myself nudging him into social chatter, asking him how he likes the course, and the reading, and getting him all caught up in book talk. Then I say as casually as I can, "So, what's up, Dillon? What made you come find me?"

He gets up from his desk and hefts his backpack over one shoulder, then slowly approaches the front of the classroom. "Now it doesn't seem like anything much. It was just a bad day. I freaked out."

"What freaked you out?" I ask, sitting back on the corner of my desk, facing him. "Seattle is a pretty tame town as far as big cities go."

"I'm probably just not used to it yet, Professor Wetmore," he says, aware that I'm encouraging him, clearly appreciating it. "I mean, you know my father. Dad did all the teaching around our house – well, Mom helped, too. I've lived all my life in a little town you've never even heard of. Admit it, you've never heard of Rose Bend in eastern Washington."

Love in the American Empire

"Hmm, Rose Bend, huh? Nope, guilty as charged."

We share a chuckle.

"I'm not used to being in classrooms with other people. I'm not used to living with strangers. I've never lived with anyone but my parents. Now I live in a rooming-house. Sometimes I feel like I'm the only one who doesn't understand all the rules."

"Well, you'll catch on to the rules soon enough, Dillon, don't worry about that. But I can tell you right now, that sensation never goes completely away, not even for a public school guy like me. And the rules are always changing. But I know what you mean."

"I knew you would. That's why I came to talk to you."

I can see that he's relaxed enough now to start revealing what's bottled up inside him. Outside the Miller Hall windows, rain clouds are heaving and shifting in the sky, causing waves and shadows in the light. Dillon is shaking a little, trying not to show it.

"Are you cold?"

"No, no, I'm fine. So, I live in a house now up at the end of Greek Row with five other guys."

I laugh. "I'll bet that takes some getting used to," I quip, but I can see he's not laughing.

"I don't know what is weird and what is normal. One of guys cries at night in his room. I can hear him. It's pretty sad."

"That *is* sad. He must cry pretty loudly."

Love in the American Empire

"And this other guy, I hear him beating off every morning in the bathroom."

"You've got to be kidding me."

"He really gets into it. Then there are these other two, they're always yelling at each other."

"Well, that can happen."

"And one guy, he has a girlfriend and she spends the night there a lot and I hear them on the other side of the wall, and everything they do. The whole thing is getting to me. It's too much. Is this normal life in Seattle?"

I can't help but smile. "Well, all the things you described are pretty normal, but it's not normal that you should hear so much. In most places, the walls would give you a little more privacy. Do you have some kind of super-sensitive hearing?"

"Not that I know of. I do have good attention."

"Attention?"

"My father taught me. What it means, really, is learning how to focus completely. When you do it right, you achieve one hundred percent awareness of data."

"No kidding! Sounds like a handy thing to know," I comment blithely. Total awareness of data sounds like something out of a pretentious science fiction movie with flying gunmen. I want to laugh, but I don't.

"Most people don't really listen and don't really see. Most people today dual-task. They pay half-attention. They talk on cell-phones while they shop and drive."

Love in the American Empire

"I couldn't agree more!"

"Attention is a perfect gaze with no distractions."

"I like that." Sounds like he's memorized his Dad's words.

"Attention is the greatest gift you can give to another person," he says confidently. "Dad can do it. Sometimes Mom and I can. Sometimes at night when I'm in bed and can't sleep, I start to pay attention." Just the memory of it troubles him, and changes his tone. "The problem is you learn too much about other people, more than you really want to know."

I'm taken aback. I've never heard a kid his age talk like this. I'm fascinated and repelled. This kid is brilliant and weird, and I think it's a major argument against homeschooling, that kids can become too original and stand out like sore thumbs, with no sense of perspective on how to behave, how to fit in, how to be one of the team, but there's also something exhilarating about his blunt honesty, his relaxed sense of knowing exactly who he is. Peer pressure has been erased from the equation. He's a natural young man who hasn't been taught social limits and boundaries.

"I don't want to know all those private things," he says with a quiet urgency. "I want people to keep their secrets. Sometimes there's so much information coming in, all my circuits jam. Most people are so sad and lonely, really. Don't you think? Yesterday I just overloaded. My circuits fried. I couldn't stand all the sadness and loneliness in that roominghouse. So I went to find you, and instead I found your wife."

Love in the American Empire

He looks at me with misty-eyed admiration, with puppy-dog earnestness. "I just hope someday, Professor Wetmore, I'm as lucky as you are. Your wife is an incredible woman."

He says the words too sincerely. That's not what he's really feeling. He's seething with envy inside, envy and something else. All I have to do is take one look at this young man, and I can see he's fallen head-over-heels in love.

9
Lucas and Grace

Boo is perched on the porch railing like a furry ornamental vase, allowing himself to be admired. He's been inconvenienced by being locked out, and he's putting up with human slowness as I climb up the hillside stairs toward him. I swing open the screen door, then turn the key in the lock and push open the front door, stepping aside to make way for Boo as I always do. Loved ones go first.

To my surprise, Boo won't enter. Something makes him baulk. He sniffs suspiciously at the open doorway, sniffs again, and backs off.

"What is it, Boo?" Usually it's a lunge through the door and a hot-footed charge straight for his bowl in the kitchen. His hesitation is totally out of character. He's giving me the creeps. I step around him and enter the dark apartment cautiously, making sure my shins and the coffee table don't connect, reaching out blindly for the little toggle-switch on the lamp by the reading chair. It blinks on, illuminating an empty living room, an empty kitchen.

"Honey?" I call.

No answer.

Something is weird here, and I can't shake off the feeling. I look around to make sure we haven't been robbed. I know it's just my imagination, but the coffee table seems to be slightly farther away from the sofa than usual. And the cushions on the sofa are arranged oddly, not quite flush.

Boo would rather not enter, but he'll never get fed if he doesn't. He charges through the door, jumps up onto the sofa and swats at me, trying to get my attention and remind me what's important. Then he runs and stares at his empty bowl, hoping he can communicate with a human being as dumb and slow as I am.

"I'm coming, Boo."

The living room positively gives me the creeps. Someone else has been here. Someone has moved the furniture, and then moved it back. I try to laugh it off – Rachel probably vacuumed the carpet and adjusted some of the furniture, and I'm turning it into a dramatic Twilight Zone moment.

While I'm popping the lid off Boo's cat food and plopping a big spoonful into his bowl, the front door swings open and Rachel comes in, closing the door quickly behind her against the cold. If she would look up, she'd see me standing in the kitchen with cat food in hand, but she's looking down at something she's clutching in her fingers until she's halfway across the living room.

She sees me, and flinches backward with a gasp.

"Hey, sorry, didn't mean to scare you," I quickly apologize. I know my wife well enough to see immediately that something is wrong. Whatever it was in her hand that she found so interesting is no longer there. She's quickly hidden it or gotten rid of it. Her usual face, the face I love, is back in place.

"I didn't expect you."

"So I see. Who were you expecting?"

It's our standard exchange, she laughs it off and hangs up her overcoat in the closet, while I put the remaining cat food in the refrigerator and Boo tucks into the juicy contents of his bowl. "Hungry?" I ask. "Anything special you feel like having for dinner?"

"I don't feel like cooking," she says, turning away from the kitchen with a groan. "I vote for take-out. Why don't we just phone China First and I'll go pick it up. I'm going to be cooking tomorrow night."

"What's up tomorrow?"

"Oh, didn't I tell you?" She's looking through our collection of paper menus of nearby restaurants. "I've invited Dillon over for dinner tomorrow night."

"Really?" I say, more than a little surprised. "Well, that was awfully nice of you."

She's already flipped open the menu for China First, and is punching the number into the phone. "Yes, I'd like to place an order to be picked up," she says clearly into the receiver, and then proceeds to list all our favorites, potstickers and barbequed pork, almond fried chicken and subgum chow mein and General Tso's chicken, along with a host of other yummy treats. I notice she's not looking me directly in the eye. This is so unlike Rachel that it gnaws at me.

Love in the American Empire

"Be right back." She grabs the car keys and darts out the front door.

I'm left standing alone in the kitchen, baffled and hurt, trying to understand Rachel's behavior. We don't keep secrets from each other. At least, I didn't think we did. It's not that kind of marriage. This is so unlike her. The house is silent except for Boo's slurpy eating sounds. I never realized until now how noisily he eats.

I grab a handful of wheat crackers and retreat to my computer room. I've been thinking about *First Person American* all day, and especially about what it means to see a story from one point of view. I've decided that a primary genre trait of first person narration is *interpretation failure*, the incorrect diagnosis of what's happening. It's used to set up storytelling surprises, and reflects the primary truth about human interaction. We're just guessing, all the time. We can never really know anyone for sure, not our own servants, not our own husband, not our own wife.

All I can do is clumsily guess at why Rachel won't look me in the eye and why she seems shocked to see me. My mind won't leave the details alone, and I keep going over the clues, and I can guess. Oh, I can guess. But how do you know anything for sure about anyone?

I'm getting more philosophical by the minute when someone knocks at the front door.

Concluding that it's Rachel with the Chinese take-out, that she must have her arms full, I rush to the door and fling it open, ready to take a few hot, white paper boxes into my arms. Instead I'm looking at a nicely dressed, middle-aged white couple who are both smiling at me as though I should recognize them at once. The guy looks like a television anchorman. His wife has long, dirty blond hair and dresses like a little girl.

"Well, hello!" I say, trying to look delighted, trying to look like I know who they are, and then while I'm staring at the vaguely familiar-looking man, he changes before my eyes into my student's father.

"Reverend Wheeler!" I'm stunned to find him standing on my front porch. We shake hands warmly.

"Please, call me Lucas."

"And I'm Colin." I'm surprised to discover how glad I am to see him. "And you must be Grace?" Of course, she is. We shake hands politely, our actual fingers and palms touching as little as possible. The idea that you can just stop in without warning must be an Eastern Washington thing, because here are the parents doing exactly what their son did. "Please, come in. Your son, Dillon – he's incredible. What a fine young man. You must both be very proud."

Grace glows, as though I'm talking about her. "Thank you. Yes, we're very, very proud. Aren't we, Lucas?"

Lucas is smiling broadly, but the man is clearly not light-hearted. He takes a deep breath of air, as though he's going to need an extra supply before going any farther. "We're very proud of him, yes. But we're worried too, Colin. That's why we're here."

They both step inside the house cautiously, as though expecting at any moment for the floor to erupt into hellfire. Lucas puts his hands in his back pockets and surveys the living room, regarding the prominent location of the bed with a raised eyebrow.

"I'm afraid our boy has outgrown Saint Agatha's in Rose Bend," he says. "We've been there five years now. Small congregation, fairly conservative, but generous, very generous. Good people, if small-minded and dull."

"Lucas!" says his wife, mildly scandalized.

"I'm lucky to have a parish. The last one asked me to leave." He hesitates for only a moment. "I married two women. They'd lived together for twenty years. My congregation wasn't quite ready for that. They'd rather I just concentrated on bingo and the raffle." He smiles and shrugs his shoulders. "It's a mistake I make, Colin. I expect people to open their hearts to God." He shakes his head. "There's so much fear. It's our new national pastime. Frightened people make frightened decisions."

Since he doesn't proceed to explain why they're worried about Dillon, I say, "Won't you sit down? Can I get you something to drink?"

Grace smiles uneasily, with an anxious glance toward her husband as she lowers herself into the armchair.

"No, no, we can't stay," says Lucas.

Grace quickly rises back onto her feet and smiles sadly in confirmation. "No, really, we shouldn't. We can't."

"We're driving back to Rose Bend tonight," says Lucas, "and we still have to visit her mother."

"We talked to Dillon last night," says Grace. This comment draws a frown from Lucas, as though the phone call were his information to disseminate and not hers. She quickly cuts off her line of thought, and diverts to, "He thinks the world of both you and your wife. Doesn't he, Lucas?"

"We feel the same about him," I assure her warmly.

"But the phone call we got last night was disturbing," says Lucas. "We've got a few worries about our boy. And I thought, if I could just mention them to you, maybe you could keep your eye out. Dillon seems to find kids his own age slightly boring. He'll relate to you, Colin, I know he will."

His simple assumption of my neighborliness and good intentions plows past all my resistance. I don't believe he has the right to marshal all this extra energy to educate his son, yet somehow his belief in me convinces me.

"He's a great kid. Home schooling really paid off. But, well…" He glances toward his wife, as though expecting a cue card. She gives him a look of blind encouragement. That's all he needs. "He's unprepared for the world, and maybe it's our fault. We may not have warned him enough. He's a man now, and he has a man's needs and a man's thoughts."

Lucas falters. We all feel awkward.

"You mean he's becoming interested in women?"

Love in the American Empire

"Interested in the world, period. He's a little too fascinated by everything that's out there. He's not as open with us anymore. He has secrets. He closes his bedroom door at night."

I'm just about to tell them that it's perfectly normal for an eighteen-year-old boy to close his bedroom door when Grace says urgently, "It's so hard to know when you're going too far. You don't want your child to be fooled or hurt, like any good parents. But maybe we're being over-protective."

"Dillon means the world to us," says Lucas, putting a hand on my shoulder and looking dead-straight into my eyes. "Just be there for him if he has questions. I want to know he has someone on his side."

"He knows he's welcome here," I say, trying to bring them some comfort. "In fact, we're having him over for dinner tomorrow night. Don't worry, I'll keep an eye on him."

"I knew you would." He puts his arm around my shoulder. "I can tell that's the kind of man you are." He glances over his shoulder at his wife. "Maybe you'd better go down to the car and phone Irene. Tell her we'll be on our way in five minutes."

"Here, you can use this phone."

"Her mother's number is on our cell." His tone is decisive. He's asking for a moment alone with me, in the language married people share.

She understands. "It was a pleasure to meet you, Colin." She hurries out the door.

Love in the American Empire

Lucas and I are left alone together. He has a good-humored sparkle in his eye. He sees something across the room that catches his attention, and strolls across the carpet to stand in front of the mantelpiece and hold up a framed picture. "Are you telling me this gorgeous woman is your wife?"

That didn't take long. His eyes are laughing at me. He knows right where to tease me. I take the picture out of his hands and restore it to its place above the fireplace. "You keep your holy thoughts off my gorgeous wife." We laugh together. His laugh is a little heartier than mine.

With a grin that's slightly sadder, he says, "I get the feeling you're still fighting the good fight against God?"

"As long as I don't believe in Him, He can't hurt me."

He's still smiling. "Some people have to fight God to believe in Him."

I grin back at him. "I fight to the finish."

His smile is a sad one, all right. "I wish I could save your damned soul, Colin. Hell, we're all damned these days, what we're doing in Iraq. It's like someone in Washington, D.C. decided that, in spite of Jesus, it was okay to commit murder, as long as you're killing Iraqis. Kill as many thousands of Iraqis as you like."

He pauses for me to say something, but doesn't wait long enough. "I'll tell you one thing for sure. If there's a draft, we're moving to Canada. My wife has dual citizenship. I won't feed my boy into this war machine. I haven't spent eighteen years of my life raising cannon fodder."

Love in the American Empire

"I don't blame you."

"Governments can be brutal idiots," he says. "I expect that. But when they drag Jesus into it, I get mad. Jesus, of all people! The man who said, "Love your enemy." Love him and shoot him? That's the one huge difference between Jesus and Mohammed, you know. Mohammed was a soldier. He was a successful realist. He chopped off Jewish heads. Jesus was the opposite. Jesus was non-violent. At his worst, Jesus overturned some temple trinket-stands. Not a bloodthirsty man. He's the love prophet. Not the Jesus of the United States of America. He's a macho savior in a military muscle-shirt, he's got an AK-47 and he fights to win. We are the most un-Christian country in the world."

He gives a deep sigh, and smiles. "I do get worked up, don't I?" He laughs at himself. "Listen to me! Once the preacher in me gets going, there's no stopping me. Colin, whether you believe in God or not, you're always in my prayers. I better get down to the car." He starts to shake my hand, then surprises me with a brief, impulsive hug. "Take care of my boy, Colin. He's a good kid, a beautiful human being. Be there for him. Don't let anything harm him."

"I'll do my best," I promise, "but Lucas, really, we see the world so differently." I force a laugh. I'm uncertain how to state the obvious. "I mean, think about it. I don't believe in God. How can you trust me with your son?"

Lucas grips me by the shoulder, and looks me in the eye like a vaudeville hypnotist. "I trust you, Colin, because you know what goodness is. You're a lazy intellectual coward and you're certainly not saved, but at least you know that goodness is the only thing that really matters." He pulls open the door and steps outside. "Don't let him make any stupid mistakes."

"I'll do my best," I call after him. "But we *all* make stupid mistakes."

10
Chinese Takeout

I'm still standing out on the porch, shaking my head in amazement at the Wheelers' unexpected visit, watching their car drive away, when Rachel pulls in down below in our ten-year-old white Volvo. She backs in too fast and bumps up on the curb. Clearly she's in a bit of a rush. She doesn't see me watching her as she hurries up the staircase from the street, doing her best not to tip or spill two plastic bags filled with hot, white containers.

She's almost at the top of the stairs before she sees me. "Sorry," she says. "That took longer than I thought."

"What happened?" I say, reaching out to help her carry the cartons. "Really, I'm surprised you didn't just have them deliver." She walks right past me. "Did they get your order mixed up, or something? Do you realize you just missed Dillon's parents?"

"Dillon's parents!" Her headlong rush comes to a dead halt. Her look is one of complete disappointment. "That's not fair!" She carries the cartons into the kitchen. I follow her, a slave to the compelling aromas. Unloading the containers into a precarious, steaming pile on the drainboard, she turns to face me, looks me straight in the eye and says, "Well, I didn't think it would take long. I just dropped off a couple orders over at Dillon's rooming-house."

Love in the American Empire

"You *what?*"

My voice goes up a notch, and she looks at me as though I've insulted her. "You heard me."

"You've got to be kidding me!"

She flinches at the edge in my voice. She was obviously prepared for some kind of volatile response. "Why would I kid you? We've got to keep our eye on him, don't we?" she offers feebly in explanation. "He's like a brave new experiment. The home-schooled child. We all need to help."

I'm so dumbfounded and angry that I want to shout at her, to say that Dillon has nothing to do with her, that he's my student and I'll be the one to take care of him, thank you. Instead I say, "Why didn't you tell me?"

She can see that I'm upset. "I don't know," she wails, and I get the weird feeling that she really might not, that I'm being unreasonable. "We talked about nutrition. He was living on energy bars and pizza coupons. I didn't mean to upset you. I wanted to surprise you."

"Well, you certainly did *that*. When exactly did you two discuss food?"

"The afternoon we met. The day he came here looking for you. We talked about a lot of things. He poured out his little heart."

This only makes me more uncomfortable.

"Don't tell me," I say. "I don't want to know."

She'd do anything to get us off this painful subject and back to the matter at hand. In self-defense, she snaps open the white flaps of one steaming carton. A dribble of brown sauce escapes from the General Tso's chicken. "Are you still hungry?"

"I'm starving." The aromas now fill the house. I put plates on the kitchen table, silverware and a couple serving spoons, and we begin unfolding the flaps and diving into the boxes. Fried rice, egg rolls, mu shu pork, soon I've got a plateful and I'm shoveling it in. I'm going into food bliss. I'm blocking out unpleasant thoughts. I'm trying to forget that my wife just delivered Chinese food to one of my students.

I can't get it out of my head. Something's wrong with this picture. I mean, this throws me. I never saw this coming. I'm delighted that she cares about him, I care about him too, but why the secrecy? She's not being straightforward with me, or I would have known what she was feeling and where she was going.

For some reason, she's not telling me the whole truth.

We both shake our heads, smiling sadly at the mishap, commiserating that Dillon's parents and Dillon's takeout happened simultaneously, that one caused her to miss the other. Underneath the sad smiles, however, I'm baffled. For a long, awkward minute or two there's nothing to say, just the horrible wet crunch of chewing.

"And you had no warning that they were going to pay you a visit?" she remarks at last. "I'm surprised they didn't call first."

"They're just staying down at the Silver Cloud Inn."

Love in the American Empire

"Well, they've clearly elected you to watch over their son? Do they want you to tutor him, too?"

"Now, now, of course not." I suppose it is an imposition, but I didn't take it that way. I like noticing how people act when they become parents. Maybe it's because I'll never be one myself. I don't mind lending a hand. It's a privilege to shape a young mind. "They're just nervous about their kid going to school on the other side of the state," I say, wrapping another mu-shu pancake around a heaping spoonful of filling. I'm making a bit of a mess, but it tastes so good, I don't care. "They're very protective. Lucas just wants me to keep an eye on him, that's all."

"You'd think he'd turn to a Christian friend." She thinks about that for a moment, spearing a chunk of eggroll. "But I suppose if a man needed to trust someone," she says, and then instead of popping the eggroll into her mouth, she catches me by surprise with a kiss, "you'd be a good man to choose."

I poke around in the last of my fried rice. Boo would lighten things up nicely right about now, but he's nowhere to be seen. Finally I can't take the awkward stillness. I ask the question that's gnawing at the corners of my mind. "So, um, how did you know where he lived?"

She tips her head back, giving me a curious look. "He told me about his rooming-house the very first time he came here," she says, shrugging it off with a smile. "He just mentioned it in passing, but I remembered the house because

Love in the American Empire

I've seen it on the corner there, sort of a faded yellow with a big porch. Do you know the one I mean?"

I didn't. "So, what's it like inside?" I try to take a deep breath and skip over the exasperating secrecy of it all. I'm curious what kind of place Lucas would allow his son to rent.

"Well, there's a cross on the front door, for starters," says Rachel. "So it's got some kind of religious affiliation, but I didn't stop to ask. Once you get past that, it's pretty normal. Smells like a boys' locker room, looks like you would expect, newspapers lying around with pizza boxes, not enough furniture. The kind of place where no one stays long enough to put up a poster. Three of the guys were in the living room watching a basketball game. Dillon's room is upstairs, the smallest room."

How did she know that? Did she ask someone? I wanted to ask if she'd gone up to his room. I was afraid to ask. Of course, she didn't go up to his room. I'm being ridiculous. How can I seriously think for one second that my wife could be interested in a student?

"You should have seen his face when he opened the door and saw the Chinese food."

"The door?" I repeat lamely. "You went up to his room?"

"How else was I supposed to give it to him? I couldn't very well leave it with his housemates, could I? You should have seen him. His eyes got this big." She smiles, remembering. "He was like instantly twelve years old and starving. He pretended like he was a big dog, barking and panting in excitement." She cracks up. "Then he tried to do the whole chopsticks thing, but he wasn't getting enough in his mouth that way, the rice kept dribbling out between the sticks..." She's laughing. His failed efforts strike her as charming. I don't find them so delightful. It's just the uncomfortable clowning around of a nervous adolescent male, courting and enjoying the attentions of a beautiful woman.

I'm wiping my hands, finger by finger, on one of the crumpled paper napkins stuffed in the bottom of the plastic takeout bag. The house around us suddenly seems so vast and empty that it echoes. She's wiping her hands, too. She's about to rise and take our plates to the kitchen sink. This is the time, if I'm going to ask her. When you've shared complete openness with someone, anything less feels fake, and both of you know it. We know there's something unspoken between us. I'm the one who cracks first. I always crack first.

"Rachel, are you hiding something from me?"

She's smiling with a look of complete amazement, but I also notice that she's not looking straight at me, but at another Colin just over my shoulder. What does she think I'll see if she lets me look directly into her eyes?

"Hiding something?" She makes it sound completely far-fetched, like I've asked if she's from another planet. "What would I hide?"

Which, of course, doesn't answer my question.

Love in the American Empire

I'm frustrated that I've mentioned it, but now that I've started I want her to understand me and answer me. "Usually we're on the same page. We don't have any secrets. Lately I keep feeling like you're holding something back, like there's something you're not telling me."

"Really?" She's up and on her feet, clearing the table, emptying the last of the white cartons into little Tupperware containers. "The only things I don't tell you aren't worth telling."

The topic is dropped, but a few minutes later she interrupts the scraping of serving spoons and the snap of Tupperware lids with, "What made you think I was hiding something?" She sits down in the kitchen chair and pulls it up close to me, so that her knees are bumping against mine.

How do you sum up a dozen clues and make sense? "You don't look me in the eye anymore when you talk to me."

She looks straight into my eyes. "Don't I?" A smile is hovering on the edge of her lips. "How's that? Look in my eyes right now. What do you see? Go on, tell me."

I don't have an answer, so I kiss her.

"Is that what you see, or what you *want* to see?"

I kiss her again.

"Colin, I try to always be honest with you, but no wife tells her husband everything. People who love each other lie all the time. That's part of love."

"But that's so wrong," I interrupt her. "If you love someone, they deserve the truth."

Love in the American Empire

"If you love someone," she replies, eye to eye, "you don't want to hurt his feelings. You protect him from every unnecessary heartache. Do you want to know each time I get a sexual heat wave from some guy with a hunky body?"

I gulp. "I didn't know you did."

"I rest my case. You're better off not knowing."

"But that can't be true." I'm too idealistic to accept it. "Honesty is the greatest gift you can give someone. I want to believe that you're always telling me the truth."

"How can a smart man be so blind?" she says in exasperation. She regrets it at once, and takes me into her arms. "Listen, sometimes you can know a person so well you realize they don't really want to know the truth. Deep down inside, they can't take it. Why torture someone with the truth if they don't need to know it? Do you think I want you to worry? I love you, Colin. I want that anxious little heart of yours to be happy."

We go to bed early.

I can't sleep.

I lay awake long into the night, pondering this new conviction that a secret place inside my wife is now closed to me, that there's a part of her I'm no longer allowed to see, or worse, that it's been there all along, that this is only the first of many deceptions opening up beneath me like treacherous potholes of deceit.

I try to believe in her, as we curl up into our usual spooning position. Sometimes we talk in bed, but not tonight.

Love in the American Empire

She's all tangled up in thoughts of her own, thoughts she's not willing to share, and they're clearly too heavy to sustain consciousness, because she's soon breathing heavily and deeply. I'm left with her sleeping body in my arms and my own preoccupations.

Like Dillon, for instance. What am I going to do with that boy? How can I explain to Lucas that his son can't write papers that come to a conclusion?

After all of our talking, after two long office meetings, his third paper, "Sexual Betrayal as Confessional," was just more of the same. Eleven bright, original insights into five books, unrelated. Did Lucas not teach him how to think for himself? Why can't I reach Dillon when I try to tell him how to shape a literary argument?

His first paper, "The Justice of Noir," was excellently written. And it certainly contained a number of provocative thoughts, but it was just bright chunks of literary thinking on Dashiell Hammett, Raymond Chandler, and Jim Thompson that didn't add up to anything. His second paper, "Honesty in the First Person," was better written, with several startling observations, but it was another Frankenstein of sewn-together parts, an arm from Henry James, a leg from Mark Twain.

That's when we had our first conference. I remember he was actually nervous in my office. He kept warming up his hands by boyishly rubbing them back and forth between his knees, as though sufficient friction could ease the prickling of his nerves.

Love in the American Empire

"Dillon, you're not listening to me. The point of writing a paper is for you to take a position on a work of literature, and show how you reached your conclusion. It's meant to be stimulating and provocative, but most of all it's meant to be arguably right."

We chuckled together. That was good.

"Which means you need to think about an author's choices, and why he makes them. You point out fascinating observations on these books, each in their own way, but for some reason, you don't put those thoughts together. You don't arrive at a truth. You don't come to a conclusion. And that, my friend, is what papers are all about."

He didn't seem to grasp a word. It was like trying to explain how an abacus works. Now I lay here staring up at the dark bedroom ceiling, trying to think how to reach him, warmed by Rachel's body up against me, listening to us breathing together, our hearts pounding together. Slowly Dillon fades from my mind. There's just Rachel.

I don't ever want to let go of her.

I feel something wet on my hand. It's her cheek. She's crying in her sleep again.

11
Bed of Coats

It's a dark, overcast Friday morning, the heat has just turned on, and I know from going to the bathroom during the night that the floorboards are graveyard cold. Either I'm sleeping very deeply or Rachel is extremely considerate getting out of bed for her daily run, because I don't wake up until she's back and I hear the shower turn on, the gurgle in the pipes, the drone of splattering. When she comes out to the bed, still drying herself, to wake her sleepyhead husband, she's unprepared for my suddenly grabbing her and dragging her down under the electric blanket.

"Colin, don't, I just showered."

"I'm not going to get you dirty. Well, not too dirty."

"You've got to get up so we can go to work."

"Let's not go to work. Let's stay home and play."

She laughs at me and tries to point out logical objections, but I kiss those sweet objections right off her lips. She feels so good I want to be all over her at once. The idea of leaving my warm, naked wife and facing the morning, of giving up our bed to march with her into that icy November wind on our way up to campus, has never seemed less appealing. Why leave behind what life is all about?

After seven years together, the rightness of our marriage has become painfully clear. I'll never want anyone else. Rachel is the one. I remember the exact day when our months of dating came to an end.

We were at a party, I remember, a girlfriend's house, someone who used to work at the bookstore. The party was winding down, but our craziness for each other had mounted to the breaking point. We were faster and skinnier then, hotter and prettier, ripped on *something* but it's hard to remember exactly what, out of our minds with desire for each other.

The party had been slowly ending for several hours. Rachel and I had kept ourselves patiently under control, but then we had one last drink. We couldn't hold out any longer. We'd retreated as far as we could get, to an upstairs bedroom, ostensibly to get our coats so we could leave, and that's where we jumped each other. A poor choice, since it was the one room where everyone would have to go, sooner or later. There we were, grappling and thrashing on a mound of overcoats, with the last of the guests tiptoeing in and out, discreetly removing their coats from our tangled limbs before they could leave. We were unstoppable. We couldn't get enough of each other. It was the kind of wild crazy sex where it's like you're stuck in gear and there's no off-switch. We were both dripping with sweat and gasping for breath when she got a serious look on her face and said, "Colin, would you ever cheat on me?"

That brought us both to a screeching halt.

"Why in the world would you ask me that?" I laughed in shock. "Of course not! I'd have to be insane to even *think* about cheating on you. I'd be lucky to have you."

Love in the American Empire

She was obviously pleased to hear my answer, but that was not the one she was looking for. "Oh, come on, now. You're still a man, sweetie, and we all know what *that* means. Don't pretend you're a saint. You've got a penis just like any other man."

"But my penis would be the slave of Yours Truly."

"Surely your eye must wander once in a while."

Many men would have taken this as permission to tell the truth and confess their sins. I would have stepped right up to the plate myself except that I didn't have any sins to confess. I had no motive. Why would I want to risk losing perfection? "Really, Rachel, there are many things I could want in life, and I do, but a smarter, kinder, sexier woman I could not possibly find. I've found the perfect woman for me. I'm smart enough to know that. You're the one I want for the rest of my life."

We kissed and snuggled, and rolled around in the last of the coats. She was aroused. But she wasn't satisfied. She was chewing something over inside, I could tell, and her lower lip trembled as though she were fighting not to break into tears. She pulled away just enough to say, "If I ever found out you were cheating on me, I'd be destroyed."

Her quiet passion left me shaking.

"Well, I think I can honestly say you never will, sweetheart – never, ever, ever." Had someone at the party been telling lies about me? I couldn't figure out what was causing this or where it was leading, but I kissed her on the nose, on the lips, on the chin.

That was the worst thing I could have done.

Now tears were running down her cheeks. She grabbed the sleeve of someone's coat and wiped her eyes. "Don't ever lie to me, Colin. I'm begging you. Don't ever, ever lie." She opened her mouth like she was going to go on and tell me something else, extract some further promise, and then got choked up and couldn't talk. She was extremely troubled about something, and nothing I said could bring her peace.

"If you ever... ever..." Her voice was wet with emotion. "I don't know how I could forgive that."

"You'll never *have* to forgive that," I assured her, and then repeated it a few times. "I've never lied to you, sweetheart. And I never will."

But my words didn't comfort her. The more I reassured her, the more miserable it seemed to make her. "If you ever cheat on me, Colin, I'll never forgive you. Never! Once you break your word, I'll always wonder if you're lying."

"But I'll never break my word," I said ardently. "Listen, you're the one I want. I've made my decision. It's you. It will always be you. Marry me, Rachel."

She smiles at me. "You big dummy, we're already married."

I blink. The bed heaped with coats is gone.

It's morning, I'm in my own bed seven years later, and my wife is pulling away from me, scrambling out of the blankets. "Now, come on," she says, hurrying down the hall toward the bathroom. "Start getting ready, or we'll be late for work."

I shower and dress, but my mind is elsewhere. We walk up to campus together without exchanging a word. We took a vow to tell each other the truth. Up until now, we always have. Haven't we?

Love in the American Empire

12
In the Shower

Some days teaching is pure joy.

Today is not one of those days. First of all, half the class is missing. Why? Because it's Friday. Many teachers don't teach on Fridays, a shabby habit of lazy teachers in general and the English Department in particular. Well, I teach five days a week. If you're not here, you miss out.

Unfortunately, those who actually come to class all too frequently arrive late. They interrupt my lecture. They drop water bottles. They bump the knees of their neighbors. They step on pens. Their cell phones go off. My patience quickly comes to an end. No one is learning. No hands go up.

To make matters worse, Dillon is mysteriously absent. A strange way for your evening's guest to behave. So, now I'm talking to myself, because as for the rest of the class, no one is listening. No one is thinking. No one has read the material. And no one cares.

My graduate seminar is no better. My graduate students are so full of their own importance they don't need to read the text anymore. Why let the facts get in the way of creative thinking? Then a department faculty meeting reaches unprecedented levels of stupefying boredom and mismanaged time. My office hours are wasted on students who aren't interested in literature in the slightest.

Love in the American Empire

I come home in a funk. My career feels ridiculous and useless. A teen slasher movie sounds refreshing.

I hope the victims are students.

The living room is too dark – Rachel forgot to pull the drapes this morning. I grab the drawstring and yank them open, letting in a tidal wave of light. Her clothes are in a mess on the floor. I try not to notice them. Then I hear the sound of the shower running in the bathroom.

"Honey?"

Obviously with the shower running she can't hear me. Another shower! My, what a clean wife I have. A shower is a great idea. She beat me to the punch. After a stressful day, a stream of hot water can be so physically soothing, so redemptive.

Not to mention a shower with Rachel in it – that sounds like heaven. The day has been frustrating enough that the thought of holding the naked body of my wife in my arms under the shower is instantly arousing. I'm getting hard. Nature knows best.

I drop my backpack on the bed, quickly pull off my shirt, kick off my shoes, drop my pants outside the bathroom door, tug free of my underwear, leave my stockings behind in hot little wads, and walk quietly barefoot across the linoleum tiles of the bathroom floor. The mirrors are steamed. The splattering conceals all sound. I can see her shadow on the other side of the shower curtain. She has no idea that her husband is in the bathroom with her, separated from her only by a translucent sheet of wet plastic.

I step up to the curtain and yank it aside.

Standing naked in the shower is Dillon.

I shout, "Aaaah!"

He shouts, "Aaaah!"

Horrified, I jerk back the shower curtain between us. My heart is pounding so loudly I can hardly think straight.

"What the hell is going on?" he shouts.

"What do you think you're doing?" I shout in reply. I stumble backward, nearly falling on the slippery wet tiles, rushing out of the bathroom to snatch up my pants off the floor, nearly tripping in my eagerness to get my feet into the pant holes and tug them up my legs and somehow get them buttoned shut without hurting myself.

He turns the water off. A dreadful stillness grips the bathroom. Neither of us budges. I should get out of there immediately, but I can't until I explain myself, and I'm so angry and embarrassed I can hardly think straight, much less speak, so that we're both waiting for the other to talk first.

"Please, will you hand me a towel?" he says at last, from behind the shower curtain.

"Of course!" I pull a towel off the rack, and three more towels tumble off the rack with it. One falls into the toilet bowl. I ignore it. His wet hand reaches out from behind the curtain, and I put the towel into his grip without human contact.

Love in the American Empire

"Dillon, please, tell me at once what you're doing in my shower," I manage to say with some dignity and authority.

He looks out from behind the shower curtain, and I can see that he's got tears in his eyes, he's so mad. "What am I doing? What am I doing?" He repeats this several times. He's trying to laugh, but he's more upset than that. "What do you *think* I'm doing? I'm taking a shower!"

"Well, how was I supposed to know that? I thought you were my wife. Speaking of my wife, where is she?"

The shower curtain bumps and jiggles as he dries himself industriously. "Gone to get butter and mushrooms, Professor Wetmore. You scared me. I thought for sure I was being attacked. I just saw a movie last week about a man who went after boys. I wasn't sure I'd like it."

Oh, God. "Well, of course you wouldn't like it. No one likes being attacked."

He yanks the shower curtain aside. The towel is securely wrapped around his waist. "Were you attacking me, Professor Wetmore?"

"Lord, no! Please, let's change the topic. We can discuss this some other time, Dillon."

He steps carefully out of the shower, keeping his steps small so as not to loosen the towel. "I thought maybe you were gay, Professor Wetmore."

Ouch. "Oh, really?" I clear my throat. Okay, take it in stride. I'm lean and well-maintained, I don't have a gut and care what I look like, I read books and have feelings, I can talk

English. Sure, I can see that I might confuse some people. "Well, even if I *were* gay, that's not the point, Dillon. Attacking someone in the shower is just plain wrong, whatever you are."

"But you *weren't* attacking me, were you?"

"Of course not!"

"Well, then," he says, and shrugs.

Somehow I don't feel I've made the situation any clearer. What's worse, I feel like I've cornered him in the bathroom. I need to pull on a shirt and some shoes, and get out of his way. I take a step backward toward the door.

"Dad says there are lots of gay men in Seattle."

Ah, so Lucas has been warning him! "Well, yes, your father's right, there are." I wonder what exactly Lucas has told his son.

He runs his fingers through his wet hair, regarding himself in the steamed mirror. "Do you know many gay men, Professor Wetmore?"

"Well, yes, I do," I say in answer. This appears to be the subject that's troubling him, and I need to be clear with him right from the start. "Gayness is nothing to be afraid of, Dillon. I know your father is religious, but I hope he never told you that gayness was a sin."

"Dad was the only guy who voted for gay marriage in our church," he says proudly.

"Good for him. Okay, well, a boy who looks – well, who looks like you, for instance, will always attract a lot of gay attention. And you may be surprised to find some gay men turn out to be the best friends in your life. Always take it as a compliment. And if one ever gets a little carried away, you can always tell him no in a polite way."

"Why do you think I should tell him no?"

"You should tell him no if he makes you feel uncomfortable," I try to clarify, trying not to look too carefully at my own past. "You can tell him whatever you like." He's leaving little puddles of water on the floor where someone could slip and fall. "Uh, Dillon, this is an odd conversation to be having while you're standing naked in my bathroom."

He laughs. "You're funny, Professor Wetmore."

I smile tightly. "I don't mean to be. If you don't mind my asking again, why exactly are you taking a shower in my house?" I try to ask this in a casual, civilized manner.

"Sorry, Professor Wetmore." His cheeks get redder. "It was your wife's idea, really. She's very kind, and she knows – well, that it bothers me what happens in our bathroom at the rooming-house which makes me not want to shower there."

I don't want to know what happens in the bathroom at his rooming-house.

"And so Rachel offered to let you shower here? Well, that was very kind of her." I'm trying to believe it. It's possible. She's kind-hearted. She's maternal. It could easily be the truth.

"You've got a very nice shower, Professor Wetmore," he says. "And a very nice wife. Thanks for letting me use it." He immediately clarifies, "The shower, I mean."

It would be funny if it weren't so pathetic. "You're very welcome, Dillon. Okay, well, I'm going to leave the bathroom now." I back out the door and start down the hall, toward the shirt I pulled off and tossed on the bed

Tightening the towel securely around himself, he follows me out into the living room. I pause at the bed until I'm dressed, but he heads straight out past the coffee table to where the curtains are wide open. At first I don't know what he's doing, but he's sure making no attempt to be discreet.

I snatch up my shirt off the bed, and as I'm tugging it down over my head, I say, "Hey, man, the curtains are wide open. What are you doing? Dillon, get back here. You're practically naked."

"Yes, I know."

"But the curtains are wide open."

"Yes, I know. They were closed before. Someone's opened them." He points helplessly toward the clothing-strewn armchair by the front window. "My clothes are right there."

"I'll get them for you."

"That's all right. I can get them."

"But I've got clothes on!"

We both lunge toward the clothes at the same time, and collide. "I'm sorry, Professor Wetmore. I didn't know you'd be coming home, or I wouldn't have left my clothes all over the place."

I'm rattled and irritated and, quite frankly, unnerved. "Well, this is all my wife's idea, but it's too late now." I snatch pieces of his clothing off the armchair – his undershorts, his jeans, his turtleneck pullover. He grabs them out of my hands.

"Sorry," he says. He starts to pull on the turtleneck, but it's inside-out so he has to pull it back off again.

"Get over here, Dillon! What are you thinking? You don't walk around like that in front of open windows…"

He's pulling the turtleneck off his head, but for a brief moment it's stuck on his chin and during that moment he's actually heading toward the window rather than away. I'm trying to tug him in the other direction. I'm gripping his arm and give him a yank.

One foot catches on a leg of the coffee table.

He seems to lose his balance and comes with the yank. I'm ready to catch him, but not expecting to catch him quite so hard, so it knocks me off-balance and his towel pulls loose. It drops to the carpet. He shouts. I shout. Then I hear the dreadful sound of laughter.

Slowly I turn.

With little mittened hands pressed up flat against the glass, with red noses squished to the window, Ilya and Vanya are trying to get a closer look, giggling at the sight of their neighbor wrestling with a naked boy.

Love in the American Empire

"Oh, God, no. Please, Dillon, immediately put on your clothes.'

"They're just kids."

"They're my landlord's kids. I don't want them telling their father that I've got a naked boy down here."

"Why?"

"Why?" I'm sputtering in frustrated disbelief that he can ask such a stupid question. His innocence is losing its charm. "Because I don't want them to think I'm cheating on my wife and playing with boys, that's why. It matters what your landlord thinks."

"Even if he's wrong?"

I sigh. "Let me tell you something, Dillon. You will have many landlords in your life, and your landlord will almost always be wrong. That doesn't matter. What he thinks still matters. Right or wrong, he's your landlord. And what your wife thinks, that also matters. And what the English Department at the University of Washington thinks, that also matters. So please, please, please put on your clothes."

13
Dinner with Dillon

Fully dressed like a normal dinner guest, Dillon joins me in the living room to have a normal conversation.

It's way too late for that.

Just the sight of his wet hair reminds me of our incident in the bathroom, which promptly short-circuits every other thought in my mind. All we can do is try to get through the time until Rachel gets back from the supermarket. Unfortunately, we're off to a very bad start.

"How do you like the feeling of being in a classroom?"

"It's fine."

"Do you like learning with other students?"

"I'm getting used to it."

"Has Seattle been treating you a little better?"

"Yeah, it's been better."

Finally we both just give up trying. I make myself comfortable on the sofa. Dillon settles into the depths of the armchair. We're both reduced to smiling at each other politely and hoping that Rachel will walk in the door with the butter and mushrooms any minute.

"How long can butter and mushrooms take?"

Something black and white comes hurtling at the window.

Love in the American Empire

It's Boo landing on the windowsill, demanding to be let inside. The minute I unlock the front door and open the screen a few inches, he wriggles through. But instead of bee-lining for his food bowl, something else has gripped his feline attention. Boo heads straight for Dillon, audibly purring. He jumps up on the table beside him, butting up against Dillon with his head, boinking Dillon's cheek with his nose, poking at Dillon's forehead.

"I can't believe what I'm seeing," I have to admit. "He's never this friendly to anyone except Rachel and me."

Boo has made himself comfortable in Dillon's lap.

"Cats like me," says Dillon.

"So I see."

"I've got two. Yin and Yang. They taught me how to be still. Cats love stillness." Boo has rolled over onto his back, his paws extended in feline bliss. Dillon massages the cat's tummy, scratches his jaw and the back of his ears. I've never seen Boo react like this to anyone. "I didn't know what language was, really, until Yang showed me how to talk with his tail. My cats and I have worked up a secret language together. Sit here, go there, scratch here. It's all language. Cat-watching is a science. Believe me, they're watching *us*. All the time. Did you know a cat's senses are just as alert when they're asleep as when they're awake? And that whole thing about them being scaredy-cats? Bullshit. They're not scared. They're just hyper-vigilant."

If Boo purrs any louder he'll be singing.

Love in the American Empire

I'm tempted to get him off the subject of cats and ask him why he never showed up in class this morning. Ultimately I decide it's none of my business, but nevertheless hope he'll offer some explanation. None is forthcoming.

We keep waiting.

"Can I offer you some wine?" I say, knowing he'll refuse but desperately needing a glass myself.

"Yes, thank you."

His polite acceptance catches me by surprise. That doesn't slow me down reaching for the bottle. I pour a chilled white. We click our glasses. "To your new life in Seattle." I raise my glass to my lips. Dillon downs his wine in five big swallows, and puts the glass down empty.

"Well, I see your father has introduced you to wine," I say, refilling his glass.

"Not really. My father doesn't drink."

I watch him knocking off his second glass. He tips back his head and drains it. He holds out his empty glass for a refill. Okay, now this is starting to worry me. I wonder if he'd be insulted if I warned him not to drink quite so fast. I certainly hope I'm not introducing him to alcohol. Good professors do not get their students drunk. Mercifully the phone rings and interrupts this train of thought.

While I'm reaching for the phone, he pours himself another glass.

"Listen, eat without me. I'm not coming home."

Love in the American Empire

"You're *what?*" I try to keep the sheer exasperation out of my voice, but this was Rachel's idea in the first place. "Why not? Dillon is here. We're waiting for you."

"I can't get into it right now, but I'm at Dario's house." She says something to someone in the background, and I hear another voice. Then she's back. "Okay, I can talk now. Dario got very depressed today after I left work. I got a call from the bookstore just as I was leaving to pick up the mushrooms and butter. Dillon was already in the shower. I figured it would only take a minute or two. I drove Dario home. He was in pretty bad shape. I'm going to spend the night here."

"You're sleeping at Dario's? But why?"

"He needs someone tonight, Colin. It's just for one night. I'll be home tomorrow morning. Everything will be fine, hon. I'll explain it all to you later. It's a very sensitive subject." She whispers. "I just don't trust him alone right now."

"Another one of his dramatic performances."

"Oh, come on, don't be so hard on him, Colin. I don't know for sure, but I think Dario has a crush on someone."

Dillon has just drained his third glass of wine. I notice he's looking at the wine bottle. I need to get off the phone.

"A crush? That doesn't make sense. Why would a crush make anyone depressed?"

"Maybe he's got low self-esteem. Maybe he's fallen for someone he can't possibly have. I'm just guessing. You'd think it would make someone happy, but that shows how little

Love in the American Empire

I know. All I can say is he needs a friend right now. So I'm going to spend the night here."

It's a huge re-arrangement, and a lot of baloney to swallow. I manage to swallow it. "Okay, hon. I'll explain to Dillon. I'm sure he'll understand. We'll have him over for dinner some other time."

"Don't be silly. You don't need me. Dinner is all ready for you boys. You can fix the rest of it yourselves. Half the garlic bread already has butter, so just use that half. There won't be any mushrooms in the salad or in the sauce, but he probably doesn't like mushrooms, anyway. All you boys have to do is boil water and put in the pasta. I'll bet you're up to the task, aren't you, chef?"

"I think we can manage that much." I feel abandoned, like an understudy forced to go onstage with his lines only half-memorized. To spend an evening with a student rather than with my wife makes me feel desperate, stranded, abandoned. "I love you."

"I love you too, sweetie. Don't be mad at me."

"I'm not mad. I'll just be lonely in bed."

"Tell Dillon he can spend the night."

"That's not funny, Rachel, not funny at all. Don't even joke about that, please."

We say a few other endearments that are no one else's business, and then say good night. I can feel Dillon's eyes on me as I beep the disconnect. "So, do you do much cooking?"

"None," he says, with a grin and a shrug.

Love in the American Empire

"Just as I thought. Well, you're about to get some free tips on survival as a healthy bachelor. College 101: Boiling Water for Pasta."

He manages to dislodge Boo from his lap and follows me into the kitchen, where we make a go of it. I've had worse dinner companions. He's a good kid, a little in-your-face, a little exasperating, no social finesse or conversation skills but he doesn't have a bad intention in his heart.

Our pasta-boiling is a success. Rachel's sauce is one of her best. We take the garlic bread out of the oven at exactly the right time. Our cooking efforts are complicated by Boo, who is constantly underfoot and will not leave Dillon alone. Together Dillon and I set the table. I try to treat him the way Rachel would have treated him. I give him a super-big serving, showing him how to apply the freshly-grated pecorino romano, warning him not to splatter sauce on his clothes since the stain will never come out.

For two non-Italians, we eat like kings. We both have second helpings, and limit our comments to the simple, honest patter of dining.

"Here, go ahead, there's one piece left."

"Thanks, Professor Wetmore."

"How about some more salad?"

"No, no, I couldn't. Really. Well, okay."

"There's enough for us each to have one more glass of wine."

"No thanks. Besides, I'm one ahead of you."

Love in the American Empire

I'm just pouring the last of the bottle into my wineglass when the rubber tricycle begins rolling around and around upstairs above us on the hardwood floors. It's an unpleasant reminder.

"I wonder if they've told their parents yet?"

He pretends like he doesn't hear me.

"Tell me, Professor Wetmore," he says, using his napkin to wipe stray flecks of tomato sauce from his lips, "what is it like to be friends with a gay man?"

Occasionally this young man startles me, as he just did now, but I find his candor refreshing. "Well, for starters I would say, I've had many gay friends, and I can tell you right now, Dillon, every single one of them is different. Some are silly and some are smart, some are like girls, some are like truck drivers. Why do you ask?"

His crackling bite into the garlic bread leaves crumbs on his lips, which he brushes away with the back of his hand. "Did having gay friends give you gay thoughts?"

"Hardly." I smile indulgently. "As you can see for yourself, I'm a married man." My words sound unconvincing, even to me.

"Did you ever try anything with your gay friends?"

"You mean, something sexual?" I try to say it casually, to sound worldly and experienced, but my voice squeaks like a nervous teenager. I'm panicking because I realize I have no intention of lying. "Most guys, sooner or later in life, try something. I had one pal back in my college days, a couple of times we beat off together."

"Was he gay?"

"Actually, no. Neither of us was. Just two horny straight boys whacking off while we talked about girls. Any time you make friends with anyone, you're liable to end up in bed with them. The older you get, the more you learn about boundaries. You don't let those kind of things happen."

"Why not?"

I think this conversation has gone far enough. "I hope you saved some room for dessert."

Dillon acts like he didn't hear me, or like I'm speaking a different language. "The reason I'm asking you," he persists, "is that I think I may have attracted one."

"One what?"

"A gay person," he explains patiently. "What does it mean when some guy keeps staring at you, no matter where you go in the room, and sometimes he gives you little looks, and sometimes little smiles, and sometimes scowls, like you're bugging him, and sometimes acts like he's going to jump you at any minute."

"Well, you're right," I say. "Sounds like you've attracted one. Those are all the signs."

"Do I have to be careful?"

"Usually there's no danger at all. In fact, usually the greatest danger is that the gay man's feelings will be hurt."

Love in the American Empire

"I won't hurt his feelings," says Dillon. "I mean he seems nice. It's just that he's always watching me, and he keeps smiling at me and asking if he can help me every time I go in the bookstore."

"Did you say in the bookstore?"

"Do you know the guy I mean?"

"Oh, my God."

With all the wine he's been drinking tonight, I know it's only a matter of time before Dillon will have to use the bathroom, and as soon as the door is closed behind him I grab the phone to call Rachel and tell her my unexpected discovery. Dario's phone number is easy to find, listed on the front page of her little book.

The phone rings and rings. No one answers.

I must have dialed wrong. I hang up and dial again.

No answer.

There's no reason to panic. I'm panicking. Where is my wife? If she isn't at Dario's, where could she be? Stay calm, Colin. There's some perfectly logical explanation for this.

"Professor Wetmore, should I go home now?" Dillon is back from the bathroom and standing in front of me, Boo nestled in his arms.

I snap out of it. "Dillon, forgive me," I say quite sincerely, and hang up. "Yes, you should probably go home and study now, but I haven't been a very good host. My wife is the friendly, outgoing one. I'm the unsocial one. But I want to say that I do like you. You're smart and honest. I appreciate that. Sometimes I'm a little shy with people, but it's not your fault. You're always welcome here. And next time you use our shower, I won't attack you."

We both burst out laughing. The laugh is short and surprised, but utterly genuine. It's the best moment of the night.

14
A Walk to the Rooming-House

The minute Dillon walks out the door, I feel exhausted. But at least the week is over, the ordeal of lectures, the business of wisdom. I turn on the electric blanket, sweep the electric toothbrush through my mouth for a once-over, pop out my contact lenses, and beat Boo to the best place in the middle of the bed.

I try to pretend that Rachel is stretched out beside me.

I wake up Saturday morning whispering to Rachel how much I love her. The woman in my arms listening to my romantic whispers turns out to be part pillow, part cat. Rachel will be home soon, and then heading right back out the door on her morning run. No need for me to waste this opportunity to sleep in. I leave Boo nestled between the pillows, take a quick piss, and I'm heading back to bed to join him when I notice an unusual light in the kitchen.

Barefoot and naked, I pad down the hallway.

The kitchen is dark, but the laundry room door is open. The light comes from inside. Somewhere water is running, but no footsteps or rustling about. Nothing but an open door.

"Rachel?" I say in a steady, reasonable voice. I step cautiously into the brightly-lit laundry room.

The washing machine beside me suddenly sloshes into violent life.

Love in the American Empire

I shout in fear.

Utterly shamed, I realize that Rachel must already be home. She must have started a load of laundry before jogging out the Burke-Gilman Trail. That my suspicions and nerves have reached this level of jumpiness is fairly indicative of my mental state. I've got to snap out of it.

I'm on my own. Rachel won't be back for some time yet – on weekends she often runs to Gas Works Park, a six-mile loop with a twenty-minute pause up on top of the mound, looking out over Union Bay. I get tired just thinking about it. For my idea of a workout, I take a quick shower, make some coffee, and bring up on my monitor screen one of my toughest chapters, "Techniques of Misunderstanding."

I don't have to worry about Rachel. She never takes my need to write as a personal affront. For this I adore her. She's not one of those needy human beings who demand constant attention. All she has to see is the computer room door closed, and she will keep her own company quietly and happily until I'm ready to leave the monitor.

That's what she does, at first, and what I expect her to continue doing, which is why her interruption this afternoon is so noteworthy. I'm deep in the bliss of complete concentration, the joy of thinking in words. I'm so lost in cerebral by-ways that I don't even hear her enter the room.

She puts her arms around my neck and kisses me on the side of my throat. Any last thought about first-person narrative

Love in the American Empire

not typed on my monitor at that point is lost forever. "Would it be possible to lure you out of your den?"

"Oh, hi there. Is something wrong? What time is it?"

"Relax. Nothing's wrong. I'm just lonely for my husband. Come take a walk with me."

"Now?" The electric heater hums comfortingly. The monitor beckons.

Rachel nibbles the side of my cheek. "It's so lovely in the fall. Let's walk through the ravine. Come on."

So, of course, I'm not an insensitive idiot, I want to believe my company matters to my wife, I go. It's bright but cold, and we bundle up warmly. We hold hands through our gloves, and stroll down the street to the south end of Ravenna Park. Across the grassy lawn and around the soccer field, we head down into the tree-crowded depths of the ravine, heading out the main trail through a mile of cedars and pines and maples along the fern-covered banks of the creek. It's one of our favorite walks, and just being there together makes our hands grip each other tighter.

"Did you happen to talk to Omar yet?"

"Talk to Omar? About what?"

"About the unlocked door in the laundry room."

"Oh, that. Well, yes, I did mention it."

"What did he say?"

"That he'll be more careful. And so will we."

We're taking a different route home this afternoon, for some reason. Did Rachel suggest it? I think she bumped my shoulder and nudged me away from our usual path back into the ravine. We wander down the winding grassy islands of Ravenna Boulevard and then turn up the avenue. It's a pretty walk, and another way of getting home. I'm not expecting Rachel to point across the street at the yellow house on the corner with a covered porch.

"That's his rooming-house."

I'm not used to knowing anything about my students, including where they live. "Really?" I say, and I'm perfectly willing to just keep on walking, but already I get a bad feeling when she wants to cross the street toward the house. "Rachel, where are you going?"

"Come on," she says, "he's home, I just saw him in the window. He probably never has anyone visit him. Let's ask him to dinner tomorrow."

"Dinner?" There goes our student-teacher relationship forever. I'm against the idea, right from the start. "Tomorrow? It's Sunday, our day off. Do we really want company?" I want to lounge around in my underwear. I want to enjoy my wife's company.

"Open your heart, Colin," she says, heading up the walkway between the juniper bushes.

"But it's not right to just drop in on someone," I protest, lagging behind on the sidewalk. "We don't do that in Seattle. Don't you see, you're putting me in a very compromising position. I'm his professor."

Love in the American Empire

"Well, I'm not," says my wife, "and a hot Sunday dinner is just what that skinny boy needs. I've seen his cupboards. He's living on cold cereal and ramen noodles." With that, she knocks on the door. When no one answers, she opens the door and peeps in. "Dillon?" Then she gestures for me to follow her.

"No, Rachel, don't," I call after her in a discreet voice, but it's useless. Have you ever told an Italian woman not to do something she wants to do? I follow her reluctantly.

Names and room numbers are posted on the mailbox by the door, but I notice Rachel doesn't even glance at it. She already knows where to go, and leads me across the dinky lobby and up the staircase to the second floor. By the time I get to the door she's already knocked, and it's swinging open on Dillon in striped boxer shorts, his face flushed red.

"Oh, hi," he says. His jaws are working, but at first no words come out. I can't look at him. Far too much bare pinkness. "Um, it's really nice to see you. Now is, um, not a good time."

"Dillon, we're so sorry," gasps Rachel as it dawns on her that he might have a private life and that he might be in the middle of it. He blushes even redder as he retreats back into his room. We fumble our goodbyes toward the closing door, and then Rachel and I are stumbling over each other to get down the stairs and out of that place. We're both thoroughly mortified. As we're hurrying away down the street, Rachel doesn't look back at the rooming-house. I do. Which is why

Love in the American Empire

I'm the only one who sees a second face in the upstairs window.

Peering down through the glass is that annoying bookseller.

My foot hits the curb. I stumble. Oh, my God. What did we interrupt?

"Are you angry with me?"

"Uh, no."

"I can tell from your face that you are," she says as we walk up the avenue together. "I really owe you an apology for that. What a terrible idea."

A cold gust of wind rattles the maple branches overhead. A crow begins complaining loudly and bitterly about the unfairness of life.

We walk half a block in silence.

"You're not going to believe who I just saw in Dillon's window."

"I can guess."

She doesn't look at me. All of her energy is focused on getting away from the rooming-house as quickly as possible. She strides down the sidewalk, which is cracked and buckling from the underground subversion of tree roots.

"How could you know? You didn't look."

"I saw him through the door. Part of him. He was sitting on the bed. But it was him." She speaks with the conviction of a medium who has made certifiable contact with the dead.

"You're not surprised?" The thrill of discovery dissolves. I've been looking forward to bringing the all-knowing Dario down a peg or two in Rachel's esteem, to exposing him as the sexual predator that he is. "You already knew?"

"I didn't know Dario would actually be there, of course, or I never would have knocked."

"But you knew Dario was after him?"

"After him?" She almost laughs. "That's not exactly how I'd put it."

"Sexually pursuing him."

"Oh, Colin, it's not what you think."

"But you knew."

"I just spent the night at Dario's house. Of course I knew. Does he strike you as the kind of man who keeps his problems to himself?"

"But you never said anything?"

"I haven't had much time, have I?"

"But we've gone on this entire walk, and you haven't said a word."

"I was waiting for the right moment. I would have broken down and told you, sooner or later," she says, after a moment of pondering. "But it wasn't my place to tell you."

"But that boy is my student."

"So what? That doesn't make you the moral police. Their behavior is none of your business. And now you've found out naturally. It's better this way. Life took care of it for me, without my having to betray anyone's trust."

She would like to let it go at that.

"That's not the point. Rachel, are you keeping secrets from me?"

"It's Dario's life, not mine, Colin. It's not my secret to pass along. Now that you know, that makes it easier. But it wasn't my role to tell you."

We're at loggerheads. The conversation sputters to an end, leaving us both entrenched in disagreement. The end of our walk is ruined. We return home without much to say to each other, and soon split up to our separate parts of the house. For an hour I sit in the dark at my computer, staring at the monitor, my thoughts racing in circles.

When I finally reach out for my pen, it's not there.

I turn on the light and check the floor – a lone pen has high entertainment value for Boo. I wander through the house looking in all the usual places. Boo is sleeping in the armchair, but as soon as he spots me within ten feet of his food bowl, he heads for the kitchen at a gallop. Not until I've given him a big, wet spoonful and prepare to jot down "cat food" on the shopping list do I discover, lying beside the list, my $100 Crown fountain pen.

Neither Rachel nor I would ever put it there.

15
Evacuation

"But does that mean you can't believe him?" I ask, and for once I feel I've got their attention. I'm standing at the blackboard in the front of the classroom, pacing back and forth, from door to windows and back again, being careful not to get white chalk dust on the shoulders of my black sweater. "Miles Coverdale holds one fact back till the very end. Does that throw everything else into doubt? Does that mean he's not telling the truth? Does that make you wonder what else he's not telling you?"

In answer, the building buzzer ends class with a jolt.

"Don't forget, your papers are due at the end of the week," I announce, but no one hears me. It's a gray, drizzly Monday morning. I clear my throat, and shout out, "If I could have your attention, please?" This time they hear me. I talk slowly and loudly, directing each word all the way to the back of that third-floor classroom in Miller Hall.

"I've decided to modify the format of your final term paper, which is half your grade." Okay, that finally got their attention. Mention grades, and suddenly all eyes are to the front. "I'm going to add an additional choice. If you choose not to write a formal paper, and instead to record a dozen or so thoughtful speculations on the texts we've been studying, I will allow that option. The paper needs to be the same length, ten pages double-spaced, and you will be judged on the quality and depth of your thinking."

When nothing else will untie the Gordian Knot, get out your sword.

Only one student in the classroom understands what I'm saying and why I'm saying it. That's all right, because the new rule applies to only one student, anyway. Dillon beams at me radiantly. The problem of fairness is solved. The morning seems bright with hope. I've made a sane and refreshing decision. I feel like I'm getting my life back under control.

Which just goes to show how wrong a man can be.

Four hours later, I'm in my campus office stubbornly trying to make the last of the afternoon count, doing my best to concentrate on Nathaniel Hawthorne and instead listening to the wail of sirens outside Padelford Hall. My coffee is cold, my rain-dampened sweater is almost dry, and the warm office smells of both.

Another siren is starting to sing. Bright red fire trucks are blocking the campus drive outside my window. The glass is rippling and dribbling with rain. The sky is dark and getting darker. It's a miserable afternoon, and all this ruckus is making it worse. There will be no more thinking today. There will be honking and congestion and revolving police lights, firing their red and blue beacons through the downpour.

Love in the American Empire

Sirens aren't unusual on campus. Several times every year some desperate student will try to stop a test or break up a date by setting off a fire alarm. The big red trucks come rumbling, sirens wailing, costing the university a tiny fortune, blocking the street, and making everyone in the dormitory or the chemistry lab or the lecture hall stand miserably outside. I get up from my desk reluctantly, and go look out my office window to make sure the bookstore hasn't caught on fire, that my wife is safe. The student union isn't the problem. Three men in safety gear come trotting up the A-Wing ramp and through the door into Padelford Hall, directly below me.

Not a reassuring sight.

I return to my desk and try to concentrate on the monitor screen, try to wrestle with unreliable narrator Miles Coverdale in *The Blithedale Romance*, try to penetrate what his motives could be for keeping that damned secret from the reader till the end of the book, but it's no good, my thoughts are with the fire trucks outside.

Soon the little French office assistant who wears such strong perfume comes hurrying down the hall in her noisy wooden clogs, clackety-clacking from one doorway to the next announcing that we all have to lock up our offices and leave, we have to evacuate Padelford Hall.

"I can't leave right now."

"The gentlemen say we must," is her curt reply.

"But it's raining out there."

Love in the American Empire

"I am not in charge of the weather." She moves on to the next office. In spite of her irritating manner and lack of explanation, her urgency is persuasive. I click on Save.

It's probably nothing, but dark thoughts go though my head as I grab my back-up disk, my grade book, and any other important papers that catch my eye. My beloved book collection of American first-person narratives must remain behind, to burn or be blown to smithereens. Shoving my arms into my rain jacket, I click off the light and lock the office door behind me. I may never see the contents of this little room again.

Other faculty members are hurrying nervously toward the stairs. Could some deranged student have made a bomb to get revenge on a hated professor? Or have we been exposed to deadly bacteria causing irreversible brain damage?

We all hustle down the stairs, around and down, around and down, in an inane exercise to make ourselves believe we're still in control, to fool ourselves into thinking that being prepared can trump chemical warfare, that sensible behavior can avert catastrophe. It's just one more example of modern security hysteria, the psychological scars of 9/11.

Nevertheless, though it's probably nothing, we're all huffing and puffing down those stairs as fast as we can make our neglected bodies move. No one's making small talk or jokes. The intention in every mind is simply to get as far away from this hall of offices as possible.

Love in the American Empire

The rain has been coming down in a gray drizzle all day, but it's coming down harder now as we rush out of the building, and the sky is oppressively dark with a promise of more to come. The gloomy afternoon is bright with glaring headlights, and at the bottom of A-ramp we plunge into the white light. People are spilling from B-ramp and C-ramp as well, crossing the street between backed-up cars.

While I'm standing on the curb, half-sheltered by umbrellas mushrooming on every side, caught between people trying to escape and people trying to see what's happening, I notice a lavender beret amid a cluster of heads, getting bumped back and forth but not moving. I'm working my way toward her when Gloria Goldberg gets whacked by a passing elbow and nearly goes down. I grab her just as her legs are sliding out from under her. She's so light-weight that what I really have is an armful of woolen pea coat. She almost loses her cocky little beret, but manages to hold it on her head while she regains her balance.

"What the devil is causing all this?" she complains. "I'm trying to teach a graduate seminar. This is not helpful." Gloria is an associate professor in Cinema Studies. She's teaching a three-hour course this quarter called "The European Painterly Visualists: Fellini, Almodovar and Jeunet."

"Nobody seems to know," is the best I can answer.

A breathless, pretty young grad student overhears us and turns around. "Terrorism," she says.

"Terrorism?" wails Gloria, tripling the volume of the word. "What the hell are you talking about?"

"Don't yell at me!" cries the upset grad student. "All I know is it's a mysterious white substance. It was delivered to the Romance Languages Department in a plain white envelope."

"A white substance? Like sugar? Like flour?" rails Gloria, but all three of us are thinking the same thing – you mean like a deadly contagious virus that will cause the entire campus to be quarantined.

I leave Gloria behind in the midst of the crowd, arguing with the grad student, trying to encourage people around her to refuse to stand out in the rain any longer, to return all together to their offices. I have no desire to return. I hurry across the rain-slickened parking-lot, through the dripping evergreens, toward the student union building.

Halfway down the hall is the bookstore. I poke my head into the doorway, and immediately hear my name shouted across the store. I get the feeling Dario has been waiting for an opportunity to talk with me, and he wastes no time steering me off toward the art board in the corner of the bookstore.

He gets right to the topic. "Listen, Colin, I know you saw me there."

Until this moment, there has been that tiny, fuzzy shadow of a doubt. "I thought it was you," I say lamely. Why bother pretending I don't know what he's talking about? "It's really none of my business, Dario, and as far as I…"

Love in the American Empire

"Don't get anything wet," he interrupts me, distracted by my dripping rainjacket.

"I'll be careful."

He clutches my hand. "I just want you to know that I don't usually go after boys his age." His eyes are way too wide and vulnerable. "Boys aren't my thing. But, well, he's like no one I've ever met."

"Yes, I know," I concede to him. "You're certainly right there, he's a case unto himself…"

"You don't have to worry," says Dario. "Nothing's going to happen."

"It's a little late to say that now. I mean, I saw him. He was undressed."

"He was just changing his clothes."

"That's not what it looked like."

"But it was. Listen, Colin, really, what you're thinking is impossible. It's a dream. At first I believed it, too. I thought it was the real thing. But he's straight. He's just super openminded and weirdly uninhibited. But as far as, well – there's not a chance."

I don't want to know any more about Dillon and Dario. I lunge for a different subject. "So, have you seen my wife?"

Dario gives me a very odd look. "She left early today."

"Did she?"

Dario seems to be watching my face. "She went home for lunch and never came back to work." There's a sickening pause in the conversation.

Love in the American Empire

I try to show no reaction. On the other side of my show-nothing face, however, I'm howling with frustration, frantically trying to remember why she might have needed to go home, what she could be doing that's so important. I'm scrambling for an explanation to my wife's odd behavior. Well, there's an easy solution. Go home and find out. Chances are I won't be allowed back into my office this afternoon. Half the work I do there I can also do at home.

"Oh, that's right," I say, with a snap of my fingers, lamely attempting to give Dario the illusion that I've just recalled something. "I remember now. Yes, she wouldn't have come back." I wish Dario a good day.

He doesn't believe me for a second.

The fifteen-minute walk across campus and down the winding boulevard home is enough to get me thoroughly soaked. The sky appears to be confused, dark clouds turning the afternoon into night.

I hardly notice. I'm too busy working myself up in anxiety, trying to prepare myself for what I'm likely to discover at home.

I don't feel good about this.

The suspicions I've been ignoring for a week now come back to me all at once, besieging my imagination, conjuring up all kinds of deceptions and betrayals. I've got this terrible knot in my gut. I'm very much afraid I'm going to find Dillon in my house.

That boy is somehow involved.

Love in the American Empire

I'm about to see something I don't want to see in my own home, and I don't know what I'm going to do when I see it. Flashes of anger burn through me like prairie fires. Why is my own life such a mystery to me? Don't most people know themselves better than this? I don't want to know what's happening to my marriage.

I'm going to make myself find out the truth.

16
Fight in the Dark

I reach the top of the stairs and cross the porch to the front door.

As I do, I glance in through the front window to see if I can catch a glimpse of Rachel. To my surprise, the drapes are closed, something Rachel and I never do. Now my heart is seriously pounding. I see no lights inside, no sign of my wife. The key turns in the lock. The door swings open.

"Honey?"

I step inside. Though it's still afternoon, the dim interior is further darkened by the closed curtains. The furniture is reduced to silhouettes. The house is hushed. No music, no soft clattering of a keyboard, no washing machine churning, no smells of cooking. The heat isn't on.

Rachel hasn't been home.

I shrug out of my dripping raincoat and hang it up to dry on the rack by the door. I'm reaching out for the light switch at the bottom of the nearest lamp when I realize there is a shadow in front of me that shouldn't be there.

"Leave it off."

My hand freezes halfway to the lamp switch.

Someone just spoke to me. Someone is sitting on my sofa. The silhouette of a man is seated here in my dark living room with his back to me, and this stranger just instructed me not to turn on my own lamp, and that is not the voice of Dillon.

It's like a nightmare. I can't move my feet.

If this guy is crazy, if he just chose this house at random to commit murder, these could be my last few moments alive, my last chance to catch him off-guard and make a difference. Act, act, act! How much do I want to live? My mind is roaring with choices. Which choice is the one that wins?

I bolt for the front door.

I move suddenly, risking everything. I'm not ashamed to run for it, even though I'm pissed at this stranger thinking he can just take over my house. He springs from the sofa and comes after me. His hands grab me from behind by the shoulders. My arms flail out in indignation.

"Get your hands off me!" I can feel one of my arms hit him in the face. I'm not a fighter. I'm not violent. But I've got my self-respect.

I lunge again for the door, and this time his hands come too close to my throat. I manage to get out a shout before his other hand claps over my mouth. He's pressed me up against the wall. Part of me can't believe this is really happening. He's got a fistful of sweater. I hear the fabric ripping down the seam. He's lugging me by it, stumbling. I pull away, yanking it inside-out, tugging free of the sleeves. My elbow bangs into the phone. I'm experiencing very real pain. The receiver is beeping in distress on the floor. He drags me over to the bed.

Love in the American Empire

He forces my face down into the pillow, and gets his mouth close to my ear.

"Colin, stop fighting me."

He knows my name. Okay, now I'm truly scared, and almost flipping out I'm so mad. "How the fuck do you know my name?" I shout in the most menacing way I can muster. "What the fuck do you think you're doing in my house?"

Without another word, he drags me over to the window, where enough light filters through the drapes that I can see him clearly.

I don't know this man.

He's exactly the same height I am, but probably weighs twenty pounds less. He looks like he's been dehydrated and then flattened by a steamroller. In his gray T-shirt and khakis, he's pure lean efficiency. He's got short hair, a buzzcut somewhere between sandy brown and gray. Piercing blue eyes, smart eyes, an unflinching stare. A few freckles across the nose, on a face that looks slightly younger than my own. He's still got a boyish quality. Maybe it's the big cheeks, the open forehead. But his skin looks old and tough and weathered, like he's been slow-fried in the desert. Only muscle is left on his bones.

Something about those eyes makes me think that happiness isn't even an option for this man anymore. He smiles, and it's hard to look at because the smile has so much sadness and pain.

Love in the American Empire

Then I get it. I see the face of someone I know submerged in the features of this weathered survivor.

"Oh, my God!"

The recognition hits me like a slap. But it doesn't make sense. How can it possibly be him, if he's in Iraq? How can my old college buddy of twenty years ago be here in my home this afternoon, gripping me by the shoulders, holding me up against the gray brightness of the window drapes?

"Jake?"

"Atta boy."

"Jake Bagley, it's you?"

"Yeah, it's me. Hey, what's going on, man? You look like shit. What's all this?" He jabs me in the gut. I wheeze. "Are you trying your hardest to look middle-aged?"

"Jake," I whisper, going into shock. "The very first thing you do is insult me. You asshole."

"Colin, you prick, you're always complaining."

"It's you, all right." Defiantly I turn on the lamp by the sofa, and this time he doesn't stop me. We stare at each other in dumb amazement. Then we both start laughing our heads off. I hold him at arm's length. He knocks my arms away, and grabs me in a hug. I can hear my bones pop. I can't conceal how glad I am to see him. "You haven't changed."

"Oh, I've changed, all right." He puts me down and laughs at something, his own grim, private joke. "Yup, you could say that I've changed a tad. But at least I'm not getting fat like some people."

Love in the American Empire

"I am not fat." In college Jake Bagley had been an expert in needling me. He clearly hasn't lost any of his skill. He pokes me again in the belly. "If that's not fat, what is it?"

"It's just a natural mature softening."

"Right. That kind that natural mature softening, pal, is symptomatic of too much prosperity."

I smile. "Okay, okay, lay off. I've packed on a pound or two, so what? How the hell did you get into my house? This your idea of a fun visit – breaking and entering?"

"Well, I'll tell you, Colin. I didn't have to do any breaking at all. You've got a real problem. That basement door of yours is always unlocked." He winks at me, as though we're sharing some kind of private joke. "Something really ought to be done about it."

"No. You've got to be kidding." I try not to show him how much he's rattling me. "Are you telling me you're the one...?" I'm remembering the muddy footprints, the opening and closing basement door.

"I needed a place to leave my stuff. I figured it was safe with you, so that's why I came here. It's just temporary. So what have you got to drink in this place?"

I snap to my senses. I quickly evolve from assault victim into host. "Right. Sorry. Of course." I head for the kitchen, and he follows me. "We've got some scotch. There's some beer in the fridge. I think there's a little tequila left." I snap on the kitchen light. The kitchen feels like reality.

Love in the American Empire

"Say no more," says Jake, right behind me. "Tequila will do."

"Here, you can finish it off. Let's see now, lime, salt..."

He takes the tequila out of my hand. "Forget that shit." He takes a swig straight from the flask and winces. "Ah, yes. This'll do just fine." He raises the flask in a toast. "Here's to old pals."

I pour myself a shot of scotch. I have so many questions I don't know where to start. "To old pals." I drink. I wince. He straddles a kitchen chair and I sink down into one across from him. "I thought you were in Iraq."

"I was," he says. "I definitely was. And now I'm here."

"You finished your stay?"

"Damn straight I did." He smiles. "Of course, that depends on what you mean by finished."

"But when...?"

He's on his feet. "You don't need to know any of that, Colin," he says, his big hands taking me by the shoulderblades, gripping me at arm's length. It's an affectionate grip, but it's also a powerful one. "Think of me as home on leave. That's the simple version." He sinks back down onto his chair, like a cowboy lowering himself into a rodeo chute. "I'm here now, alive, slightly sane, looking into that beautiful mug of yours again. Do you realize how many years have snuck past us? Your friendship meant the world to me in college, man. More than you will ever know."

He looks at me long enough to make me uncomfortable.

Love in the American Empire

"Those were the days." I purposely avoid thinking about how our friendship ended. Instead I remember all the great times we spent together, the movies and plays and coffee houses, the stoned parties and late night book talks, always with his military service hanging over our heads. "It'll be great to have you back."

"I wish." He rises to his feet again, rolls his eyes, shrugs his shoulders. "Sorry, buddy. I won't be here for long. Can't be. Gotta keep moving." He gives me a long, assessing look, as though wondering how far he can trust me, how much I can possibly understand. "Just in town for a day or two. Looks like I'll be heading up to Canada for a spell."

"I thought your parents and sister lived down in the Tri-Cities."

"Can't go near my family." He paces to one end of the kitchen and turns back. "It wouldn't be good for them and it wouldn't be good for me." He keeps watching me, weighing the effect of his words.

"Jake, I don't get it. I thought you were home on leave. You're not going to see your family?"

He gives me a sad, pained look. "I know, I know. It totally bums me out, too. But that's the only way my plans can work. I don't know how to tell you this, buddy, so let me just say it. I'm not returning to duty."

My mouth is hanging open. I don't know what to say. Down on the street that seems to still exist outside, a car drives

Love in the American Empire

by with a remote whoosh, as though it's happening on a different planet.

"I've served in the United States Army for nine years," he says. "I was in the assault on Baghdad. I have a flawless record. I've won three merit awards. I have completed my deployment in Iraq with the 4th Infantry Division."

"Listen, you don't have to tell me if..."

"No, I need to talk about it." He stands behind his chair and grips the back of it as though it anchors him. "Because I'm not happy about what I was doing in Iraq. About what the American military was doing there. No, not very happy at all. I enlisted to depose Saddam. We did that. So why aren't we leaving? Now we're fighting civilians, people like you and me, people defending their families against the invaders. I'm ashamed. Colin, men in my unit were instructed by our Captain to fire on children throwing rocks."

A silence rings through the house. The boiler goes off. The refrigerator stops tingling.

"You've served your term there?"

"Yes, but it's not over," he says with a quiet sigh. "My unit has been re-deployed."

A light goes on in my thick, slow head.

"You're being sent back for more?"

"Those are my orders." His eyes say it all. "They are not going to happen. I've served my time in hell. They thought I was going home on leave. Well, I never arrived, did I? I vanished. And here I am. The less you know, the better."

Love in the American Empire

He's giving me the chills. "Okay, I don't need to know any more. You're welcome here, Jake, you crazy man, however long you need to stay."

He smiles at me, that sad smile. "My unit leaves in three days. I've applied for conscientious objector status. I was informed that my papers won't be processed by the time my unit leaves. Since I will not be re-joining my unit, I'll be considered absent without leave. I'll be subject to court-martial. I don't have any choice. I can't go back there. I can't do that anymore."

"I'm so sorry, buddy," I say. "That's such a fucked situation to be in." I mean it from my heart.

He's got tears in his eyes, but he's the kind of guy who would never let them spill over and run down his face. "Some guys can do it just fine. I tried. I can't do that shit, and still look at myself in a mirror. I can't go storm trooping into one more house. I'm sick of scaring the shit out of people. Do you know what people look like when they're really, really scared? I'm going to see that look on their faces in my nightmares for the rest of my life. They look at you like you're a fucking heartless monster. Pretty soon you realize that's exactly what you are."

He's shaking. He's pacing again. The kitchen has never seemed so small. He grips his arms across his chest as though trying to keep himself from exploding.

"The only thing I hate is leaving my men behind. They're my boys. They're family. They're counting on me coming back. They're gonna feel I deserted them. And they'll be right. I don't have any choice. I know I'm doing the right thing. That part of my life is over. Some doors you have to close. I've seen too much, pal."

At first I think he's waiting for me to say something. Then I realize, from a catch in his breathing, that he's just waiting to get his emotions under control enough to speak without his voice breaking. It cracks a little, anyway. "I have seen sights no one should ever see."

"Forgive yourself, man," I say to him. "You were doing what you were ordered to do."

"Treating people like shit is treating people like shit," he says sharply, impatient with my rationalization. He takes another long swig on the tequila flask, tipping back his head. "Killing is killing. Don't be fooled into thinking anything else. Don't give me Iraqi Freedom. Dead men aren't free."

"You didn't have any choice, Jake. That's what being a soldier means. You are not the one making the decisions."

He hardly hears me. "I'll tell you something, man. The dead win in the end. Because you never forget the people you kill. Taking someone's life, it's the ugliest thing you can do, the lowest, the meanest, the nastiest, the foulest. It's the deed that doesn't wash out." He almost stops there, wants to stop there, and goes on. "Take it from me. I know."

He finishes off the last of the tequila, and sets the empty flask down on the drainboard. I'm afraid to hear any more. I'm so sad I'm speechless, so I just grab him and we hug each other. When we went to college, we believed in things. Some things were worth fighting for.

"I'll do anything for you, Jake. Just say the word, man. Whatever you need is yours."

He hugs me. "I knew I could count on you. So, here's the situation." He holds me in front of him, looks me in the eye. "For just a day, or two, or maybe three, I need to hide here. It would be such a relief to stop lurking back there in your appliance graveyard."

"Please, move inside. I'll make up a bed for you in the computer room."

"Sweet, man. I'll be getting my ID papers any day now. I know someone who knows someone who knows someone. Then I'm off for Vancouver. I've already got a place to stay there. I won't be in your hair for long."

"Don't worry about it," I say. "Stay as long as you need to. Whatever you need, it's yours."

"You shouldn't be in any real danger."

I laugh. "Why would I be in danger?"

Then the picture shifts into focus and becomes clearer, and my laughter dies in my throat. I feel my cavalier confidence draining out of me. Maybe this is a little more dangerous than I thought. Are we talking federal crime here? Are people going to come in shooting? I mean, how serious is this? Jake seems to be telling me that he deserted from his military service, but is there more he's not telling me? Will I be guilty of sheltering a criminal?

Love in the American Empire

Maybe his staying here is not such a good idea, but it's too late now. I'm committed. Does this mean that from now on I'll be under surveillance? Probably. Is my phone going to be tapped? I wouldn't be surprised. Will my emails be scanned? Will I be accused of treason?

He's looking at me like he's waiting for something.

"Do you want to clean up a little?"

"That's the most beautiful thing anyone's ever said to me!"

"How about a nice, long shower?"

"Have I died and gone to heaven?"

"The towels are hanging on the bar."

"I only need one." He smiles, and then blatantly regards my body with such interest that I nearly panic. "Just eyeballing, but you look like you're about my size. Well, at least in the shoulders. Maybe not in the gut."

"Okay, enough of that."

"How about some clothes?" he says, teasing set aside for the moment. "I wouldn't ask this, but I'm in sort of a jam. You have anything I can borrow?"

"A closetful."

"Mind if I...?"

"Help yourself." I gesture toward the clothes closet next to the bathroom. "Go ahead and take a shower, and then you can poke through my stuff and see if I've got anything that looks decent on you."

Love in the American Empire

"Thanks, buddy." He's heading for the bathroom, but he pauses, turns around and grips my forearm. "A lot of things I believed in turned out to be bullshit, Colin," he says, eyebrows furrowed. "I've fallen for a lot of crap in my life. But I also believed in you, pal. I've always believed in you. And you're the real thing."

17
The Lying Wife

I yank open the drapes, dispelling the shadows of the living room. Enough of this claustrophobic gloom. It's dark enough outside without making it darker inside. I'm still shaking. A man doesn't expect to fight for his life in his own living room. I stand alone here, my eyes adjusting to the troubled gray light coming through the picture window. In the stillness of the house, I hear the shower begin splattering.

My elbow stings from hitting the phone. I massage it. I pick up my sweater off the floor. It's hopelessly torn. There'll be no repairing that. I drop it in the waste can.

Until an hour ago, I was a law-abiding citizen. Funny how a man's whole life can flip-flop in a single moment. Suddenly all my comfortable habits have just been thrown out the window. I have an illegal houseguest. I have just given up police protection. I have said goodbye to privacy. Not to mention that I'm giving up all casual displays of physical intimacy with my wife. I have just offered my entire wardrobe to a military criminal.

I change my mind. I reluctantly pull the drapes shut again, returning the house to its gloomy secrecy. The days of open windows are over.

I go into the kitchen, looking for a snack to munch on besides my poor fingernails, wondering what I'll make for dinner tonight, and most of all how I'm going to explain this whole thing to Rachel, when I happen to glance at the door into the laundry room. So that's where he's been hiding.

I can hear the shower running.

He'll never know.

I open the door, and pull the light cord inside. I can see from here that the stroller and an old microwave oven have been moved away from the water heater. I go farther inside, and stop on the other side of the boiler. Beyond the skis and empty appliance boxes, tucked away under the stairs and half-hidden, is a backpack somewhat the worse for wear, a sleeping bag, dirty on the outside, half unrolled, and a pair of muddy boots. That's all I need to see. How long have they been there? With quick and stealthy steps I retreat from the laundry room, pull the cord dangling from the light bulb, and return the cement tomb to darkness. I'm carefully dodging the cat's food bowl, pulling the laundry room door shut, when I bump into someone standing behind me.

I shout.

"My, my, expecting Count Dracula?" says my wife with a welcoming smile.

I'm embarrassed and rattled. "Hi, honey. I didn't hear you come in."

"Apparently." We kiss. She slips out of her raincoat, drapes it over a kitchen chair, and gives me a second glance. "Look at you. Wild hair. Shirttail untucked. You look like you've been in a fight." I chuckle, but before I can tell her how right she is, she adds, "What were you doing in there? More noises and footprints?"

Her teasing rubs me the wrong way. The explanation on the tip of my tongue stays there. "Something like that." I avoid her probing look.

She notices. Using that irrepressible Mediterranean avoidance technique, successful for three thousand years, she gives me another kiss. "Nice to see you. I didn't mean to startle you."

"Forget it. I've had too much coffee." I'm studying her face, trying to read her expression, trying to see how much she knows, how much she guesses, what she's thinking, what she's hiding. She's unreadable. "Where were you this afternoon? You missed all the excitement on campus."

"Doctor's appointment," she says. "I've been having this weird ringing in my ears. He thinks it's too much aspirin."

"Too much aspirin?"

"Headaches," she says simply, as though that explains everything. "I've been having a lot of them lately."

"Since when?" I ask, and what I don't ask is, "Why don't I know this?" My wife has been suffering from a succession of headaches, enough to prompt her to go to a doctor, and her loving husband is completely in the dark? My mental wheels are spinning. This doesn't compute. My wife scorns being sick. She acts like it doesn't happen to Italians. She goes into instant denial at the first stuffy nose or sneeze.

Love in the American Empire

Generally, I would be the one *insisting* she go to a doctor. Rachel avoids doctors.

Rachel doesn't have headaches.

"By the time I get home I don't mention it, because it happens at the bookstore." That's all the further she gets before Boo wanders into the kitchen. "Well, hello there, Mister Boo, and how was *your* day?"

In that effortless way cats have, he immediately draws complete attention to himself, doing nimble circle-eights around our feet, marking our ankles, rubbing up against our legs, looking meaningfully toward his empty bowl.

"Looks like somebody's hungry," says Rachel, popping the tab on a can of cat food. The sound immediately secures Boo's complete attention. As she bends over his bowl, spoon in one hand, can in the other, lowering a glop of chicken bits in gravy, there's a momentary hush in the house and that's when she hears it. She pauses and listens. I can hear it, too, the drone of splattering water from the bathroom.

For a moment, neither of us moves. Neither of us says a word. We're both engulfed by the incontestable fact that someone else is in the house with us. Rachel turns to look into my eyes, the can of cat food gripped like a souvenir from a lost era of trust and innocence. Her look is not an innocent one. Her eyes betray an uneasy flicker of knowledge.

Boo meows impatiently.

"Sorry, Boo." She lowers the food to his bowl and says, as casually as she can, "Is someone taking a shower?"

"Yes, actually, there is…"

"Don't tell me Dillon has come over again?"

I have to smile, remembering. "No, this time it's not Dillon. It's that old college friend of mine. I know I've mentioned him…"

"You mean Jake," she says.

"Yes, I hope you don't mind," I answer, and that's all the farther I get before I realize she's said his name too easily. If I could, I would go on to explain that it's a complete surprise to me, too, and apologize for the short notice, watching to see her reaction to finding out we have a guest, knowing that a guest is always a hassle, extra cooking, bedclothes, entertainment, not to mention that helping him is against the law. I expect her to be a reluctant good sport, to accept the inconvenience, to be ready to bravely help any friend of her husband who's been victimized by the war.

Instead, as I watch her, confident that she's the human being in this world that I know best, a mask seems to fall off, her features appear to relax into a more honest expression. That first face, the familiar, reliable face I know so well, is shown for what it really is, a deceit. The look on her face at that moment leaves a scar on my mind that is not yet healed, even to this day. It's a subtle change, but what it means is that my sense of reality is wrong. Watching this transformation, I realize how completely I once believed in that mask. For the first time, the woman I think of as Rachel isn't here. Someone else, deceptive, wiser, more complicated, is in her place.

"You know about him?" I can hardly get the words out of my throat.

"Yes," she says. "We've met. Sounds like you two have finally talked." She sighs. "Thank God." She gives a brief, nervous laugh and looks at me, waiting for some kind of acknowledgment, but I'm speechless.

You think you're standing on solid ground, and then someone you love jerks the rug out from under you. How can a secret I've just discovered be old news to my wife? I can't stop myself from asking. "How long have you known?"

"A week," she confesses.

"A week!"

She's looking directly into my eyes, but I can't tell if she's watching to see if I really believe her, or if she's monitoring to see how much she's hurt me. "He made me promise not to tell you. He wanted to tell you himself. Then he had to leave town. I never dreamed he'd be gone so long."

Wait, back up, I don't think I heard right. "You've lied to me for a week?"

"I lied as little as possible, Colin."

"You left things out."

"I suppose I did, yes. It's not actually lying."

"You knew something I didn't know. You didn't tell me. What do you call that?"

"It wasn't my place to tell you. I gave my word. I'm so sick of hiding something, but he made me promise."

Love in the American Empire

The kitchen is way too small for a conversation like this. For one thing, there's not enough air, and I feel faint. For a week I've been thinking my wife is acting a little odd, and now I find out she's keeping a secret from me. She knows that my old college pal has hidden his stuff in the laundry room, and she doesn't tell me. I thought I was on solid ground with her. I thought I knew who she was.

I head for the open center of the living room. I can hear her behind me, talking to my back, but I can't seem to stop my legs from running, some kind of reflex reaction of my body to extreme pain.

"That is so lame," I turn around and snap at her. I'm shocked when the words come viciously out of my mouth, but I can't stop them. "How can any promise to a complete stranger mean more to you than honesty to your own husband?"

"Colin, when I promised him, I never dreamed it would take so long. He came here looking for you. You're the one he wanted. He just found me instead. He poured out his secret to me because he was all alone and he had to trust someone. You just weren't here yet. That's the truth. I hate hiding anything from you."

I want to believe her, but I don't.

"I'm sure that's another reason for all these headaches I'm having."

Fine, and so why did she promise, then, for even an hour, to give up being truthful with her husband? Even an hour. I find it strangely satisfying to think that keeping secrets from me causes her headaches.

I notice a small paper bag on the chair. "What's that?"

"Oh, that. On the way home I stopped at Bartell Drugs in University Village to get my prescription filled." She pauses long enough to take a good look at me. "Actually, it's my prescription but it isn't for me. It's for Jake. I couldn't just stand by and watch him hurting. You can tell how much pain he's in. I figured I could get him some good meds."

"Pain? He didn't mention any pain." I'm feeling about as dumb as I sound.

"Of course not! Well, he's your friend, you must know what he's like, Mister Tough Guy." I appreciate having a wife so sensitive and considerate, but it bugs me to think she knows my friend better than I do. She takes a plastic pill bottle out of the little white bag.

"What a sweetheart you are!"

"I feel bad for him," says Rachel. "Face it, he's a ruined man. Physically, mentally, spiritually, you name it. He's been gutted. Can't you feel it, Colin? No one should have to do that much for his country."

"He looks like he's been through it, all right. You probably know that he needs to stay with us for a few days, right?"

At first she doesn't answer. She doesn't need to. "I was sure you wouldn't mind," she says at last, "but he wanted to ask you himself. He wanted to talk to you first himself. He insisted. Maybe it's a guy thing, maybe it's just a personal issue."

"Any more secrets you want to tell me about?"

Her look is not reassuring. She seems to be considering how much I can take. She smiles sadly. "I think you've had enough secrets for one night."

I listen. The shower is still running. "I think he's a good man."

"Yes, I think he is, too."

"You realize there's some risk involved, obviously."

"Well, yes. We're breaking the law."

"I think he's worth it."

"I agree." She looks at me like she's waiting for me to say something else. When I don't, she begins probing. "I know you too well, sweetheart. I know this is upsetting you. Try not to imagine the worst."

"Oh, I'm not," I'm quick to assure her, "I'm fine. I realize you were put in an awkward position. Really, I don't think badly of you. Ever. And I'm not imagining things. I'm sure it's all fine."

She tips her head slightly, in a funny way she has when she's re-evaluating. "What is it then, Colin? Something's bugging you. You're holding back. What is it?"

"It's just that, well, you've never lied to me before," I say, and even as I say it a dreadful thought occurs to me. "Have you?"

Love in the American Empire

The splattering of water abruptly ceases. We hear the tinkle and clink of the shower curtain rings being tugged across.

"I try very hard to tell you the truth, dear, always," she says, and she touches the side of my cheek with her fingertips as she says it. "But the truth sometimes has a bad effect on you. You over-react."

"I do not."

She smiles and nods. "Oh, you do. You brood on small things. You worry and fuss and stew and make a lot out of nothing. I don't mean to hurt you. I always want to tell you the truth. I want to be a good and honest woman. But sometimes the truth is hard."

We both look toward the bathroom door as it opens.

18
Roast Chicken Dinner

"You have no idea how good a shower can feel," he says, coming out of the bathroom shirtless and fastening his pants. He's flat and firm as a board, and I momentarily hate him for parading around that way in our house where my wife can see him. Which is exactly what she does.

She sees him. He sees her. They both freeze.

"I didn't know you were home."

"I just got here."

I look from one to the other.

"Colin, blame me," he says, without knowing a word of what we've said to each other. "I asked her not to tell you that I was hiding out here. I wanted to tell you myself."

"That's what she said," I say noncommittally.

"I didn't think it would take this long, but it did. Something came up." At first he's going to skip this part, he's not going to tell us, but he makes a conscious decision to continue. "I had to make an extra trip up to Vancouver. Things fell apart, then things came together a little quicker than we thought. Payments were due. I had a lot of strings to pull, had to do a lot of running around. I didn't know I'd be leaving so soon."

"That doesn't explain why you made my wife keep your being here a secret."

"I was afraid you wouldn't want to get involved. Maybe you didn't trust me anymore. I didn't know how things stood between us. It *is* against the law, you know. It's not without danger. It's participating in a crime. That's why I wanted to tell you myself. I wanted to look you in the eye and know you trusted me, and that I could trust you."

I try to swallow it. "I think we're okay on it, Jake."

Do I believe it? Am I swallowing this crap about a promise and giving her word? Not for a minute. My mind is roaring with possibilities, none of them happy ones, all of them marriage-threatening. If she loves me so much, why would she lie to me and keep her promise to a stranger?

"I don't mean to disturb things," he says.

"Well," I say, pretending to laugh, "you can't very well hide in someone's laundry room and not disturb things."

"We're glad to be able to help," says Rachel, with a glance at me to show that my humor is ill-timed. I watch their eyes. They're both very aware of each other.

"Whatever we can do," I say lamely.

"Here, I got you some decent meds," says Rachel, handing him the little plastic pill bottle.

Getting painkillers clearly means a lot to him. I can see he's choked up. His eyes are bright with gratitude. He takes them without a word.

"Dinner will be ready in an hour," she says, heading for the kitchen.

"Thanks," he says at last. "I could eat a horse."

Love in the American Empire

She cooks a delicious roast chicken dinner, Jake puts on a shirt, and the three of us talk for an hour afterward over glasses of wine. By unspoken mutual consent, we keep it light. We don't mention our devastation at the election results, or the horrors of the war. I'm dreadful with small talk, but Rachel has enough social skills for the both of us. She keeps his plate full and always has a new topic to introduce.

They talk about Seattle. They talk about campus. They discuss their favorite authors. They discuss Venice, my wife's favorite place in the world. I get a word in now and then, but I'm not really trying. The two of them have a natural rapport, a kind of similar animal chemistry. They both love running and swimming. They're both very much into their bodies. I'd forgotten how charming Jake could be. Every time he's charming to Rachel, I watch his magic working its effect on her. He wants to know all about us. She tells him about the bookstore. I tell him about the English Department.

"You're my book friends," he says. "Some of the guys in my unit read books, and they're different from the other guys, they see more, they can talk about things. I like to hang out with book people. They communicate better, know what I mean? They go into other people's heads easier. I start to notice the people I enjoy the most, the ones I can talk to, they're always readers. Like you." He admires the overflowing bookshelves. "It's like your house is a temple. What beautiful walls you have, walls of books."

"Did you read much over there?"

Love in the American Empire

It's the first time either of us have dared to mention the war. "As much as I could. Whenever I could get my hands on anything worth reading." He falters, starts to say something and then doesn't. Then he starts again. "I know you want me to tell you about it. You want to know what it's like over there. I know. But that stuff, it's hard to talk about. It's hard enough to see it. If I put it into words, I have to remember it. The memories are the worst."

"We totally understand," says Rachel.

"Don't say another word about it, Jake," I say, "not until you want to."

"I don't mean to bug you by avoiding it. But the one thing I do not want to do right now is remember what I saw in Iraq." Even saying this much, I could see tension coming over the features of his face, his neck muscles straining. "If I talk about what is going on over there, I'll get too upset." He manages to get those words out, then fakes a laugh. "So, if I'm real careful, do you mind if I read a book or two?"

"I insist," says Rachel warmly. "My library is your library."

"And help yourself to any of my clothes," I add sincerely.

The subject of the war is successfully avoided. The night is young, but the poor guy is worn down, and so are we.

"We're pooped," I tell him. "We're going to retire early. You should have everything you need. If not, holler."

Love in the American Empire

He stands regarding us both for a moment. "You two are real friends. Thanks for putting up with all this – this invasion." We smile at his reference. His smile is brief, mere punctuation. "I'd appreciate it if you wouldn't tell anyone about me. I don't want to leave a trail that leads to you. No one is going to suspect a thing until the day I don't report for duty. Then they'll find out from my parents that I never went home. That's when the search will start. By then, with luck, I should be living in Vancouver under a different name."

Rachel and I glance at each other nervously.

"We won't say a word," says Rachel.

Jake retreats into the computer room and closes the door behind him, leaving Rachel and me to ourselves. I undress first, then sit naked on the side of the bed, waiting for her to hang up her clothes. "Tell me how you found out he was here," I say, as she slides under the covers.

"Not tonight, hon, I'm exhausted," she says. "I'll tell you the whole story, I promise. Ask me tomorrow."

That will have to do.

Peacefully holding Rachel in my arms will get me through the night. I'm too confused and insecure to be horny. We're wrapped up together, and Rachel has almost drifted off to sleep when I finally get up my courage, brace myself for unpleasant surprises, and move my lips closer to her ear.

"I tried to call you the night you stayed at Dario's."

She snuggles against me, spoon to spoon. "You did?"

"No one answered."

Love in the American Empire

For a moment there's only the steady drip of the kitchen faucet. I'm waiting for some kind of explanation. The silence demands it.

"Dario must have turned his phone off," she says at last, sleepily. It takes her another moment to murmur, "Why did you call?"

I'm about to tell her my reason for calling, that I had discovered the root of Dario's melodramatic distress, that he was head-over-heels infatuated with Dillon. Of course, I have no intention of letting her know the other reason for my call, to make sure she was really spending the night there.

"And you called because…?" she says, waiting.

I smile feebly. "Just wanted to say I love you."

"You big silly," she mumbles, and falls asleep.

19
Death Cry

That's the sound of someone being killed. It cuts through the stillness of the house. Whatever I was dreaming is forgotten in an instant. I've never heard a death cry before in my life. I just heard one now.

Boo leaps off the bed and there's a thump as he hits the carpet running.

I'm sitting bolt upright in bed, wide-eyed, my mouth open and ready to shout for help. Rachel is sitting up beside me, tense, one arm braced against the headboard. Her eyes are huge. The living room is gray from the porch light and streetlamps outside, and both of us are looking in all directions, toward the hall, toward the kitchen. The house has become deathly silent.

"Oh, my God, do you think that was him?"

"Who else could it be?"

"Do you think he's hurt himself?"

"God, I hope not." I really don't know what to do. Could the poor guy have been suicidal? My pulse is pounding too loudly in my ears to think straight. After hearing a sound like that, checking on the health of our guest is the last thing I want to do. I fold aside the covers.

Rachel reaches out and grabs my hand. "Wait. What are you doing?"

Love in the American Empire

"I'll be fine."

"I'm going with you."

"No. Stay here. I'll be right back."

I rise from the bed, but she won't let go of my hand. Rachel is looking at me incredulously. "Do you think someone else could be in the house?" she hisses through clenched teeth. "Do you think someone's hurt him?"

The idea of being invaded again is almost more than I can bear. We both listen, not daring to budge. Not a sound. That's when I smell it. Just faintly, an acrid hint.

"I think I smell something burning."

The thought of all these books catching fire makes my mind spin. I can smell it now, stronger. "I'll be right back." I listen for any other noises in the house. Then I jump out of bed and walk quietly down the hall. I'm more intent on being ready for anything than remembering I'm only wearing my jockey shorts. By the time I realize I should have grabbed my bathrobe, I'm there.

The door is open, like he's expecting me. A thin trail of smoke is coming from inside. I step into the doorway. Down on the carpet in front of me is the improvised bed that Rachel and I rigged, an air mattress with a goosefeather quilt wrapped around it, with plenty of sheets and a couple of pillows.

The bed is torn apart. No one is in it.

I see the glow of his cigarette before I see him. He's sitting in the chair at my desk, but the chair is turned around, facing the door. The cigarette tip blazes temporarily brighter as he sucks the fire down into him.

"I know, I know, I probably shouldn't be smoking in here," he apologizes the moment I appear before him. He won't let me get in a word. "I'll air it out tomorrow morning, I promise."

"Are you all right?"

"I just had to have a smoke, man," he says, still focusing on the cigarette. He puts it out, crushing it against the side of the trash can beside the desk. "I just desperately needed one right now. My sanity was on the line." He tries to pretend cigarettes are the topic, not screams in the night, but gives it up. "Sorry about being so loud. I'd give anything to not do that."

"Nightmare?" I ask. I put a hand on his shoulder.

"Bad dream." He pulls away.

I snap on the little gooseneck lamp that perches beside my computer. He winces at the light.

"Don't worry, I'm okay."

"You sure?"

"Go back to bed." He snaps off the lamp, returning the room to shadows. "It won't happen again, I promise. It's the wine. It makes me soft. It lowers my defenses."

I go back down the hallway to where Rachel is waiting for me in a little puddle of light by the bed, and switch off the night lamp. "Poor guy, he's got demons he can't shake off," I say, sliding under the covers. I accidentally bump into Boo, who's already reclaimed his place on the bed. "Sorry, Boo."

"Is he all right?"

"He'll be fine. He just woke up from a nightmare." I wrap my hands around her bare body.

She squeals. "Warm up those freezing hands," she cries softly, wriggling deliciously. I'm perfectly willing to warm them up. We smother our laughter under the covers. A long, slow kiss from her and I'm hard. She wraps her arms and legs around me.

But there's something wrong with us tonight. Our lovemaking is self-conscious. We're not swept up in it. We're trying to prove something, to find our way back to each other. We're pretending, and we do it silently, like the sound has been turned off.

Mercifully, sleep intervenes. The next thing I know, she's jiggling my shoulder, telling me it's time to wake up.

Rachel is wrapped in a bathrobe, and she's handing me one. "No more casual nakedness around here."

"Oh. Right."

The door of the computer room remains shut. Jake shows no sign of life, and doesn't join us for breakfast. I figure he was up much of the night. He probably didn't fall asleep till morning.

"He'll be fine," says Rachel, grabbing her overcoat as she nudges me toward the front door. "Come on, we're going to be late. It isn't like it's his first time alone in the house."

Love in the American Empire

Her comment brings to the surface memories I'd rather keep buried, that retroactive feeling of being the fool, the one who didn't know, excluded in my own home from my wife's secret. Whatever could have possessed her to conceal his presence from her own husband? This doesn't ring true, but I don't want to think about it now.

As we leave him sleeping and walk up the winding boulevard toward campus together, she takes hold of my arm. "It'll be fine," she says, "and then it will all go back to the way it was."

"Yes, of course," I say. "It's just for a couple days."

"Whatever happened to him over there," she says, "it's our responsibility. He's just one of thousands. It's the least we can do."

"The least." I want so much to believe her. I want to simply have faith and love her insanely. I don't want to think too closely about this last week. It doesn't bear scrutiny. But at least it's over now, the mystery solved. At least I have an answer now for that terrible sensation that she was keeping secrets from me. I wasn't imagining things. She was.

I know my wife that well. That's how close we are! Hopefully her deceptions have now come to an end.

20
Dario's Boyfriend, Gloria's Date

I'm tired but good-humored this morning, still nervous, maybe a little paranoid, but at least I'm on good terms with my wife as I kiss her goodbye across the street from Padelford Hall. I'm no longer feeling quite so confused. At least I know what's going on now.

Dillon is already in the room when I get there, entertaining two spellbound sorority girls. Throughout class he's at his charming and intelligent best. He gets my energy going. Between the two of us, we actually succeed in sparking an interest in the rest of the class. He gives me a thumbs-up sign as he walks out the door. It touches me.

I even manage to fire up my grad students a bit out of their post-lunch lethargy, and am feeling pretty good about the teaching profession when I notice that I'm leaving Padelford Hall about the same time Rachel gets off work.

I cross the street and catch her just coming out of the bookstore office, bundled up in her overcoat. She looks genuinely happy to see me. The doubts that have been tormenting me for a week are finally loosening their stranglehold. Right there in the hall outside the bookstore she kisses me on the lips, and it's a lot more than a hello kiss. It takes my breath away.

"Thanks, I love you, too," I gasp.

Love in the American Empire

"Does that answer any questions you might have?"

She knows I've got a pretty powerful imagination, which is why I worry so much. I've been working it overtime, pushing it to the limit. But really, what is there to worry about? My wife loves me. That's obvious.

A burst of laughter causes us to pull away from each other. Dario steps out of the office, just finishing off a bag of Cheetos, his fingers caked with orange cheese flavoring, flashing his thousand-kilowatt smile with orange flecks on his teeth. "Hey, Colin," he says. "You're looking mighty good today, as always. You two have a nice evening."

Just seeing the old bookseller so cheerful and flirtatious puts a grin on my face. "Someone's in an awfully happy mood," I mutter to my wife as we turn to leave.

"I think someone had a very good night," says Rachel confidentially, sweeping me away from the bookstore.

"Good for him," I say.

Oh, my God. It's really happening.

My wife goes on talking. I don't hear a word. I remember Dillon this morning in class, rested and alert, witty and perceptive, discussing Jim Thompson's lying, murderous sheriff in *Pop. 1280*, the ultimate unreliable narrator. The boy radiated wholesomeness. Am I to believe that cherubic face belonged to a young man fresh from his first gay experience?

I find myself in the middle of the student union hallway, caught between two bicycles trying to go in and out of the bike shop door at the same time. Rachel laughs at me, her absent-minded professor, and pulls me along on our way, but my mind is roaring with all of Dillon's questions about gayness, and now they seem to have a different meaning.

"I didn't think Dillon was gay," I offer feebly.

"He's not," says Rachel decisively, as though she knows. "Doesn't mean he might not try something. Funny what a little love can do. It's the best medicine."

"I could use a dose myself."

Rachel pats my hand discreetly. "We'll both have a great big spoonful when we get home."

She squeezes my arm and we walk along happily together, past the dormitories and Russian House and the sorority with the cupola, rubbing and bumping shoulders like two people in love. The closer we get to the house, however, without a word between us, without a mention of his name, Jake Bagley comes to dominate our thoughts.

"Obviously we can't tell anyone about our secret guest."

"Absolutely not," she says, quite seriously. "It's just for a few days, but I think we'd better decline all invitations and keep everyone away from the house."

"Which includes Gloria. And Dario."

"Especially Gloria and Dario," she agrees.

"Not even your mother."

"Above all, not my mother." We laugh. The boulevard winds down the hill toward home, lined by apartment buildings with banks of windows on both sides. From every window, someone seems to be watching us.

"It's going to be very different, not having any privacy for a few days," I caution her.

"We can handle it," she says. "We're adults. We know how to close the bedroom door."

"Do we?" I like her attitude. "I think I'm a little rusty on bedroom door-closing. I could use some practice."

I already know what her body will feel like in my hands when I peel away her clothes. I'm bounding up the stairs with the key to the front door already out of my pocket, in my hand and ready to insert in the lock, when I'm stopped mid-bound by a bittersweet New Jersey voice with a nasal twang saying, "Just like I figured, you forgot."

A short, skinny figure with tight curls crushed under a jaunty beret pops up from the porch seat.

"Gloria!" I exclaim, unable to keep the disappointment out of my voice. She doesn't appear to notice me, anyway, so no harm is done. Gloria only acknowledges the existence of my wife.

"I didn't hear from you today. I figured, 'She forgot.'"

Rachel gasps. "Oh, my God! I *did* forget. Are we late?"

"Not if we hurry." Gloria takes her arm. Suddenly my wife is being escorted away from me, away from the door.

"Hey, what's going on?" I cry, losing my cool, reaching out for my wife's hand and bringing her forward momentum to a halt.

Love in the American Empire

"Colin, I'm so sorry, I've got to leave," she tries to explain, extricating her hand from mine, finger by finger. "*Law of Desire* is playing at the Varsity, and I promised Gloria last week I'd go with her. I mean, it's written on my calendar, I just didn't see it this morning. I have to go. It's the one key Almodovar film that I've never seen."

"And it starts," says Gloria, pushing up her bulky overcoat sleeve and checking her watch, "in twenty minutes."

"Love you, sweetheart," says my wife. "Don't be mad, please."

She kisses me goodbye on the cheek and then hurries after Gloria down the stairs toward our car.

"What about me?" I want to call after them. I've already seen it twice, but it's such a fine film I could easily watch it again. Both women have already forgotten about me. They clamber quickly into our car through opposite doors, the doors slam, the engine growls, and they're gone up the avenue. I'm left standing on the porch alone.

Sometimes I hate Gloria.

21
The Price of Love

As I glumly turn away from the porch railing toward the door, I notice the scrape and scratch of raking.

Omar Volkonsky and his wife Odette are in the side yard cleaning up all the fallen leaves. I have been so distracted being ambushed by Gloria that I didn't notice them. Omar has amassed a crackling mountain of autumn debris in the patio. Odette is carrying leaves to the pick-up barrel, and she does so without getting a speck of dirt on her, like an expensive European fashion model.

Four-year-old Ilya is trying to use a rusty old rake which is much too big for him. As he tries to manipulate the claw end, the handle end swings out of control behind him, nearly blinding and then braining his two-year-old brother, Vanya, who miraculously avoids his older brother's deathblows, playing in a pile of leaves and occasionally shrieking with happiness.

I'm about to rush forward to intervene, probably confusing and alienating my landlords for all time but at least saving Vanya's life, when something attracts Ilya's attention, something that makes him drop the rake, thus sparing his little brother's skull, and head straight across the patio to the window into my apartment. Vanya is right behind him.

Love in the American Empire

What do they think they're doing? I stare in disbelief at these two junior spies. This has become a new game for them. Odette looks up and sees them, scolds them in Russian. They ignore her. She has to drop an armful of leaves and physically haul them away from the window.

I step back out of sight. By now they've told their parents about the naked young man. Clearly the two little boys are hoping to see more entertaining spectacles. Odette feels they've seen quite enough.

I retreat back toward my own porch, while the industrious raking continues. I hope Ilya and Vanya were thoroughly disappointed. I hope there was absolutely nothing to see.

The front door is unlocked. I step inside.

"Who are those annoying little kids?" asks Jake from the sofa. He's reading a slender volume called *The Art of Living*, a modern translation of Epictetus. He's stretched out on the sofa wearing one of my favorite shirts, a form-fitting black sleeveless, along with my new gray trunks. Admittedly, the shirt was getting a little tight on me, and I've never had much to show off in the bicep or chest departments. Since Jake is well-equipped in both, he looks better in my clothes than I do.

"They're my landlord's kids."

He glances piercingly at me over the top of his book. "Why do they keep looking in the window?"

Love in the American Empire

I lamely avoid answering the question. "Kids always look in windows, don't they?"

"Those kids have been encouraged." He's watching me carefully, waiting for me to spill the beans. "What's with all this giggling? They must see some pretty funny stuff in here."

"Yeah, I live a wild life." I gesture toward the book he's reading. "So, what do you think of that?"

His face lights up. "I've never read Epictetus before. I thought I knew the classics pretty well, but this guy's incredible."

"The original self-help book, two thousand years old."

It's exactly the kind of book this old college buddy of mine would love. I'm delighted to be the one to introduce him, glad to see the philosopher in him is still alive. I think he's about to go back to his reading, and instead he casually goes on, "Met a young friend of yours this afternoon. Said he was one of your students."

My heart shrivels in dread. Now there's a complication I never considered. "Oh, God."

"So now we've already got one person who knows I'm here."

"I'm so sorry. Listen, keep him out of it."

He raises an eyebrow in concern. "Little late for that. We had a nice talk."

"Watch yourself with him." I settle into the armchair at the end of the coffee table. "He's a good kid, don't get me wrong, but he's Mister Space Cadet, a total babe in the woods."

"He told me he was home-schooled up till now," says Jake. "Imagine that. Never in a classroom before."

"That's what I'm trying to say. He's naïve, totally sheltered. He's going through a lot of changes, and he's very unpredictable. I wish he didn't know you were here."

I can't read Jake Bagley's face, I never could, and that certainly hasn't changed. He's as inscrutable as ever. "Those kids out there sure seem to like him. They went wild when they saw him. They think he's *real* funny."

"Yeah, I'll bet they do.'"

He lays the slender book down open on his chest, and folds his arms behind his head. I wince, because it's my book and that breaks the spine and I don't treat my books like that. Still, I appreciate the gesture, his willingness to pause in his reading, because suddenly we're just two old pals hanging out together, chilling. Bright, cold sunshine is spilling through the windows. The afternoon is peacefully hushed.

"Keep the book. I knew it was right up your alley. I can easily get myself another copy."

"You're too good to me." He smiles that killer smile. "I need to ask you something." Now he isn't looking at me, he's looking at the ceiling, as though he's talking to God.

I notice his feet are up on the sofa, and I'm hoping they're not muddy. Rachel has very few rules, really, but one of them happens to be no shoes on the sofa. "Ask away."

Love in the American Empire

"It's a thought question."

"I'm braced."

He can tell I'm trying to clown around, to pull away from serious mode, and so he just shoots. "If you fell in love with someone, how much would you risk to have that love? Would you risk everything you had for her?"

I don't know what I was expecting, but it wasn't that. "Whoa, now that catches me by surprise. What a weird question."

"What I mean is," he says, trying again, "how far would you go for love, if you thought you really found it?"

The question makes me uneasy, right from the start. First of all, the terms. "Well, I *do* feel I've found it. With Rachel."

"Fine," he says. "Good. So, how far would you go for that love? If you thought your love for her was threatened or endangered. Would you fight for it?"

I'll admit, I'm not much of a fighter. But if someone were to threaten a person I love, especially Rachel, I'm sure I could become suitably aggressive. "If she were in danger, I would."

"Would you kill for her?"

His question gives me the creeps. "To protect her, yes. To possess her, no. No, of course not. No sane person goes that far. Killing to possess love, that's buying your happiness with evil."

Love in the American Empire

He crosses his legs, and when he moves one shoe, it leaves a smudge on the armrest. Damn. Rachel will be furious. I want to shout out a warning to him, but it's too late now. I keep my mouth shut.

"Okay, no killing," he says, like a patient teacher explaining the alphabet. "How about lying? Would you lie for love? How important really is this love business?"

I decide not to look at his shoes on the sofa any more, and instead to look up at the ceiling, just like he is. "I see what you're saying now. You're right. It's one of our most cherished myths, this coming together with the ideal partner. The ending of all good fairy tales. Everyone wants it. Would you cheat to get it?"

Because I've come so close to achieving true love with Rachel, I've got many friends who can scarcely hide how jealous they are. They can't help it. In their lives, with their luck, that urge to find an attractive mate has been frustrated. Why have I been lucky, and not them?

"Because really," I continue, "let's be honest, it's just an irrational glorification of that old built-in biological urge to reproduce."

"Well, sure, that's part of it," qualifies Jake. "Maybe that's what we start with, that biological urge, and then we romanticize it and call it love. But what I'm asking is – do you think true love is so important that, given the chance, I should snatch it at any price?"

Love in the American Empire

His persistence on this topic is spooking me. "Well, you're lucky if you get a chance to love at all. So it can't be very smart to throw chances away."

My answers aren't quite satisfying him. "But is love really so valuable that no other moral considerations apply?" Jake's face couldn't be more earnest. "Is all fair in love and war, or do moral judgments still count? What if the only way you can have love is to betray a friend?"

Sometimes, if you're scared enough, the only way out is to laugh. I laugh. I look at him stretched out on the sofa, half a dozen small pillows scrunched under his head, his pale, hairy legs crossed, the philosopher made comfortable. "Jake, you crack me up. You are such a thinker!"

I'm giving him too much attention, and that embarrasses him. He doesn't want personal attention, he wants me to take a stand. "Okay, but humor me, Colin, answer the question." When he's tracking an idea, he can be relentless. "What if Rachel were my wife, and not yours? What if you were in love with Rachel, would you take her away from me?"

He's testing me, he's pushing me to the very edge of self-doubt. "That's a hard one. I'm as selfish as the next guy, but I don't think I could screw your wife. Friendship is sacred for me."

He gives me a skeptical look. "Come on, Colin. You're talking to another man here. Are you telling me you consider friendship so sacred you'd give up a once-in-a-lifetime opportunity to have sex with perfection itself?"

Love in the American Empire

A trickle of sweat slides out of my armpit and down the side of my body. "Okay, so I'd probably at least consider it."

"What if she wanted you as badly as you wanted her?" He rolls over on the sofa and looks straight at me. *The Art of Living* slides off his chest and flops to the floor.

I'm flustered now. It's hard to think clearly. I pick up the book, smooth out the bent pages. "Being wanted intensely is part of the addiction."

He gets up off the sofa and walks toward me. "You're a funny guy, Colin. You never answer questions." He regards me thoughtfully. "Now, answer me. Would you risk wrecking a family to have the passionate love of an extraordinary woman? Would you run away with her to Canada? How far would you go? What is it worth, Colin, this love thing?"

He's standing there looking down at me. I feel like a pinned specimen of beetle. I'm kicking, but getting nowhere. The more I poke at his question, the more I prod it and turn it over, the less I want to answer it. It's a scary question he's asking me.

"Well, I know that if winning the love costs too much, if the guilt gets too strong, it ruins the pleasure." I can manage to say that much. "So every person draws a line on the value chart where, say, the moral cost of getting something outweighs the pleasure gain of having it."

He folds his arms across his chest. "And so?"

"So maybe if you were my best friend in the world, because of the extreme value I place on that, I would sacrifice my passion for your wife and instead honor the bond of trust between us."

"You think so, huh?" Jake smiles. "That's what Sir Lancelot thought. And you see where it got him."

"Yeah, well, Sir Lancelot betrayed King Arthur because he over-estimated his self-control. I wouldn't."

"Let me get this straight. You would live in sexual misery for the honor of a friendship?"

"Maybe."

"You're a better man than I am," says Jake. He returns to the sofa as though he got what he came for, and drops back down onto the cushions. He punches the pile of pillows under his head. "As far as I'm concerned, life is so pathetically short, so full of pain and unhappiness, that any chance you get at love should be snatched up immediately at any cost. Burn the bridges. Take no prisoners."

He stretches again, baring his belly and fondly slapping its flatness, and then says, "Hey, I gotta tell you, I owe you an apology. I sorta lost it the first time I walked in your bathroom and saw that electric toothbrush."

He grins at me, his eyes bright with mischief.

"Wait a second," I cry, "Are you the one who…?"

"Who do you think?" he says. He gives me a dopey, apologetic smile. "Sorry. I had a little psycho moment and forgot my manners. Never throw your host's electric toothbrush in the trash. It's rude."

"What's the big idea?"

Love in the American Empire

"I couldn't help myself."

"What have you got against electric toothbrushes?"

"I get impulsive sometimes. I gotta watch it." He's acting like some kind of dry television comedian.

I'm not laughing. "You felt an impulse to throw away our new electric toothbrush?" I can't hide my irritation.

"You don't see it at all, do you?"

His condescending smile smokes me. "See what?"

"It's such an unnecessary luxury! Seen in a global context, it's obscene."

"What are you talking about?" I say, trying not to sputter in frustration. "What's obscene about it?"

"Some people have to drink impure water every day of their lives because that's all they can get, and eat fly-covered meat and wear threadbare rags and spend a week's wages to buy aspirin for their kids. We're fighting and killing those people. While we, the mighty Americans, we don't even have to put out the energy to brush our teeth, the whitest on the planet, because for that we can harness hydroelectric power."

A laugh bursts out of me, unchecked. He ignores it.

"Okay, so what if it doesn't make sense? I was having a hard day, my pal had ditched out on me, I'd just made a trip to Vancouver for nothing, I was tired and I needed to piss and nobody was home, so I decided to borrow the facilities and pee like a civilized man instead of in the weeds behind the house, and there it was, white and slick and unnecessary, the latest in overpriced pharmaceutical gadgetry. I lost control."

Love in the American Empire

My mouth is hanging open. I can't believe I'm hearing right. "Well, I sure hope you won't lose control again." For one hair-raising moment, we look each other in the eye.

Then the front door is shoved open. Rachel blusters into the warm house out of the chilly evening. She waves from the open doorway, and I can hear Gloria's car chugging away up the street.

Rachel quickly presses the door shut behind her on the cold. She's looking flushed and beautiful, so very alive, and a little rattled.

"Good evening, boys."

She can tell she's interrupting something. I want to include her. "So, what did you think?"

"Whew, that is some movie," she announces. "Never seen anything quite like *that* before. The Varsity was packed." She shakes her head, smiling. "Took my breath away." She turns to Jake. "Do you like Almodovar?"

"Never seen anything by him."

"*Talk to Her*, his last one?"

"What a movie!" I chime in, to remind them I'm there.

"Well, in this one – it's called *Law of Desire* – a gay movie director flirts with this gorgeous young straight guy, who falls insanely in love with him."

Jake looks amused. "Well, there's a reversal."

She beams. He got it in one. She rattles on euphorically, completely distracted by the very thought of Almodovar's cinematic genius, unable to think about anything else, pacing, mugging, talking with her hands. I love Italians.

"There's an actress named Carmen Maura who plays a man who's had a sex change into a woman. And then, there's the young Antonio Banderas. Ai yi yi! There should be a law against being that handsome."

She continues non-stop, and while discussing all the wonders of the film, the movie-within-a-movie-within-a-movie that opens it, the pieta that ends it, and so on, she's taking off her pale blue raincoat, her green woolen neck scarf, her shiny black boots. Watching her I fall under the spell of a striptease, I can actually feel myself getting turned on. I only hope she's not having the same effect on our guest.

We never get back to discussing the price of love. My wife's arrival puts an end to that. The conversation becomes film talk, rapid and witty. When Rachel gets worked up like this, all animated and expressive, she's at her most lovely.

As for Jake, he listens to every word she says. He studies her every move, asks her one question after another. The more I watch them together, the more ill at ease I become.

He's acting like he's fallen in love with her.

Love in the American Empire

22
Rachel's Version

"Good night, you two," says Jake.

The door to the library clicks shut behind him.

My wife and I look at each other. The house belongs to us again. She goes into the bathroom and shuts the door. I get in bed first. It's embarrassing to admit, but I'm shaking. My body is literally trembling with anxiety. I'm not blind. I see where this is leading. I see that everything I hold most precious is on very shaky ground right now. I'm not sure about anything anymore.

I'm going to ask her tonight. I'm just waiting for her to get into bed. I want to know what I have to know.

The bathroom door opens. She's in her bathrobe. I listen to her footfalls and watch her shadow from under the electric blanket, which is turned up to HIGH and yanked up around my neck. She moves back and forth, in and out of sight, turning off the reading lamp by the armchair, getting a last drink of water from the refrigerator, folding something unseen and tucking it neatly into its drawer, doing some last minute private things in the bathroom. When she drops her bathrobe at the foot of the bed and slides under the covers, she doesn't wait for me to make advances. She cuddles right up against me, backing up into me and taking my arms and wrapping them around her.

Love in the American Empire

She knows me so well. My body stops trembling.

"You don't have to ask me," she says, pulling my arms closer around her. "I'll tell you everything tonight."

One of my tears falls on her shoulder. I'm so afraid of losing her. A tremor goes through my body.

I can't help it. She knows that.

"It happened the Saturday you took the train down to Portland, remember, for that MLA conference. I was putting in some extra hours up at the main bookstore on the Ave, so I didn't get home till that afternoon. I remember I spent my lunchtime reading Russell Banks' incredible new book, *The Darling*. I had thirty pages left to go."

"The one about the Sixties activist who gets caught up in the Liberian revolution?"

"That one, yes. I'd saved the ending to read that night. So I tuck into it, I've got Boo in my lap, he's in heaven, I'm in heaven. There's a knock at the door. I get clawed. Boo's pissed. I'm pissed, ten pages from the end of the book, all choked up, and interrupted.

"It's this uptight, nice-looking guy with psychopath eyes. He's asking for you. He looks military gone bad, slightly grubby. He's a little too much in your face, and he keeps looking back over his shoulder. It's pouring rain and he asks if he can come in and leave his phone number for his old college pal. Am I supposed to leave your friend on the porch in the rain? The first thing I know, just because he says he knows you, I'm alone in the house with a strange man and his

Love in the American Empire

backpack and traveling bag. He's dripping on the carpet and leaving wet footprints.

"I should ask him to write down his phone number and send him on his way, and instead I say, 'You look like you're starving.' And he says, 'You're right, I am starving.' So I fix him some bacon and scrambled eggs."

"You *cooked* for him?"

"He said he was your college friend. I admit, when I turned my back on him cooking, I could feel his eyes on me. You should have seen him wolf it down. He even asked for more toast and a refill of orange juice. He's slightly pushy. I'm thinking to myself, what if this guy's a nut case? What if I'm frying scrambled eggs for a rapist who asks his victims to cook for him first?"

We chuckle together under the electric blanket, but it's the nervous laughter of dread.

"There's a knock at the door. It's Omar. He asks in that formal Russian way if he can have a moment of my time."

"Which means you had to let him in?" I add, knowing my landlord's Russian traditions. I have learned, though trial and error, mostly error, that it is an insult to go up to a Russian door and not step inside. Odette has repeatedly tried to teach me this. To give them my rent check, I must cross the threshold of their home.

"So Omar must be invited in, and in he comes. 'You should know that a neighbor has phoned us,' says Omar. "There has been someone, a homeless man perhaps, seen around our house today. I just wanted you to be aware of that.' Then he looks up. 'Am I interrupting something?'

"I turn around to introduce your friend, Jake Bagley, and I say, 'Omar, this is…' and there's no sign of him. He's vanished. Which communicates one thing to me immediately. Your friend is hiding. I decide, on the spot, to protect him. After all, he's your friend. 'No, you're not interrupting anything, Omar. Thank you for the warning.'

"As soon as the door's shut, Jake comes in from the laundry room. He's got this edgy smile, and he straddles the kitchen chair again and goes back to finishing up his eggs, no explanation given.

"I won't be intimidated in my own home. 'Sounds like you scared one of the neighbors,' I say.

"He shrugs. 'I don't care about her. I care about you. Are you scared?'

"So, now I'm getting scared.

"But he's already inside my house, and I have to just deal with it. I didn't tell him exactly when you'd be home from Portland. I said early evening because I was scared to admit I'd be alone so much of the night.

"So he finishes eating, and then gets a flask of Southern Comfort out of his backpack. He takes a swig and offers me one. I say no, but that doesn't stop him. Suddenly I've got a stranger getting drunk in my living room."

"Oh, my God."

Love in the American Empire

"Then he starts crying. Just sitting on our sofa, with tears running down his face, and he starts telling me one horrible story after another. They just pour out of him. The things he had to do in Fallujah to "secure" a neighborhood. The things he watched other guys in his unit do. How scared people were of the soldiers, and how much they hated them, and this guy is quietly falling apart in front of my eyes.

"Colin, maybe I was insane, I couldn't help it, I took him into my arms."

"You did *what?*"

"It had nothing to do with sex or bodies. It had to do with a damaged human being who needed some kind of contact and comfort. I didn't know what else to do. You can't just ignore misery like that. Fortunately, he was on the sofa, so there was plenty of room. Unfortunately, once I was holding him and he was clinging to me…"

"Oh, my God."

" I mean, nothing happened, Colin, really, seriously, but…"

"But? What do you mean, *but?*"

"Well, it was pretty obvious. I mean, I could feel it."

"Oh, my God."

"But I'm your wife, sweetheart. I told him he had to let go of me."

"You did?"

"And he did let go."

"He did?"

Slowly I stop hyperventilating.

"He apologized. I suppose I could have been more scared, but by then I wasn't. I could see he was a good man with very troubled thoughts. He needed someone, Colin, and he was reaching out, and it had to be me. He asked for a place to stash his things. He asked if we could leave the laundry room door unlocked."

"So that's it."

"And he asked me to let him manage his own introduction to you, face to face. He said you two had parted on a bad note, many years ago. Until he could talk to you, he needed to get his papers in Vancouver and keep out of sight. I could see he was in serious trouble. So I told him he could hide his things here. Was that wrong?"

"Of course not."

"It seemed the right thing to do. And I said, sure, he could tell you himself. I figured that meant when you got home that night.

"But you came home late from that conference, remember? The train got delayed for two hours, remember?"

I repress a shudder. "I do remember."

"And the next day when I looked in the laundry room, he was gone. I thought he'd be back, but he wasn't. And there you were, and you started hearing things and seeing things, but I didn't know whether he was there or not, and I've been waiting for him to tell you ever since."

Love in the American Empire

The living room is hushed. A car drones by down below in the street.

I look at her lying beside me. I want to ask her, "Are you attracted to him?" I want to ask her, "Did you kiss him?" I want to ask her, "Did you two have sex?' I don't.

"Does that answer your question?"

"Yes," I mumble, and kiss her good-night.

"No, it doesn't." I'm surprised when she takes my face in her hand and turns it toward her. "I know you too well," she confronts me. "I haven't put your heart at rest. Now, don't lie to me, Colin. What is it that's troubling you, sweetheart?"

I try to tell her, and it's pathetic, all over the place. I like to think of myself as eloquent. Put me in an uncomfortable situation, and I can hardly put three words together.

She laughs at me. "You're not making a lick of sense. What is it I don't understand?"

"When we were best friends in college," I say, trying again, "Jake and I were pretty loose with each other." I'm not looking her in the eye. "Closer than brothers. He was ready to take it one step farther than I was. That's why we stopped being friends."

"You're saying he came on to you?"

"Sort of."

"Then I really don't understand what you're worried about," says Rachel matter-of-factly. "Women don't interest him. I couldn't be with anyone safer. You have some pretty foggy notions of sexuality, Colin. To my experience, men are one thing or another. Jake isn't interested in both you and me."

I laugh in surprise at her. "Why ever not? Men are people, too. Don't be fooled, sweetie. Listen, it is one of the best kept secrets of the male gender. We act as straight as we can, but we all know that, under the right circumstances, our crazy dick can make us do just about anything."

"And that's what worries you."

"It worries most men. You never know what that crazy thing is going to do next."

She smiles sadly. "You just like to worry, Colin. It distracts you from life." A moment later she's dead to the world, far over on her side of the bed.

Not me.

Sleep won't come anywhere near me. No position in bed is quite the right one. It's going to be a long and hellish night. He's come back into my life, this man I rejected so long ago. And now he wants my wife. Am I going to just step aside? Or am I ready to kill for love?

23
Losing Madeline

By the first meager light of morning I'm watching Rachel sleep.

I notice pointed ears perk up from the little bagel of fur curled beside me. Boo yawns when he notices I'm awake. I scratch him behind the ears and under the chin. He purrs loud enough to wake her. She doesn't budge.

Maybe it's impossible to ever really know anyone, but you always think you know your wife. How can this woman sleeping beside me, the true center of my being for the past seven years, be a stranger? Do I have to wonder from now on if she's telling me the truth? Because where there's one surprise, there are more.

She moans in her sleep and rolls toward me, snuggling up against me. For a moment the sheer pleasure of closeness with her blots out all the dreads and suspicions coursing through me. How could this affectionate partner ever want to deceive me? Boo decides to investigate, touching his cold little nose to the tip of Rachel's nose. Her eyes blink open.

"Good morning, Boo," she says, fondly stroking his head, then she rolls around in my arms and gives me a kiss on the nose. "And good morning to you, too." She looks immediately into my eyes. I could never fool this woman for long. She knows every dark little corner of my mind.

Love in the American Empire

I try to hide the fear inside me, but she can see that she's rattled me. She'll give me time. I need to get my personal pride back in place.

"You remember I'm going to my parents for dinner tonight?" she murmurs into my ear, as our arms and legs go about their business seeking out pleasure.

I've forgotten. "Oh, right. Right."

Occasionally she likes to go visit them in their condo up north. Sometimes I go with her, but often it's their time to be a little family again. She proceeds to tell me what's in the refrigerator and what I can make for dinner tonight, enough for Jake and me, but I hardly hear a word. I don't care if I eat a hot dinner or not. Jake can take care of himself. What I care about is this dear woman in my arms. I can't quite shake this worrisome sense of doom.

Jake doesn't join us for breakfast this morning, and we don't question it. The man has demons, and clearly has to wrestle with them. Who knows when he actually gets to sleep? We slip out of the house quietly and head up the avenue toward campus. When I say goodbye to her outside Padelford Hall, I won't see her again until later tonight.

"Is everything okay between us?" she says, kissing me goodbye.

"Everything is perfect," I say.

Dillon seems preoccupied in class, not his usual self at all. I'm curious to know what he thought of the guest in my house, but don't want to ask him for fear of giving it too much importance. Better to blow it off, and hope he does, too. He only raises his hand a couple times half-heartedly, and leaves as soon as the bell rings. I find myself wondering if he's heading for the bookstore to visit Dario. I suppose he could have made a worse choice for his first experience. I try not to feel parental concern for a young man who is not my son.

Young people are clumsy in love, but they survive. He'll be fine.

By the time I head home, I'm tuckered out and hungry and trying to remember what exactly Rachel told me I should be preparing for dinner tonight. It's been a moody gray day with an icy breeze warning there's much worse weather to come. As I walk home, I decide that tonight I'll borrow Rachel's reading armchair while she's at her parents' house, get into some comfortable clothes, put my feet up, and enjoy a good novel with a glass of wine. Then I remember that Jake will most likely be there, and that my reading fantasy probably won't happen.

The front door, however, is locked and no one's home. Boo races around a bit in excited circles, alone too long, a can of cat food long overdue. He's got his head happily in his food bowl and I'm halfway through adding tortellinis to a thick cheddar soup when I hear the front door open.

"Dinner's almost ready."

"Sounds good to me," says Jake, who disappears into the bathroom for a while. He emerges after about five minutes, the sound of the flushing toilet following him out the door. He disappears into the computer room, where he's got his stuff arranged in a little nest in the corner. I've got to concentrate on turning down the heat, keeping the cheddar soup stirred, adding the crumbled hamburger and olives. Suddenly I realize someone is standing behind me, barefoot, watching. I drop the ladle. It clatters and splatters to the floor.

"Sorry," he says. He snatches up the fallen ladle before I can get it, and rinses it off under the faucet. "Didn't mean to make you jump," he says, handing it back to me. "Looks mighty tasty." When he sees I'm going to be taking the pot off the stove, he gets out of my way, straddling a kitchen chair and watching me with a look of amused interest. It doesn't take me long to get my quickly-improvised concoction on the table and in our bowls.

We're both hungry. We go at it. As we gradually ease up into more leisured dining, he pauses momentarily and smiles that toothy smile.

"You can't imagine some of the simple stuff you miss. Like the pleasure of being alone. The pleasure of just being quiet. The pleasure of a hot shower in the morning. The pleasure of a toilet where you can just sit with nobody waiting for you to finish. The pleasure of a day without standing in one fucking line after another. I experienced pure joy today, man. I sat in your living room, and I listened to Mozart's *Requiem*, and I read *The Symposium*."

I can see from the features of his face that he's remembering. Only his body is still in front of me. His eyes are seeing stuff I'll never see. I watch his face slowly become sad. I'm convinced he doesn't even remember I'm still there until he speaks. "You ever lose someone you love?"

The question totally catches me off guard. By answering quickly I accidentally tell the truth. "Once."

"What happened?" he says, sensing he's struck a vein. "Tell me."

"I don't want to. Why should I?"

"Go on. It'll be good for you."

"She was my high school sweetheart. Her name was Madeline. She was skinny and wore braces and thick, clunky glasses. Maddy lived a block away. We were inseparable. We could read each other's minds. We would kiss for hours."

I don't go on.

"How did you lose her?" he asks.

"She changed," I say. "Over the three years of high school, she changed. She got contact lenses and her braces came off and she gained weight in all the right places. She got so pretty the school jock asked her to the prom. She accepted."

"Ouch."

"I went crazy. We had a fight. She dropped me. The morning after the prom she died in a car accident. I was in therapy for a year."

He's looking at me like he actually cares. That much attention unnerves me.

"Never thought I'd love anyone again until Rachel walked into my life." I eat a little, pull out of the spell. "I never think about high school now, because that means thinking about Madeline. Don't get me wrong. It was puppy love. It was nothing compared to what I've got now with Rachel. But it was the world to me then. The world. And it slipped through my fingers."

Enough memories. "How about you?"

After all, that's what this is all about. He's got something he's trying to say, which is why he brought up loss in the first place. He's having a hard time getting it out.

"The guys get to be like your brothers. There were a couple guys…"

That's all the farther he can go. Something is left out here, left unfinished, and I'll never know the loss he's trying to get off his chest.

"That's the only thing that hurts right now," he says. "The guys I'm leaving behind. They're my boys. I'm their Sarge. They're going to be fucking pissed at me.

"They're kids, Colin. They believe what you tell them. I was like them. It's like, you're in one world, and you believe it's real, and you're ready to fight for that world, and then you get your face pushed into another world that was there all along, and you realize you were believing a lie. And there you are, stuck in fucking Iraq, killing for something you don't believe in, dying for it.'

I can't stand it anymore. I keep waiting, but I'm never going to find out unless I ask. I just want to know the truth.

Love in the American Empire

"Jake," I say, trying not to sound desperately urgent, "what exactly is going on between you and my wife?"

"Me and your wife?" That gets his attention. "What are you talking about, Colin? There's nothing going on." He looks me straight in the eye. "Nothing! Other than, well, I mean, she's told you, hasn't she? You do realize that Rachel and I knew each other before?"

24
The Handwriting on the Envelope

I remember to breathe.

I say, "Sure, yeah, she mentioned that." I avoid his eyes. I push back my kitchen chair and start gathering up the plates and silverware and pots. He insists on washing, I dry, and soon we've gone our separate ways.

All the time my mind is reduced to a whirling mess. The concept that Rachel and Jake have ever known each other before stuns me. The thought processes of my brain are jammed. This can't be true. This changes everything. I feel like I've been punched in the head. I can't think about anything else, unable to get past this disturbing confirmation that there's something about this whole predicament I still don't understand.

Rachel comes home early, finds me in her reading chair, smiles, and says, "Sorry, sir, you'll have to vacate. That chair is reserved." It's one of our little games, her territoriality about her armchair, and our humor feels so normal it's hard to believe this woman has brought an old lover into our house in a brazen, audacious deceit.

She appropriates the chair and finishes her novel. I get a few paragraphs written on multiple temporal positions in narrative structure. I wait until we're in bed and she's switched off the night light, until my eyes are adjusted to the darkened living room, and the light from the streetlamps has highlighted the edges of the furniture, before I ask her the question that's turning the inside of my mouth to acid. "Jake says you two knew each other before."

I can't hear her breathing anymore. I'm looking at the back of her shoulder as I say it, and she slowly rolls over to face me.

"We went on a date."

"You never mentioned it."

"One date. It's nothing for you to worry about."

"Was this before you knew me?"

"Of course."

"Why didn't you tell me?"

"It wasn't that important. I was afraid you'd think it was more than that."

"More like what?"

"Like a boyfriend or an affair. But it wasn't."

"Was it a good date?"

"It was twenty years ago."

"You should tell me the truth," I say simply and bluntly.

"Why do you think I don't?" She almost loses her temper here, but I can also see that her eyes are bright because they're wet with emotion. "Why would I want to torture you? I don't like watching you worry. Besides, it hurts my feelings. It means you doubt me. Yes, I knew him. I knew a lot of guys before I met you. Because we went on a date didn't mean anything. So why tell you, and give you something to worry about?"

But by now I'm worrying, and there's no stopping me. "But that means, when he showed up on our doorstep, you already knew him. You would have recognized each other."

She sighs. "To say the least."

"But you never mentioned it."

"No," she admits, "I left it out. It wasn't important. He wasn't here because of me. He was here to see you."

One date, huh?

I lie awake long after she's settled into the regular breathing of sleep, thinking about that date, hoping they were both inhibited and miserable and hated every minute of it. Down in the street I can hear two very drunk fraternity boys shouting at each other. Each of them thought the other one had brought the keys to the car.

I must be one distracted mess, because for the next couple days I don't remember a thing. I can see from my lecture notes that I taught two classes on temporal points of view in first person, in other words, the various stopping-points in the time-line from which the narrative is being told. I don't remember a thing about either lecture, or about my office hours or my evening, and in fact, not much until Saturday afternoon, when Mrs Vespucci interrupts the restful stillness of our home by calling her daughter in high distress. Apparently Mr Vespucci has failed to read the directions and now they can't get their new DVD player to work.

Love in the American Empire

"I'm going to head over to Mom's," says Rachel, at the end of the call. "It won't take long."

Since Jake never came home last night, I've suddenly got the house to myself. That means several hours of pure concentration ahead. Well, I can certainly use it. I'm trying to formulate an outline of where I need to go in my book. I've got a paragraph here for my chapter on "The Lying Narrator," and one for "The Deluded Narrator," and a couple others that need work. I settle into the computer room, a steaming cup of coffee by the monitor, lights dim, just me and the text, trying to label the phenomenon of reader's trust, how it's created, how the narrator gains or loses it.

My mind keeps going blank. It's like the circuits keep blowing.

I find myself standing in the laundry room.

I'm wide awake, I'm just so preoccupied I keep losing track of things. I'm loading the washer with all white clothes, emptying in the contents of the wicker laundry basket. I crank the knob, give the contents a good swig of detergent, and close the washer lid.

Then the boiler goes off, and suddenly the laundry room is hushed. It's not until then that the idea occurs to me. I try to ignore it. I pick up the laundry basket and turn out the light. But it isn't long before I'm locking the front door of the house. I know Jake has a key, but unlocking the door will at least slow him down and I'll hear him coming. I go back into the laundry room, and this time close the door behind me.

Love in the American Empire

Farther back, past the boiler, is the area behind the stairs where the circuit box is mounted. He's still got some stuff here, hidden away in the dead space under the staircase, the contents of his backpack spread out on the cement floor. I might as well admit right here that I've already looked through all his things in the computer room.

I can't help it. I need to know everything I can. I'm way beyond being polite. This is survival.

I find what I'm looking for, the stuff that was in his backpack, papers in a variety of plastic bags. I crouch over them, heart pounding. Some of them have dated entries, so they must be parts of a journal, in several small notebooks. I read through a bit. He doesn't have the best handwriting. In one he's in Baghdad. A lot of it is military talk. I remember part of one sentence. "…that little girl screaming over her dead father." That one fragment I remember. Some magazine articles on the war, some essays he was working on, one called "The Illusion of Military Justice," but actually most of it is a blur now, most of that pile of worn-out paper with frayed edges is erased from my memory, because of the letter I find.

I recognize the handwriting on the envelope.

It's hers.

The temperature in the laundry room plunges to icy cold, because otherwise why am I trembling as I slide the letter out of the envelope?

A key turns in the front door.

The lock clicks, and the door is pushed open.

Love in the American Empire

I stuff the letter back in the envelope, return everything to exactly where it was, get up off my knees and slide the baby stroller back in front of his hiding place. Just as I reach the washing machine, it chugs to a halt, and then launches itself into spin cycle.

I step into the kitchen, closing the laundry room door behind me.

"Those two," says Rachel. "Watching them try to figure out that DVD player was a truly terrifying experience. I hope we never get that bad when we get to be their age."

The very thought that she's talking about us sharing old age together prompts me to get this whole thing out in the open, but I can't quite tell her the truth, I don't want her to know I've been going through his papers, snooping through her letters.

"Mom sent you a slice of her peach pie."

Mrs Vespucci's pies are to die for. "I adore your mother," I say, diet suddenly forgotten, utterly distracted from my goal. I open the Tupperware container. Inside is a hearty wedge of glazed crust oozing gobs of thick peach syrup. "Um, did you write letters to Jake?"

She stiffens, but I get the feeling she may have been waiting for me to find this out. "I did," she says simply.

"I thought you said it was just one date a long time ago."

"That's all it was."

"But you're writing him letters. Letters aren't just one date. Letters are now."

"The letters came later. They're separate. Come on, sit down with me. Let me get this clear with you."

She takes me by the hand and leads me to the sofa, where she snuggles up close to me. "All right, now listen carefully. I'm going to tell you everything. I've been leaving out part, because it's completely unnecessary and will only bring you grief, but now I'll tell it all. About oh, what, say six months ago, I got a letter from this guy I once went on a date with back in college. And he was now stationed in Iraq, and he begged me to let him write letters to me. Now, tell me, was it wrong to write back to him?"

"Of course not."

"So, yes, I wrote to him. Writing to him was harmless. He already knew I'd married his old college pal. He already knew our address."

She takes hold of my hand and presses it between both of her own. "There's nothing more to it than that."

"Then why didn't you tell me?" I ask.

She throws my hand into the air. "For the obvious reason," she cries, and rises from the sofa. "Look at you right this minute. You've become totally irrational. You have this illusion that I am so irresistible that someone is going to steal me away."

"It's no illusion."

Love in the American Empire

"It's your own personal distortion, Colin," she says to me. "You think I'm going to do the same thing your old high school girlfriend did. So, yes, I wrote a few harmless letters to this poor guy in Iraq who I went on one date with twenty years ago. Okay? That's the extent of it. He showed up here completely without warning. He needed help, Colin. We're the only two people he knew in town that he could trust. Now you've got it all. Have I put you at ease?"

She has her arms around my neck.

"I'm trying to believe you," I tell her.

"This is where the problem lies," she says, kissing my hot forehead. "Too much gray matter in there, working too hard. You're always imagining the worst. You can't see life for what it really is."

25
Just One Date

I wake to whispering voices, my wife and a man. I can see the two of them in the kitchen, just out of my sightline from the bed. The living room is gray. It must be very early morning. I see bare legs, four of them. I jump out of bed, adjust my jockey shorts, and take a few steps to get a better view.

Rachel sees me first. "Good morning, sleeping beauty. Want some carrot juice?"

The sweaty man turns around, and grins. "Good morning, Professor Wetmore."

To my sleep-addled brain, it looks like Dillon is standing in the kitchen with my wife in his underwear.

"I think I've found a Sunday morning running partner," says Rachel, slapping Dillon on his damp shoulder. "This guy sets a good pace."

"Your wife nearly killed me," says Dillon.

I nod. "She nearly kills *me*."

Boo is doing figure-eights around Dillon's running shoes, tail straight up in the air, purring like a tractor. Dillon bends down and scratches him under the chin, then straightens up and looks at me.

"Professor Wetmore, I have a confession to make."

I swallow, with difficulty, and force a smile. "You do?"

He's beaming. "I've been working on a real paper. With one topic and one argument. I decided to try it."

"Is that so?" I'm confounded, not only completely caught off-guard but rather delighted. "Well, you're full of surprises this morning. What changed your mind?"

"I had to try thinking for myself. For twelve years, my Dad has been my teacher. For twelve years, there has been a right answer and a wrong answer. I'm just feeling more comfortable making decisions on my own, that's all. I sorta like thinking for myself. I think I'm good at it.'

We laugh. "Stay for breakfast," says Rachel.

"Nah, I can't," says Dillon awkwardly.

Rachel pushes it, which is unusual for her. "And what's so much better than my scrambled eggs?"

"Well, to be honest, I've got another running date," he says, heading for the door. He's laughing.

"My wife was just a warm-up?" I ask incredulously.

"I'm insulted," she says.

We're just teasing, but I can tell Dillon doesn't find us very funny. "Thanks for asking me, though." He's anxious to leave, and in a moment is bounding down the stairs heading for home.

There's no sign of Jake all day. When it starts to rain later this afternoon, we drive up to Scarecrow Video and check out *Winged Migration*, a French documentary film with breathtaking photography of birds in flight. The camera seems to be flying along with them. I can hardly believe my eyes. I look over at Rachel midway through the movie, and she's got tears lining her face. "They're so beautiful," she sniffs. It's hard to watch the acting out of the laws of nature without sheer awe.

We go to bed early, pooped after a long weekend.

It's somewhere in the middle of the night, and I happen to be rolling over, half-asleep, shifting my arm and leg to more comfortable positions, when I notice a shadow move in the living room.

I jerk halfway up from the bed with a gasp. It's Jake, who must have come in through the laundry room door, in an effort not to disturb us. He's trying to get down the hallway to his makeshift bed. He motions me to relax, to not say a word, mouths the words, "Sorry, sorry," urging me to go back to sleep, and I do, lying back down beside Rachel.

She appears to sleep through the whole thing.

Far too early Monday morning, while the three of us are having toast and eggs, Mrs Vespucci calls to alert her daughter to a sale on T-bone steaks at Safeway. She also informs her that the woman who used to babysit Rachel as a child has passed away in her sleep.

"I've got a funeral to attend on Tuesday morning," Rachel tells us when she puts down the phone. I know her well enough to see she'd rather not talk about it. She'll be crying enough later without starting now.

Jake disappears without explanation shortly after.

Love in the American Empire

When I come home this afternoon, after a long day on campus, I find a note on the kitchen table written in bold, black marker:

> *Meeting Gloria for coffee. Will bring*
> *back a sweet treat for my honey.*

Jake comes home after I've been at work in the computer room for an hour. I hear him in the bathroom, the toilet flushing. I hear him in the kitchen, the refrigerator door opening and closing. Then nothing at all, and I think he's fallen asleep until I realize he's standing behind me.

"Jesus! You scared the shit out of me," I blurt out ungraciously.

"Sorry, man," he says. "I just needed a couple meds, and they're here in my stuff." He fumbles around in a denim pocket, and pulls out two white pills, which he bounces once on his palm before closing it into a fist. "Didn't mean to creep up on you."

He's heading out the door when I say, "You wrote letters to my wife."

He stops with his back to me. "Guilty," he says, and then turns around. "I needed someone. I'm sorry, man, to borrow your wife." He's smiling as he says it. "She was the smartest girl I ever dated."

Something about the way he says it rubs me wrong. "I thought you guys only went on one date."

Love in the American Empire

"Yeah, one actual *date*," he says, "but obviously we got to know each other first. I mean, do you consider coffee together dates?"

"Actually, yes, I do," I say, unnerved and annoyed. "Don't you?"

He smiles at me, and shakes his head. "Then it was a little more than one date." The phone rings, interrupting us. It's a cheerful robot selling real estate. I hang up, but it breaks the spell. Before I know what he's doing, he has his jacket on and is heading out the door.

When Rachel gets home, she's not only zippy and funny from too much espresso but she's got a cluster of yummy-looking bakery goods dripping with maple frosting and nuts. "Diet restrictions will be lifted tonight," she says, "and look what else I've got. I stopped by Scarecrow Video to return *Winged Migration* and, guess what?" She holds up the DVD of *Children of Paradise*. "I saw it there, and had to check it out. I'm dying to see this again. I haven't seen it since college. Let's watch it tonight, okay? Okay?"

I love her when she gets all worked up. "Okay," I say, knowing that it's three hours long, but it's such a pleasure, that brilliant French epic of the theater world, such a heartbreaking love story. "Yes, let's," I say, tasting a few glazed hazelnuts and a gob of maple frosting on the tip of my finger. I can tell the death of her old babysitter is on her mind, and so we watch the video, the whole thing, crying together through the sad parts, loving every minute, and we finish off every crumb of our nutty baked delights.

She's dressed in black at the breakfast table the next morning, since she'll be leaving straight from work to go to the funeral. She's distracted, irritable and not very hungry, sliding half her scrambled eggs over into my plate. Now's not the time to ask her, so I try to remember that she's hurting and let it all go.

But I need to know. This is driving me crazy. Every time I almost reach some kind of peace of mind, another doubt rears its head.

By the end of the day she seems to be over the worst of the grieving and so after dinner, once Jake has slipped out the door on one of his furtive appointments, as Rachel and I are doing the dishes, Rachel at the sink lathering them with soap, me with the dishtowel drying them and putting them away, I finally say, "Did you really have just one date with him?"

My question is unexpected. For a moment she seems to not even know what I'm talking about. Then she sighs. "Are you obsessing?" she asks, without turning around.

"Oh, maybe a little." I try to be witty, light-hearted, vaguely rational and even-tempered and sane. "No, really, how long did you know him?"

She seems to ponder her reply as she rinses the last few soapy dishes, dries her hands on the dishtowel, and turns to face me squarely. "Sit down."

I do.

"Put away that dish towel, and listen to me. I'm not getting through to you. Jake Bagley and I sat next to each other in Classics and Philosophy. We talked about Socrates together. We had coffee together a few times. I paid for my own coffee. He's a smartie, and nice-looking, and troubled loners have always been one of my specialties."

"News to me."

"That's because you're a troubled loner."

"Me? Troubled? A loner?"

She smiles patiently at my bumbling about. "He asked me out on a date, yes, Colin, once." For a moment she seems to be remembering it. I try to read her face. "Let's just say it was a little too successful."

"What's that supposed to mean?"

She turns her back on me and starts wiping down the drainboard vigorously. "I don't want to discuss it. Really, hon, it's not worth it. It's the kind of thing you worry about."

"Why would I worry about it?" I say, trying to keep the worry out of my slightly-too-loud voice.

"You'll start making something out of it. I know you too well. I don't know how to describe what happened between us."

I can't remain sitting down any longer. I feel like I've got an icy, fatal dose of liquid anxiety surging through my veins. "Just try to say it. I can handle it. What happened?" I begin pacing at the end of the kitchen, watching her scrub the same places on the drainboard over and over again with the sponge, as though there might be a speck or crumb that could have escaped her.

"Please, Colin, don't. See, you're getting agitated. This is only going to agitate you more."

"Why would it agitate me?"

She turns her back on me and rinses out the sponge in the sink. Then she looks at me and sighs. "We were all over each other."

"What?"

"Yes. We were like nuts for each other. We were *too* sexually attracted. I had never felt so physically aroused."

"Okay," I say, trying to swallow, cutting her off. "I get the point."

"Sorry, sweetie," she says, with a kiss on the cheek, "but you asked. It didn't make any sense. It was just physical. It was so intense we freaked each other out. Neither of us was ready for that kind of intensity."

Now I'm afraid to go on. "How far did you go?"

She's not looking at me. "We got so worked up we were just about to take our chances without a condom."

I suck in an apprehensive little gulp of air.

"Don't worry," she says. "I came to my senses and got out of his apartment fast."

My sigh of relief is audible.

"We never saw each other again. We never called each other. We pretended like we didn't know each other when we passed on campus. Two decades later, out of the blue, I get a letter from Iraq."

I'm stunned. I can't speak.

"Now do you see why I didn't tell you?" she says tenderly, touching my cheek. It feels like my cheek has turned to stone.

What am I supposed to think? I stare down at the patterns in the linoleum. "Do you still feel the same way about him? Do you still want him?"

"I want you," she says. "Come on, get ready for bed. That funeral really wiped me out."

She no sooner puts her head down on the pillow, however, than she falls deeply sleep. I hold her. I watch her. There's no sleep for me.

This man should not be living in my house. This man is a viable threat to my marriage. Do I have to ask him to go? Would he turn dangerous? Would I have to fight him to get him to leave? I'm tormented with doubts tonight, wishing I'd never heard of Jake Bagley, cursing him for bringing so much grief and loss into my life. Is violence ever justified? Would I kill for love?

A gunshot wakes me.

It's a sound I never thought I'd hear in my own house. I'm appalled and terrified. When I turn to see how Rachel is taking it, I find myself alone in bed. I leap to my feet. Where is she? Is she in danger? My God, has she been hurt? There's something wrong with my lower limbs, like they've fallen asleep and aren't working right. I get to the hallway, and at the end of the hall I can see a light from behind the bathroom door. And I see something seeping under the door. I'm running down the hall toward the door, running, running.

I sit up in bed. My heart is pounding. Slowly I get a grip on what's real.

Fingers close over my wrist. "Sweetie, are you okay?" says Rachel beside me, gripping my arm, shaking me.

"Bad dream," I say, trying not to let my voice quaver.

Her arms wrap around me. She squeezes me. "Go back to sleep."

An hour later, Jake wakes us up with a piercing wail of terror. Both of us look toward the hallway.

"I'm fine," he calls out huskily.

We stay where we are.

26
Vespucci Thanksgiving

He hasn't left yet. It was supposed to be for just a couple days. Soon he will have been here a week.

Rachel and I are walking on eggshells. We try to pretend that everything is fine, but there's an icy wall of pain between us, and neither of us is quite brave enough to risk removing it.

Now that I know the truth, I think it's only a matter of time. I expect at any moment to come upon her and Jake whispering together, or worse. When this does happen, when I walk into a room and they're exchanging a furtive kiss, I will hopefully conduct myself with wisdom.

Once again for the entire day Jake disappears, going about whatever his murky business connections entail here in Seattle, but his presence hovers over the house, his baggage and bedding crowd my home office. His imminent, unpredictable return controls the intimacy level all afternoon, and keeps it low. Both Rachel and I maintain a guarded silence regarding him. Because he's been to Iraq, because he's personally waded through the evil, there's a special urge to protect him, to take on his sins as our own. We're implicated. His festering mental wounds are ours to heal.

We owe him something. The only question is how much.

Love in the American Empire

Tonight, the night before Thanksgiving, we invite Dillon to join us for dinner. Rachel makes her incredible tomato sauce, and we have giant ricotta-stuffed shells of pasta. All four of us crowd together around the table in our tiny kitchen, bumping knees against each other's chair legs. Jake and Dillon are cautious of each other, a bit reserved, but seem to get along. I'm used to my wife's cooking, so I pace myself and savor each mouthful, but Jake and Dillon almost make themselves sick stuffing themselves with multiple helpings.

We go through a bottle of wine, and then another. We don't mention Iraq. Mostly we sit around the kitchen table enjoying Dillon's perceptions of life in Seattle. His candid observations soon have the four of us laughing that wild, crazy, infectious laughter you can't stop. Boo jumps up on Dillon's lap as often as he can get there.

At one point, as I'm coming out of the bathroom, Jake is approaching to go in. As we pass by each other, Jake reaches out and grabs me by the shoulders. We've both had plenty of wine by that time.

"You don't trust me yet, do you?"

I offer up a surprised half-laugh of confusion.

Jake suddenly pushes me back against the bathroom door by the shoulders, and brings his knee up sharply, violently toward my groin.

I curl up like a slug, with a wince of anticipated pain. His knee never comes close to touching me. It's just a little ultra-butch military clowning around to prove a point.

Love in the American Empire

"I'm your friend, Colin. A friend wouldn't knee you in the crotch."

Other that this moment between Jake and me, it isn't a particularly memorable night, except that all four of us seem to believe, in spite of the evidence against us, that the situation can somehow improve, that happiness can be achieved.

Dillon leaves early to study. Jake has business elsewhere. Rachel and I find ourselves quickly alone together, washing the dishes. Such a simple act, one we've done so often, yet every wet plate she passes to me seems like a precious thing now that I sense, in my gut, that I'm losing her.

We have one holiday left to share together, Thanksgiving. That particular holiday for the Vespucci family is an eight-hour ordeal.

It begins the next day around two in the afternoon, at the compact, modern condo of Rachel's parents in a suburb just north of Seattle. Nick and Rita Vespucci answer the door like two happy little Italian fireplace dolls, gray-haired and twinkly-eyed and spry, she in apron, he in suspenders. For Italians in general, and the Vespucci family in particular, any holiday provides an opportunity for sensory overload, a socially-endorsed stuffing with good food and wine. Thanksgiving is the Italian-American zenith of this tradition of celebratory gluttony.

No one rivals Rita Vespucci, kitchen master. She's a wonder to behold as she brings all her dishes to fruition simultaneously, like an eight-armed Indian goddess of cooking. She's stirring, chopping, scooping, scraping, slicing and sprinkling, sometimes all at once. Everyone else, as usual, gathers around the kitchen sidelines, heady with appetizing aromas, ready to get out of the way at a moment's notice.

"Nick, where are you? Come on, this is ready to put on the table."

Her husband obediently hustles out of the kitchen toward the dining room table with platter after platter. We're all salivating by the time we take our places.

We haven't stopped exclaiming over those first spicy, flavorsome mouthfuls when the telephone rings. Rita promptly gets up from the table to answer it in the kitchen. She's back a moment later.

"Colin, it's for you."

There is absolutely no reason for a phone call to arrive for me at my in-laws' house. Pushing back my chair from the table in confusion, I excuse myself and step into the kitchen, trying to imagine who could possibly know how and where to reach me today.

"Professor Wetmore, this is Dillon," says the strained voice. "Am I catching you at an inconvenient moment?"

"Well, yes, as a matter of fact, you are."

"I should hang up."

"No, don't. Dillon, how did you know where to find me?"

"I went to your house, and Jake looked up the number for me in your phone book."

How helpful of Jake! But now a new question presents itself. "How could you go to my house, Dillon, if you're in Rose Bend?"

"I'm not in Rose Bend."

"But I thought you were going home for Thanksgiving."

"I was. That's why I called, Professor Wetmore. I had a change in plans."

I'm afraid to ask what that involves. Instead I ask, "Have you told your parents you're not coming?"

A long pause. "No."

"Call them, Dillon. Right now. Explain to them."

At first he doesn't answer, and I think he's put down the phone. Then I can hear him sniffling on the other end of the line. "I don't know how to explain. I don't want to hurt them. I'm not the son they think I am."

"Why do you say that, Dillon?"

Abruptly he asks, "Can I talk to your wife, Professor Wetmore?"

This profoundly shocks me. "No, talk to me, Dillon. I won't judge you. I care about you."

He's struggling with his voice to get the words out. The telephone reception makes it hard to understand him. "I have to do something that is going to hurt my parents very much."

I can hear him crying. This is heartbreaking. How can I reach out and comfort him? Maybe I'd better get my wife, after all. "Dillon, please…"

Love in the American Empire

The telephone disconnects.

I return to the table, more upset than I want to admit, frowning. "Sorry, it was a troubled student of mine."

Rachel looks at me sharply. She knows we'll talk about it on the long drive home to Seattle.

I've been looking forward to every minute of that drive, our time alone together. Maybe we'd be honest with each other again. Maybe we'd find a way back to a simple, relaxed trust in each other. The call from Dillon ruins it. Now we're worrying about him and not about us, just the two of us in the car, with the lights of the freeway guiding us through the vast, impervious blackness. We drive in silence, the radio turned off, just us and the drone of the tires.

"He's in love with you, Rachel. You know that, don't you?"

She smiles at me and pats my hand. "According to you, everyone is."

27
"Tell Me about My Son"

No matter how much Rachel enjoys mocking housewives who rush out to sales, I notice she finds a reason to head down to University Village on the Friday morning after Thanksgiving to check out the zillion specials spilling out of every shop doorway. Her own campus bookstore is closed due to the four-day Thanksgiving holiday, leaving Rachel free to browse through the markdowns in the mall. I'm at home, deep into writing the sixth chapter. Which is why, when the phone rings, the only one to answer it is me.

"Professor Wetmore?"

I don't recognize the voice. "Speaking."

"This is Dillon's father."

"Reverend Wheeler."

"Please call me Lucas," he says. "Because I'm going to call you Colin. I hope you won't mind."

"Not at all," I manage to squeeze in.

"I need a friend in Seattle right now, Colin, I must tell you. And although I do have many ex-parishioners who live there, none of them know Dillon the way you do. I'm having a hard time." He's choked up. It's a voice that isn't used to asking for anything, a voice that has been humbled and doesn't know how to ask for a favor. "I need some input and advice, Colin," he says, in a voice that cracks and wavers, carrying its urgency all the way from eastern Washington. "I need someone to tell me my son is all right."

He pauses, waiting for me to say the words he's hoping to hear. I can't say them. I'm trying to think of something hopeful to offer him when his patience seems to snap. "Please, don't toy with me. That boy means the world to me. Something is troubling him. What the hell is going on over there, Colin? He called us last night, and he had Grace and me so upset we could hardly understand a word he was saying."

I recognize the sound of a frightened, protective parent when I hear it. I also suspect there are some elements of his son's phone call that Lucas has tried very hard *not* to understand. I need to be patient. I click on Save. "He called us, too. Let's start with how much you do understand."

"Why didn't you tell me he called?" he demands curtly. "Colin, help me." I think he's sincere. He simply doesn't understand any of it, and is afraid to use his imagination for fear of where it will lead him. "And don't play games with me. What is he trying to tell us? It isn't as though we haven't put our very best efforts into raising him right."

"He could be troubled about any number of things." I'm sorry to admit that my first instinct is self-preservation. "Dillon didn't happen to mention anything about getting scared while taking a shower?"

A brief silence ensues, suggesting that he thinks I'm losing my mind. "No, of course not, Colin. This has nothing to do with showers. This has to do with my son's sex life."

"I know absolutely nothing about your son's sex life," I quickly lie to him. "Let's be clear about that right from the start. I hardly know the boy. Why would he talk to me about something as private as his sex life?"

"Funny, the way he tells it, you appear to be right smack dab in the *middle* of my son's sex life."

Well, that gets me so worked up that I erupt into a volley of pathetic protests and panicky disclaimers, alibis and excuses, stammering and fumbling, like a guilty priest denying how much he loves altar boys, making me look guiltier by the minute and giving any concerned parent a lot more to worry about than he had before. Lucas endures a polite amount of this, and then cuts me off.

"Fine, fine, fine. Well, I'm through watching from the sidelines. I'm flying to Seattle this afternoon. You'll be hearing from me shortly."

I hold the dead phone in my hand long after he's disconnected. What could he possibly have meant? How could I be in the middle of his son's sex life?

All my professional anxieties about sexual harassment make the claustrophobic walls of my little home office press in on me. I stride out into the living room. I need air. I need light. He couldn't be referring to Dillon's crush on my wife, could he? Could he possibly have heard about my wife's gay co-worker? That would be enough to make any religious father worry. He'll take us to court. He'll sue us.

Love in the American Empire

No, no, surely he knows that my wife would never consent to any illicit behavior – I mean, with *anyone*, much less a student.

But what if Dillon repeated back to him my liberal attitudes on gayness? That could be it. What if Dillon told his father that he's had sex with my wife's friend? That would be enough to upset any father. What if Lucas thought I had encouraged his home-schooled son to be sexually adventuresome, that I'd endorsed him having a gay sexual experience? That might explain why this very open-minded Christian father was freaking out.

Unable to focus, I give up on the sixth chapter. I work on my bibliography, instead. I place reserves on some library books and read a couple chapters in a new Salinger study. Rachel spends most of the day idly paging through a detective novel. Occasionally, when our paths cross in the kitchen or the bathroom, she gives me a kiss on the cheek and mentions how wonderful it feels to unwind, to relax, but what she really means is that her protective shield is up and she's unreadable. If what she's doing is called relaxing, it sure takes a lot of effort. By afternoon I'm about to suggest we go out to dinner and a movie when the phone rings.

It's Gloria, inviting Rachel out to dinner and a movie.

Rachel has scarcely hung up and is trying in vain to convince me to join them when the phone rings again.

"Colin, I hope I'm not bothering you," says Lucas Wheeler, and this time he's not calling long distance.

Love in the American Empire

"You don't waste any time," I say. I'm genuinely impressed. He must have caught a plane to Seattle.

"I don't know the University District too well, but I'm at the Silver Cloud Inn. Is that anywhere near you?"

"It's just down the hill. You're on 25th, I'm on 22nd."

"I don't suppose you're free tonight?"

I look at my wife, standing in front of the hall mirror, sliding her arms into her jacket as she prepares to dart out the door to meet Gloria. She blows me a kiss. "Actually, I am."

"I wouldn't mind some company, and a little help with my battle-plan. I'll buy, you drive."

Rachel gives me a questioning look. I mouth the words, "Dillon's father," and I mime downing a shot-glass. She gives a thumbs-up, and closes the door behind her. "Deal," I say. "I'll be there in five minutes."

"I'll be waiting outside."

That's where I find him, standing in the entryway under the awning.

The wind blows open his raincoat to show a white clerical collar underneath. Were it not for that, Lucas Wheeler looks more like a corporation executive hero or an Iron Man finalist, vitamin-rich, monomaniacal, whiplash resilient. He radiates a self-control that puts up with no excuses. Lucas isn't used to waiting for anyone, and his body language says so. He strides up to the car, slides in next to me, and slams the door.

"Thank you for helping me."

Love in the American Empire

"Nice to see you, Lucas." We vigorously shake hands. "So, where are we going?" I'm summoning up all my reserves of social grace and cheer. "Any requests?"

"I don't care, anywhere. Choose someplace," says Lucas, and there's so much weary heartache in the sigh that goes with it that the cheeriness goes right out of me. "I won't notice, anyway. You can just keep driving, for all I care," he says. "Just talk to me about my son. Explain him to me. That's what I want."

"Pretty big order." I pull away from the Silver Cloud into evening traffic. The sky is darkening, maybe with rain clouds, maybe it's just nightfall.

"Tell me, what is it I don't know?"

I head toward Ravenna Park. "Why ask me? Why not ask Dillon?"

"Because he gets me too upset." I glance over at him while I'm driving, and to my amazement, he's chewing nervously on a fingernail. Lit by a passing gas station, by the yellow arches of MacDonald's, he's one of those men who keep all of their hair, work out at the gym three times a week, and read *The Economist*. Right now he looks like the stock market has just crashed.

"Fasten your seatbelt, Lucas."

He complies grudgingly, yanking down the strap as though he resents any attempt to protect his life.

"So you two don't talk to each other very much?" I venture to conclude.

Love in the American Empire

"Dillon thinks he's learned all he can from his old man," he says. His smile jiggles insecurely on his lips. Obviously it's a painful subject. "That's why he insisted on going to the University of Washington, on moving to Seattle. He wants to get as far away from me as he can. Grace and I thought it was a bad idea, right from the start."

I turn west, up the winding curves of tree-lined Ravenna Boulevard. After twelve years of home-schooling, it's not surprising that Dillon might want some other teacher than his father.

"What did Dillon say that upset you so much?"

His lips are thin and tight, as though he's trying to force them to remain silent. Lucas is used to solving his problems quickly and decisively with the sheer power of his will, and this problem refuses to be solved.

"Well, for one thing, he told me that some gay man is interested in him."

The words are hard for him to get out, and afterward silence grips the car. I can hear the friction of the tires on the street beneath us, the ticking of my wristwatch. Lucas impulsively turns on the radio. It's too loud and silly and vulgar, a disc jockey who thinks he's way funnier than he is, and Lucas impatiently snaps the radio back off again.

"Dillon is not gay," says Lucas, and before I can say a word to him, he goes on, "I know my son well enough to know that much. He's just open, Colin, open and sensitive and guileless. There's a difference."

Love in the American Empire

"What do you mean, open?"

"I mean he doesn't have a sexual agenda. He's not after any stereotype in particular. He's completely open to anyone."

The headlights play over the trunks of maple trees.

"That sounds healthy and sane to me, Lucas," I concede, "and I'm willing to believe it because I've met him. The kid is extraordinary, no doubt about it. I mean, I was jealous of him. At first I thought he had a crush on my wife, to tell you the truth."

"And what makes you think he doesn't?" Lucas asks unexpectedly.

I realize that I simply don't worry about Dillon anymore. Why worry about an inexperienced eighteen-year-old boy when I can worry about a handsome Iraq veteran?

"How do you know he doesn't lust your wife?" reiterates Lucas.

There's a fine line here I don't want to cross, of betraying Dillon's confidence to help his father. But Lucas is my friend, and I can't just strand him without support.

"Your kid was asking me a lot of questions about gayness, Lucas, to be frank," I say, and the silence in the car thickens. "I might as well tell you, my guess is that last night he took a step of some kind."

I don't know how much to say, and so instead I focus on where I'm going, and at the light I turn up Roosevelt.

"Who is the guy?"

"He's older. A bookseller."

Love in the American Empire

You never know how someone is going to take this kind of information. Lucas Wheeler drums his fingers on the dashboard, as Indian restaurants and auto repair shops zip past.

"I try to be open-minded, Colin. I try to not judge. But it's hard when it's your own son."

His voice cracks, and his jaws clamp shut. The cars ahead of us are all turning into Scarecrow Video. I swerve around them.

"Nothing my kid does can make me love him less, Colin. Can you understand that?"

We turn back toward the university. We seem to hit every light. Lucas wipes his damp forehead with the back of his hand. He blows out a long sigh. Then he turns to me and asks, "Is he a good man?"

I consider Dario Foccacia with a critical eye. "Well, he's loud and opinionated and a little prone to over-dramatize things," I qualify, "not exactly my kind of person." Those traits aside, I have to add, "But he's got a good heart, he's politically sane, he's kind, he's fair. Yes, he's a good man."

The fingers of Lucas's two hands are interlacing in his lap, almost like they're trying to pray. "That's the most important thing for us. A sense of God is best, but if not, at least a sense of goodness."

"The guy's very intelligent, extremely well-read, even a good cook, I hear," I go on, listing Dario's best traits. Lucas doesn't seem to be paying attention.

Love in the American Empire

"I had no clue, Colin," he says sadly. "I never saw this coming."

"Kids today aren't afraid to try things out," I say, attempting to lift his spirits. "He may try it once, and decide it's not for him."

He's not listening to a word I say. "Isn't the 45th Street viaduct around here somewhere?" He doesn't wait for an answer. "Head down toward University Village."

Soon we're sailing down the cement viaduct ramp toward the sports fields and university parking lots, with a right turn-around into the shopping mall. It's nightmarishly crowded at the moment, with people just getting off work and early holiday shoppers.

"Liquor store," he says, pointing.

"We'll never get a parking space." I've seen drivers in this mall scream at each other red-faced over contested parking spots. I've seen a woman jump out of her car and use her own body to prevent another car from taking her space.

"Just pull up close and I'll run in."

Which he does, and emerges a moment later with a bottle of Glenfiddich.

"Back to the Silver Cloud," he says casually, with the tone of a man who is used to being obeyed.

Predatory cars surround us the moment I turn the key in the ignition, waiting to pounce on our parking spot as we escape from the mall and head back up 25th Avenue to the

Love in the American Empire

Silver Cloud. We've completed a full circle. I pull up in front of the motel awning.

"Here we are. Try not to worry about him, Lucas."

"Park the car," he says.

"Thanks, but I can't."

"Park it."

"Really, I…"

"I'm not drinking this alone. We're killing the bottle tonight, and you're going to help me."

28
Killing the Bottle

Reverend Lucas Wheeler isn't used to anyone arguing with him, and won't take no for an answer.

He doesn't want to be left alone with his sense of failure. I can feel his urgent need for distraction, for companionship. It's hard to turn away from anyone in that state. Even though it's a tad early in the afternoon to be drinking, I knuckle under to his persuasion. It's close enough that I can easily walk home if I drink too much.

"All right, all right, but just one drink, that's all. There's no way we're going to finish off that bottle."

I park the Volvo in his parking space and we walk to his room, which has an outside door. Lucas pulls off his collar, hangs up his jacket, rolls back his sleeves, and pours us each a couple fingers of scotch. I waste no time in knocking back the shot, and head for the door. He lifts the bottle again. I let him refill my glass. I sit back down. I let him refill it again. I take off my jacket. I keep meaning to call Rachel and tell her where I am. We talk about women. We talk about life. We become wiser with every hour. Next time I look at my watch, it's too late to call.

"It's anyone's guess how a smart, sensitive man like you can fail to believe in God," he says out of nowhere.

I burp. "It's not on purpose, believe me."

"You probably think I'm some kind of goofy Christian fanatic," he says. "Don't you? Admit it."

We have a good laugh over that one. There's just enough truth to his assertion to make it funny.

"Well, let me tell you something," he says earnestly. "I would have crashed and burned without it. Really, I'm being serious, I don't believe in all the hocus-pocus part, but just the words of Jesus, just the teachings themselves without the church attached to it…"

Time to divert the conversation. "I can see that you take being a father seriously. Even home-schooling!"

"It's more work than you ever dream. You have to re-educate yourself, from the ground up. But I care what kind of mind my kid has. I saw it was an opportunity. I didn't want Dillon learning all the different ways you can hate other people. I want my kid to grow up loving people, loving difference, knowing he has a soul, knowing that it's his job to take care of it."

"You've succeeded, Lucas," I tell him, lifting my shot glass in a toast. "You've raised a superb young man." I have a little trouble with the word 'superb,' but I write it off as enthusiasm, down the shot, and somehow manage to say, "I'd be proud to have Dillon as my son."

"So what is it I don't supply, Colin? What made him gay?" Suddenly he's crying. He falls against me, making this horribly sad sound. I catch him. I hold him. "I just don't understand why... why... what would make him turn to another..."

"Oh, come on, Lucas." I give him a shake. He's leaving a wet place on my shirt. "Why do some guys like big boobs and some guys like small ones? Why do some guys like asses and some guys like legs? He's just not a reproducer, that's all. You raised a smart kid. Trust his choices."

I might as well talk to the wall. Lucas goes on saying stuff like, "I tried to be a good father" and "What did I do wrong?" He cries on me. I'm not used to men doing that. Now my shirt has another wet splotch.

"Lucas, things are different these days. Being gay is not a death sentence. It's just another lifestyle."

"The only thing I care about is that my son is a good man and that he's happy," says Lucas, although his crying somewhat belies this statement. I'm embarrassed to have my arms around him, but he needs it. Mostly Lucas Wheeler just needs someone to listen to him. I'm a good listener. I'm also smart enough to know when I've had enough to drink.

Lucas clearly doesn't know this about himself, because he thinks he hasn't had enough yet and is spilling a good deal of the bottle down the front of his shirt while trying to pour.

"Here, let me do that." I take the bottle away from him.

"Good, because I need to pee," says Lucas, leaving me to put the bottle and his glass on the bed-stand.

Leaving the bathroom door wide open, he succeeds in unzipping his pants and at least audibly hitting the water of the toilet bowl. But in trying to cross the motel room coming back his feet sail out from under him and he hits the floor hard. It sounds like he's broken his head wide open. I run over to him as best I can (okay, I'm wobbling a little, too) but he's smiling and appears to be unhurt.

"No, no, I'm fine, really, I needed that," he says, and crawls over to the side of the bed, where he raises himself up, props himself against the mattress, and folds his hands in prayer. To my great discomfort, he begins praying in a voice that's suddenly urgent and uncomfortably loud.

"Lord, please don't take my son away from me," he sobs, all wet and emotional. "That boy is everything to me. Lord, give me back my boy!"

I try to reach him, to snap him out of it. "Lucas, you're making a big deal out of nothing. You haven't lost him. You haven't lost anything."

He tries to get to his feet. He stands erect for about five seconds, then sits down suddenly on the side of the bed. "Why would God take away my most precious possession?"

"He's not taken away, Lucas. Dillon is still your son. He's just not under your control."

He doesn't hear a word I say. "We tried to be so careful, to do everything right. Maybe God doesn't hear our prayers at all."

"Maybe that's the whole point," I say, trying to think like a believer. "Maybe it's all a big test. Your Jehovah is notoriously fond of them."

Love in the American Empire

"You think God's testing me?"

"Think of what he did to poor Abraham and Isaac. Think of what he did to poor Job."

"You're right," he says sadly. "Of course. God takes away what you think you can't live without. Be thankful God isn't testing you, Colin. Be thankful."

His words suddenly terrify me. I do not want to consider how they might apply to me. I'm fumbling drunkenly through a host of different conversational possibilities, intent on finding us some new and safer direction, when he interrupts my feeble diversion tactics with a snore.

I slowly get up off my knees. Lucas Wheeler is thoroughly drunk and sound asleep, his shirt untucked, sprawled across the bed like a starfish, arms flung wide like he's embracing the universe. I feel very affectionate toward him in my alcoholic fog as I quietly close the door behind me, leaving him to whatever hung-over memories await him in the morning, making my way back down the motel hallway toward reality.

I walk home. I'll get the car tomorrow.

When I can finally get the key in the hole and unlock the front door, the lights are out and the living room dark. Rachel is already in bed. I quickly scramble out of my clothes and tumble eagerly onto the bed to join her. She moans, so I know she's awake. I figure I'll charm her. There's

Love in the American Empire

a little confusion as I'm caught on the wrong side of the sheet. No matter how much I try to wrap my arms around her, there's always the sheet between us. I have to get out of bed and try again. This time I manage to slide under the sheet. There she is, and she feels so good.

"Smells like somebody has been having a good time," says my perceptive wife. "Don't tell me, let me guess." She kisses me, tasting me, savoring me. "I'd say Scotch, and a pretty good one, too."

"I love you," I say. My lips are numb and difficult to work with. Since she has no idea how hard it is to make my mouth move in just the right way to say those three words, she doesn't realize how much I want to tell her that.

She laughs at me. "You're so cute when you're plowed. Now, stop being cute so I can be mad at you. You don't tell me where you're going. You come home stinking drunk at three in the morning. What kind of partner is that?"

"I've been bad," I manage to say. I kiss her again.

She puts up with it. "Fortunately for you," she whispers in my ear, "you're not bad very often."

After another attack of kissing, as we both pull away for air, I ask, "What movie did you girls go see?"

She tells me, and I promptly forget. "Where's Jake?"

"I thought he was with you. I thought maybe you boys were measuring peepees to see who was the biggest."

I'm mildly shocked by the picture this brings to mind. "Is that really what you think we do when we're together?"

Love in the American Empire

"Among other things. For men, everything is about their peepees. You can deny it till you're blue in the face, but it's true. Men just pretend to have brains. The penis rules."

"I think you'd better speak to my ruler."

One of the great pleasures of married life is lazy sex, where you stretch out every step of the lovemaking, where you take hours administering to each other the simplest erotic joys. Without a drop of alcohol, Rachel matches me, love-stroke for love-stroke, as uninhibited as I am.

We give in to our impulses. We're like two armies of starving ants, eating each other in a thousand nibbles. We stay up half the night, and don't give our jobs a thought. Until we finally slow down to the point that we fall asleep, we're in erotic heaven, slowly pleasuring each other, the happiest we've been in months. She is very much tonight the woman I will always love, the one who makes me whole, the woman who really loves me.

Of course, I think that I finally know the truth.

29
Searching for Dillon

I'm starting to believe that I'm safe.

After such a wonderful night together, who wouldn't? I actually think we can be happy again.

The worst is finally over. We've had our rough times and, yes, I've doubted her, but the facts have always set her right in the end. Life is complex, and many things we experience we don't acknowledge, but Rachel acknowledges them, even the upsetting ones, which would confuse most people, but not me. Human motivations are murky and frequently shallow, selfish, and politically incorrect, but that's what being human means. Rachel is just herself. She's an extraordinary example of honesty and faithfulness. She's a woman who keeps her word.

I wake up alone in bed.

I glance at the alarm radio. I'm shocked to see that it's ten o'clock. No wonder Rachel isn't still here. I never sleep this late. My throbbing temples tell me that I'm going to be paying a bitter price for my little bacchanal.

I'm brave enough to look in the bathroom mirror, and immediately wish I hadn't. I'm red-eyed and puffy-cheeked, and clearly need more rest. Rachel, bless her heart, has already left on her Saturday morning six-mile run. My physical stunt for this morning is dragging my sorry body down the hall into

Love in the American Empire

the shower, hoping a blast of water will help restore functioning consciousness. What was I thinking last night? I will never drink that much again, ever.

I glance toward the computer room. The door is open. If Jake were here, it would be closed. He makes no attempt to keep us informed as to his whereabouts. I don't think he came home last night. I venture barefoot down the hall in my underwear. The house is still and empty.

On the kitchen table is a note, all in capitals:

WHAT DID YOU DO WITH THE CAR?

I laugh until I try to answer the question. I'm pretty sure I remember where it is. Sort of. I throw on some dockers and a button-down shirt, grab my down vest, and head out into the bright, cold morning. I cut through the neighborhood and cross the avenue and there it is, right where I parked it yesterday at the Silver Cloud Inn.

I consider just getting in it and driving home. But Lucas will be in worse shape than I am, that's for sure, and a real friend would check on him. I go into the main lobby through the ornate entryway, and up to the smiling, well-groomed young man at the front desk who is just about to finish assisting a very short Eastern European couple with thick accents. I'm enjoying eavesdropping on the exchange, waiting my turn, when Dillon walks past me in the lobby.

That wakes me up, all right. Has he been summoned here by his father? I'm about to call out, and then I notice that his clothes look rumpled and slightly dirty. Not the way a son would look paying a visit to Reverend Wheeler. He looks in worse shape than I am.

"Sir?"

It's my turn, and before I can try to explain to the clerk that I'll be with him in a moment, Dillon is gone out the door. I don't want to lose him.

"I'll be right back," I say to the clerk, and run out the front door after him. I look in every direction, and run partway back into the parking area. He's vanished. I take a deep breath. I'm losing it. I've become delusional. That wasn't Dillon. I'm chasing strange young men out of the hotel. I'm about to head back to the lobby, but I recognize Lucas's room from last night and decide to just knock instead.

He opens the door holding an icepack to his forehead.

"Good timing," says Lucas. "I hope you'll be kind enough to come with me and help me find my son's rooming-house."

"But…"

"I remember the general neighborhood, and could probably find it in a pinch, but you could just show me and make it so much easier on my poor head."

"Look, it won't take much guidance to get you there," I say, "and besides…"

"Good," he says, heading for the passenger door of my car. "Let's get going. I want to see my son."

"See your son?" I say. "Wasn't he just with you?"

"Of course not," says Lucas.

"But he just left the hotel."

"He *what?*"

"He just walked out the door. I saw him. He must have come to see you."

Lucas leaps out of the car and leaves me stranded idling in the middle of the parking lot as he runs around to the front lobby, looking wildly in all directions. He walks back to the car, huffing, scowling.

"Let's go," he says, fastening his seatbelt.

We pull out of the parking lot and cross the avenue, heading up toward the University District. Lucas is fumbling with a pack of cigarettes. I didn't know he smoked. He drops the pack, spilling cigarettes all over the seat and floor. He's gathering them up, saying "Piss!" over and over, angrier and angrier. Suddenly he just crushes them all into one angry fistful of tobacco confetti, with a shout.

I nearly hit a parked car.

"Reverend Wheeler, please, no more shouts!" I bark indignantly. "Are you trying to kill us?"

"Sorry," says Lucas. "I've been phoning him all morning at the rooming-house. No one answers."

I don't blame Lucas for being tense. At least we know Dillon's alive, since I just saw him. But he didn't look healthy.

Love in the American Empire

He looked like he'd had a wilder night than I had. Put that together with the desperate phone call at the Vespuccis' and I feel in my gut we need to find that boy.

I approach the rooming-house by going past the street it's on and then turning up the alley behind it. About halfway up the alley I recognize the back of the house, and pull into a gravel parking space near the foot of a wooden add-on staircase that climbs the back of the house to the second floor.

I lock up the car and follow Lucas up the stairs.

As I start down the dimly-lit hallway, Lucas is already standing in front of the far door, knocking. He continues knocking until I'm beside him. He pulls out his cell-phone and jabs in a number. On the other side of the door, a telephone begins ringing. It rings until Dillon's voice in the receiver says, "Hi, this is Dillon. Leave me a message."

Lucas waits for the beep, and says, "Dillon, this is your father. I'm in the hall outside your room. I wish you'd let me in. Dillon, I love you. I'm worried about you. I'm staying at the Silver Cloud Inn until tomorrow morning. You know my number. Please call me, son. I'm trying to be a good father. I won't desert you, ever. You know I only want to help you."

He continues standing in the hall in front of Dillon's door for another couple minutes, listening, hoping to hear some sound of life. "Well, at least you saw him today. So I know he's all right."

I did see him, didn't I?

Love in the American Empire

As we start down the steep flight of wooden stairs toward the gravel below, I find myself wondering if I could possibly have been mistaken. What if Dillon looked so haggard and not himself for the very good reason that he wasn't Dillon at all? I keep these thoughts to myself, as we drive back to the motel parking lot. I stop outside the door of his room.

"Thanks for the help," he says, sliding out of the car. "I'll let you know if he turns up. You do the same."

I promise I will and the door of his room closes behind him, leaving Lucas intent on getting a little relief from aspirin and an icepack.

Driving home, I think about fatherhood. Maybe because Rachel can't have children, I always notice what kind of fathers my friends become. Take Lucas. He's more demanding than he realizes. A steady diet of Lucas as my father and teacher might be oppressive. I see now why Dillon has trouble coming to own conclusions in his papers. Love can be a tyrant. Some people smother what they love.

I slide back into a parking place right in front of our house. I check through the mailbox to see if any of the mail is for me, but it's all for the Volkonskys, who clearly write their names on far too many mailing lists. As I head up the stairs, I'm thinking that it's still early enough for Rachel and me to make dinner plans. We really ought to treat ourselves to something, get out of that house more, try to initiate a new time of understanding each other. With Jake there and the drapes always pulled, it's been oppressive, claustrophobic.

No one appears to be home, and I'm getting out my key when for some reason I try the doorknob and it turns. I push, and the front door swings open. Someone must be home. None of the lights are on inside, so that everything is dim. Could Rachel have forgotten to lock the door? I reach out and click the light switch. Nothing happens.

Then I hear movement in the hallway.

"Rachel?" I say, and I'm starting toward the hallway as I say, "Is something wrong with the lights?" when a figure steps out of the hallway who clearly isn't Rachel.

"Jake?"

I immediately regret it, the minute the word comes out of my mouth.

A man in standing in my hall that I've never seen before, short, burly, ill-shaven, balding, with tiny little pig eyes. He's muttering something under his breath which makes no sense at all, but it doesn't sound good. Then I realize he's not talking to himself, he's talking to someone else who now also steps into sight, another man, shorter and balder and not in a very good humor.

"What are you doing here?" I bark with as much authority as I can muster. "Get out of my house, before I call the police!" But you can't call the police on the military, can you? And I already suspect they're here because of Jake, they've tracked him down. "Get out of my house!" I say loudly. "Get out, now, this minute!" Unfortunately, instead of stepping boldly toward them, I step backward and realize that a third man has entered the house behind me.

"Hey!" I shout, as loudly as I can. There's no sign of Rachel or Jake anywhere. Why are these men in the bathroom, hiding and waiting for me?

Then all the lights turn on.

Omar Volkonsky steps out of the laundry room. He calls out in Russian before he stops at the sight of me. "Oh, you're here," he says. "I'm sorry. We had an electrical problem upstairs. I think we have fixed it now. These men know electricity. They don't speak English."

The three sinister military police, now transformed into three Russian immigrant electricians, break into toothy smiles.

At the end of the hall the bathroom door is wide open, and the overhead light is blazing.

30
Lighting Up

It takes me twenty minutes or so to shake off the willies from my encounter with the Russian mafia. During that time, with nervous energy spewing wastefully in all directions, I pace, I tidy, I organize, I throw out time-honored memorabilia. I'm on the edge of actually housecleaning, but don't quite teeter that far. I'm genuinely worried about Dillon. He was reaching out for help on Thanksgiving, and the wasted, gaunt young man I saw this morning at the Silver Cloud Inn was a kid who needed help in a big way, and now where is he?

Finally I decide to succumb to the time-honored, tried-and-true remedy for anxiety – junk food. Without Rachel around to police me, I step out for a quick dash down three blocks to the nearest fast food establishment. Let's forget what I bought. When I get home the light is on in the laundry room and I can see someone moving around from the shifting shadows in the doorway. For some reason, I don't call out. I simply pop the last French fry into my mouth, wipe my greasy fingers on the sides of my pants, and quietly step into the doorway.

She's looking away from me, loading the dryer with wet clothes lifted out of the washing machine. Suddenly she senses someone behind her, spins around, and screams.

"What a mean thing to do," she says.

It's a sad state of affairs when a simple, everyday place like a laundry room can become fraught with terror. She slams shut the door of the dryer, starts the clothes tumbling, and barges past me into the kitchen, pulling the laundry room door closed behind her.

"I'm sorry," I apologize quickly. "I wasn't thinking. I had no idea I'd scare you so badly."

She's flustered, and angry that I've seen her upset. She strides out of the kitchen like there's something very important she needs to take care of, but there's nothing there that needs doing, and she's stranded in the middle of the carpet, staring helplessly at the curtained front window. "What do you expect, lurking around behind me like that?"

"Honey, really, I didn't mean to. Please, don't be mad."

Her shoulders relax. She sighs, as though she could blow the anger out of her. "All right, you beast. I forgive you."

"Where in the world have you been?" I'm more than ready to change the subject to anything else.

She's red-cheeked and radiant. "Gloria called, and we walked around Green Lake. It's cold but so pretty, and utterly refreshing." She gives me a once-over look. "And what about you? I come home from my run and you're just gone, no note, no explanation."

"I went down to get the car and drive it home. I didn't think I'd be gone long."

"You must have run into Dillon's father again. Is he converting you? Are you becoming a believer?"

"Very funny. Believing isn't exactly my long suit."

My words bring her up short, and cause an awkward hush between us. Her facial expression slowly changes. She stares down at the spatula in the kitchen sink, waiting to be washed. "What's that supposed to mean?" I've hurt her. I can hear it in her voice.

I wasn't trying to be meaningful. It just slipped out. Nevertheless, I need to be brave enough to tell her my real feelings. "It's my problem, not yours. Sometimes I'm just a little insecure, that's all. Sometimes I need to hear you say you love me."

"I wonder what I have to do to make you believe it. My high-maintenance husband, the doubter. I need a drink. I say we break open that bottle of wine my uncle gave us at Christmas."

"I'm up for a little celebration," I say agreeably. "I second the motion. But, uh, celebrating why?"

"Celebrating because we can," she says defiantly. "Celebrating to drive away the blues."

"What blues?"

"You dear thing." Suddenly she can hardly talk. Her eyes become wet, her eyelids redden. She tries to swallow the lump in her throat. "Your little universe is such a tidy thing, sweetheart. It's a little clockwork toy, and it all makes sense. Well, sometimes the universe doesn't make sense. Sometimes

Love in the American Empire

I'm standing over the toilet bowl in the cold bathroom, waiting to relax enough to pee, when I hear these soft, muffled sounds coming from his room. I pee. The sounds continue. I flush the toilet. The sounds continue.

My understanding of the masculine code, not to mention my sense of hospitality and privacy, all urge me to ignore it, because those are not the sounds of happiness. Men coming home from war have to work out their own darknesses and demons in their own way. But even though common sense tells me to mind my own business, to give Jake room to quietly come unglued in private, I don't go back to my warm place in bed beside Rachel where I belong.

I stop outside the open computer room door. I nudge it. It swings wide.

The white tanktop gives him away in the darkness, stretched out on the quilt-wrapped air mattress in the dark. "Sorry, man," he says. I can't see his face. "Sorry, sorry, sorry. Don't know why I do that. I just wake up that way. Sorry."

"Don't be sorry," I say.

He's shaking.

"You okay now?"

He blows air out his nostrils. "Okay? What's okay? You mean, can I live with it? Sure, I can live with it. I don't have any choice."

Love in the American Empire

He hooks his arm around my neck, and pulls me into the room. I feel the muscles. He could snap my neck with his bare arm. "Come in here for a second, and close the door."

Hesitantly, warily, I do. I turn around the chair at my desk to face the bed, and lower myself down into it. Jake is stretched out on the narrow air mattress, arms folded behind his head, scowling at the ceiling.

"There was this little guy named Amir. Shit, he couldn't have been more than six, maybe. He had these tiny little black eyes that always seemed to be laughing, even when the rest of his face was crying or pissed off, his eyes looked like he'd been a stand-up comic in another lifetime. He hung around us like a little fly. At first he bugged the shit out of me. I could always feel him watching me. He was always trying to make a dollar here, a dollar there. One night a guy gave him money to get us some food. He was coming back. Stupid little shit was clowning around, trying to surprise us. So I see him. And he sees me. And, uh, there was this jumpy new guy..."

Another one of those sickening sounds I'd heard from the bathroom. It's him sucking for air through a throat that's so choked up he can hardly breathe. He doesn't let the tears out. That's why he's choking. He looks away from me, waiting for his emotions to come under control again, keeping his lips pressed together, his jaws clenched. His eyes are red, but they will not cry. They stare into the dark as though they can see right through it.

Love in the American Empire

"It sounded like a ping-pong ball getting hit by a paddle," he says with difficulty. He clears his throat. "One minute he's there, next minute he's a little lump of rags by the wall." He words are so soft they're almost inaudible. "You'd be surprised how fast it can happen. I see his face every night."

There's nothing to say, and for once I'm smart enough to know that.

"I refuse to go back there," he whispers. "I refuse. I'll put a bullet through my own brain first."

We remain together in the silence, him stretched out on the floor, me slumped down in the desk chair, sharing the darkness of the room because there's nothing else we can do.

"Thanks for putting up with me. You're a real pal."

He snaps on the small lamp by the computer, and ruffles through his backpack on the floor. He pulls out a little plastic container, a lighter, and a pipe, and raises his eyebrows as he looks at me.

"Like old times."

I can't believe I'm seeing right. "Not for me, thanks," I say. "Really, haven't for years."

"Good," he says. "Tonight will be special."

He's not accepting disclaimers or excuses. Before I can get up on my soapbox, he snaps his lighter into flame, and makes the bowl of the pipe crackle. Then he passes it to me.

"Go ahead," he urges, poking the pipe's stem at my mouth. "You need this more than anyone I know."

Love in the American Empire

I feel like objecting, and instead I grudgingly open my lips. I still remember how to toke on little pipes like that. Unfortunately, my lungs promptly protest in body-wracking coughs.

He watches me hack and wheeze. He shakes his head.

"You are sadly out of practice," he says, tapping out the ashes and re-loading the pipe. I'm trying to think of exit lines. I don't like where this is going.

"Just got back from Vancouver," he says, toking on the pipe himself. Holding his breath, he says, "Setting the whole deal up. All the little steps."

"How is it coming?"

He blows out what's left of the smoke. "Oh, fucked, as usual. Plans are made to fuck up. Then you make new plans. That's how plans work. I'm begging for your patience, man. It's gonna come together, I promise, any day now. I know I'm bugging you here. I'll be getting out of your life soon, really soon, as soon as I can. You've both been great to me."

I don't know what to make of what he's saying. He sounds like he means every word. He passes me the pipe. "Try to look less like a teenager on his first try," he says.

His goading prompts me to inhale heartily, just to show I can do it. I suck in too much, and entertain him with another bout of coughing.

"You are truly lost," he says. "You've become a stuffed shirt, Colin. You've let yourself become middle-aged and boring."

Love in the American Empire

"Thanks, pal," I say, and laugh, but his words sting.

"You know how you act, Colin. Like a dog who's been hit in traffic. Now the mutt stays away from cars. The owners think, see, he's learned his lesson. Smart doggie. But the truth is, he's also crippled."

I have to laugh. "You're saying I'm a crippled dog?"

We laugh together.

"Buddy, there's one thing we've never talked about," says Jake. "Maybe, before I walk out of your life here, we should get that out in the open. What happened between us that night back in college."

I should have seen this coming, that inevitably we'd need to discuss it. Well, I didn't and I'm completely thrown. I rise to my feet, stricken with embarrassment and anxiety. "I don't think we really need to go into that, Jake. I mean, why? Leave it in the past. After all, that was twenty years ago. We were kids. We were inexperienced. A lot can change in twenty years."

He has to smile at my feeble dodging of an awkward moment. "Yeah, a lot can change, all right."

I'm getting dizzy standing up. I sit down abruptly. We both laugh.

"So, what are you, Jake, really?" I have to ask. "You dated my wife and you came on to me, too. Straight or gay? What the hell are you?"

He grins at me, and winks. "What a fuss over nothing, man. A little difference in the plumbing. Listen, I fell in love with you, Colin, not because you were a man with a dick, but because you were the bright, kind, modest, literate best friend of my college days, that's why. I'm not hung up on bodies. True, you didn't have breasts, and breasts are nice, but you had your own pleasures, and most of all, you had you. Colin, sometimes I smile just thinking about you. For me, that's what counts. So, yes, I came onto you, and Rachel, too, for exactly the same reason.

"I'm going to make a new life with good people like you, buddy," he says, and draws deeply on the pipe, holding his breath while he says, "But it never works out right for everybody. Some people are going to get hurt." He exhales. "Some people always get hurt."

I look into the face of Jake Bagley, my old friend. We hug each other. I can feel his sadness clinging to him, a personal grief reeking of unhappy midnight thoughts and unbearable regrets.

"I've always relied on my mind," he says. "You know me. The mind is king. Philosophy is the only subject worth studying. Yadda yadda yadda." We both smile, remembering college, those sweet times when you could believe in things. "I like to *think* my way out of my problems. I used to be good at it. This old mind could tackle almost anything. Iraq cured me of that. Permanently. Some things I cannot understand. I have brought pain and grieving to so many people, Colin. They didn't have much happiness to begin with, and I ended what little there was, and brought sorrow. And I can leave it behind, I can run away, sure, but I can't stop remembering. I can't. I can't. I can't. I can't stop hurting people. How do you stop wrecking people's lives? I can't seem to stop."

A lump in my throat prevents me from forcing the words out of my mouth, from asking the dreaded question, if my life is on his hit list, if he's about to take away my joy and add me to his list of regrets.

A firm rat-a-tat on the door.

It swings promptly open on Rachel in a bathrobe, sniffing the air.

"Shame on you two!" she says, fists planted on her hips. "Didn't you boys ever grow up?" She shakes her head as she regards the two of us. She can't help smiling. "Pathetic." She points at Jake. "Next time you share that pipe, I get invited or I'm throwing you out." She points at me. "You, knucklehead. You have a job. You work tomorrow. Get out of here. Back to bed!"

I leap to my feet, immediately regret it, and almost pass out. She catches me wobbling by the elbow. "My husband is a very poor stoner," she says. She escorts me out of the reeking, pot-smoked computer room like a juvenile delinquent.

My last thought as I'm marched down the hall toward bed is: we're starting to become just like her parents.

31
Gloria's Favor

"Professor Wetmore!"

It's bright and early Monday morning, and I'm caught mid-stride in Padelford Hall just outside the open English office doorway. I've spent most of the weekend correcting mid-term essays, they're done, and as I head for the stairs leading up to my office I'm feeling like a righteous professor who earns his keep.

"Professor Wetmore, someone is trying very hard to reach you," calls the woman at the English office front desk.

"Did he leave a name?"

"He didn't," she says. "He just called for the third time. I gave him your voice mail, and told him to leave his phone number."

"Thanks, Martha." Something about that message agitates me even before I know what it's about. Maybe it's the three repetitions that give it a sense of urgency. I head for the stairs, and take them at a heart-pounding clip. I'm in no mood for the snail's pace of the elevator.

Striding down the corridor to my office, thrusting open the door, I play back my messages. They're all from Lucas Wheeler. He's learned nothing new about Dillon. He's a lost man, reaching out.

I erase them. I have nothing to tell him.

Love in the American Empire

The first knock on the door isn't long in coming. It's a sorority girl whose paper on *The Great Gatsby* was copied word-for-word out of Cliffs Notes, which would be bad enough, except that it has nothing whatsoever to do with Nick Carraway as narrator.

She's chewing gum nervously and glances at her expensive watch. She doesn't want to be here. Neither do I.

It's going to be a long afternoon.

She is followed by a chain of unlucky students who ask me to show them, in turn, how to revise their papers, how to present their evidence, how to organize their argument, how to spell, how to think, so that by eleven o'clock a silent scream is building inside me and I'm ready to throw in the towel and consider office hours officially over. I cannot humanly read one more poorly constructed, poorly written essay.

I push back my chair and shove my arms into my jacket sleeves. Time for me to administer this quarter's midterm exam. I hope Dillon has managed to squeeze a little studying into his dramatic new life.

I'm just locking my office door when I see Gloria coming down the hallway toward me, acting like she doesn't see me. This is her usual style. I know perfectly well that she sees me, and I'd like to avoid her, too. Unfortunately, we're the only two people in the hall so it's going to be impossible not to acknowledge each other. We mumble at each other as our paths cross, and then find ourselves stranded together waiting for the elevator. I pray for any of my most boring colleagues to appear. I would encourage them to monologue mercilessly. None do.

Gloria is hunched over a steaming ceramic mug of coffee, like a sibyl waiting for her message. No message is forthcoming. She glances at my face, and scowls. "You look awful."

"Thanks."

We could let it go there, and we *would* if this pokey little elevator would arrive, but it doesn't. "Let me ask you a question," she says. "I'm just curious." She scrunches her eyebrows, and gives me another brief, penetrating glance. "Do you have any idea how lucky you are?"

"Lucky? Lucky?" This is my usual style of repartee when caught off guard.

Gloria tips her head sideways, regarding me intently. "The whole time Rachel was at the movie, she was worried that you felt left out. She was stewing so much that she hurt your feelings, she could hardly concentrate."

This information floors me.

I'd go for more, but the elevator doors whoosh open and we're making room for three sleepy-eyed grad students reeking of coffee and deodorant. We all have an existential moment as we slowly groan down toward the earth. I casually mention, to fill the silence, that I'm on my way to waste an hour twiddling my thumbs babysitting my morning class through a midterm exam.

Love in the American Empire

"But that's exactly what I'm going to do," says Gloria. "Third floor of Miller Hall."

"That's the place, all right." We compare rooms.

"I'll be right across the hall," says Gloria, "doing exactly the same thing."

"Well, if you hear me snoring, step across and wake me up." I attempt to put a polite end to the conversation.

"What a way to waste two first-rate minds!" says Gloria. "Listen, I'm in better shape than you are. The way you look, you should go home and get some rest. Scram. I'll give your students the test."

It's one of those empty gestures that should never take place. "I couldn't let you, Gloria."

"Of course, you can," she persists. "Take care of yourself. Those are bags under your eyes. Tell me one thing *you* can do that I can't do just as easily and probably much better from across the hall."

This is awkward. "I shouldn't."

"Of course, you should."

I really don't want to do this. I don't like being indebted to anyone, least of all Gloria Goldberg. But there's no graceful way out. It does make a kind of sense. "Really, Gloria, it's not your burden."

"It's effortless. Consider it done."

I'm out of arguments. "Well, I guess I did have a pretty full night last night."

Love in the American Empire

She smiles tightly. Once again Gloria has effortlessly taken control of the situation. "Good, then it's settled. I'll leave my classroom door open, so I'll know if there are any shenanigans. I'll stroll in every five minutes or so. You can get a little rest, which you obviously need."

And the deal is done.

The elevator doors jerk open outside the English Office. We both head out into the morning. It's a sudden, unexpected window of freedom. I thank her, and we part ways. That cocky, annoying little beret disappears into a bumping, jostling crowd of backpacks. That's it. I'm free. Suddenly I have a beautiful fall morning to myself, and with a little luck I can share it with Rachel. There's nothing I'd like better than to take my wife to lunch.

Instead of heading for Miller Hall, I swing by the bookstore. Dario is working the cash register. When he sees me, he abandons a line of customers to come directly over to me and say, "How is she?"

"Rachel? Isn't she here?"

"We figured after the doctor, she'd go straight home," he says, turning his back on the shocked faces of the abandoned line of customers. "Didn't she?"

Dario is watching me. He doesn't miss a thing. He doesn't look nearly as happy today, and unfortunately I feel my own happiness diminishing rapidly. "Oh, right, of course, she probably did, sure. After the doctor, she probably just went straight home. That would make sense. Right."

Love in the American Empire

My wife's annoying co-worker goes back to the line at the cash register and I walk out of the bookstore knowing Dario didn't believe me for a second.

Doctor?

Doctor?

What is this about a doctor? My pace is quickening. How can this be the same woman who made love to me last night? Today she's a stranger. Today she's a woman with secrets. I walk swiftly in a preoccupied daze past the dormitories and down the leafy walkways toward home.

Why does she keep going to the doctor?

Not until then does the horrible thought first occur to me. What I have mistaken for the mysteries of sexual attraction, first with Dillon and then with Jake, might be something completely else, a reason that has nothing to do with sex, a reason that is far, far worse.

32
The Crack in the Curtains

The thought has never occurred to me until this moment. What if a test has come back with bad results? What if she's sparing me the anguish of waiting until she knows for sure whether she's facing some horrible medical diagnosis?

Suddenly so much makes sense. You would think a man would know his own wife, if she were being eaten alive from within. I've had this gnawing conviction in my gut that she's hiding something. I sense it, and I also sense that confrontation will be useless. She won't admit a thing. Is this how relationships begin to die? Or is this how a heroic woman faces death alone? What if it's breast cancer? What if it's ovarian cancer? What if it's inoperable?

I'm so preoccupied as I reach the stairs to my home that I don't even see Boo watching me. The instant I set foot on the stairs leading up to the house, Boo jumps down from the porch and bounds down the staircase to meet me, complaining as he comes about all the things going wrong in his world, scolding me for all the inconveniences he's had to endure.

I scratch him under the chin, with promises of catnip and a big can full of fishy-smelling food. He gives me a little genuine purring and a couple full-body ankle rubs, then remains behind to inspect a couple interesting blades of wild grass, waiting till I'm almost at the top of the stairs. Then he dashes all the way up the stairs, bounds onto the porch and gets to the front door ahead of me.

I'm having such a good time watching Boo's antics that I don't notice we're not alone. A movement in the back yard catches my eye, and I look up to see the two little Volkonsky boys silently giggling over something, standing in the middle of the red brick patio, their hands clapped over their mouths. They don't see me, and while I'm watching them, they sneak over to the side window of my apartment, which appears to be the epicenter of their amusement. I can hardly believe my eyes. Not again!

I feel an icy chill in the pit of my stomach.

Instead of going up onto my porch to join Boo waiting by the door, to Boo's great disappointment I turn away from the front door and continue around the side of the house, slowly, not making a sound. Ilya and Vanya are just beyond the woodpile, their little faces pressed up to the glass, watching something inside my apartment that causes them to suddenly explode away from the window, gasping in delight.

Then they see me standing there.

The hilarity vanishes from their faces. They take off running around the back, Ilya towing his little brother Vanya away from me like I'm the Creature from the Black Lagoon. I don't notice where they run, because they no longer interest me. The only thing that interests me is that crack in the draperies so poorly drawn across the side window of our apartment.

Love in the American Empire

Usually during the day those curtains would be open, letting in the late afternoon sun. Those are the curtains into my world. My world has no secrets.

I'm home early. I'm unexpected.

Something very funny is happening on the other side of those curtains. Something that can send two little boys squealing off in fits of giggles. If I want to know what they were looking at, all I have to do is use my key to the front door and in one quick thrust, swing the door open and stride into the living room. I can look for myself, confront head-on whatever is so uproariously funny.

Of course, there *is* one other option. I can be less bold, less confrontational, less vulnerable, and walk up to this window in front of me right now and sneak a look through that crack in the curtains.

I choose this second, more discreet, more cowardly approach. Across the flat red bricks of the patio, flawlessly laid by Old World immigrants, I step across a forgotten green plastic robot lying face down, a raygun and a red rubber ball, and around the corner of the covered sandbox.

With one knee braced on the windowsill, trying not to get it dirty, I can lean forward to the glass and peer inside. The space between the two curtains isn't much, barely an inch, but it's enough to see into the main room. I'm looking down on the bed. I can see a pillow. I can see a crumpled sheet. I can see part of a blanket flung back.

I can see bare skin.

Love in the American Empire

That has to be part of a human back, because I can see no nipples, no belly button, just muscle and skin.

A man's bare back. Then I see a little more, the back of an arm, a neck, a hairline, and I realize I'm looking at the naked back of Jake Bagley, who is in my living room completely without clothes, stretched out in my bed, and softly talking to someone.

No, no, no.

I see a third bare arm. Now another shoulder. I can't see her face, but I can see that she isn't wearing anything. All I can see is that smooth, lovely skin. And then he blocks her from view, stretching out on top of that perfect body I used to think was mine.

I jerk away from the glass, like it's burned me.

I go into shock.

I stand up, dusting off my knee as though a clean knee were still important. I keep forgetting to breathe, and then gasping for air. There are no tears. My emotional switchboard is jammed.

I was just in that same bed with her. I just made love to her through half the night. Obviously it meant a lot more to me than it did to her.

But now one mystery has been solved. Now I see why she lied to me to protect my old friend's hiding place.

She's in love with my old friend.

Boo rubs against my leg, reminding me that I'm standing in the Volkonskys' patio staring into my own

Love in the American Empire

window, spying on myself. Boo looks at me in sheer exasperated frustration – his poor dumb human being has forgotten that someone very important is waiting to have the front door opened.

His human being has forgotten a lot more than that. To Boo's horror, I turn away from the house. He meows after me in annoyance, unable to believe that I can ignore him, that I don't realize the importance of his wanting to go inside, that he's hungry and needs to be fed.

Instead I go hurrying like a criminal down the stairs in a reckless rush, wanting to be invisible and escape undetected, wanting to run away from my own house, wanting so very, very much to not have seen what I just saw.

33
The End of the Line

I know too much to doubt any longer.

This is the darkest moment of my life. I always knew I'd been given more than my share of happiness, that no one could have a wife like Rachel and live happily ever after. I always knew I might lose her in the end. But I feel like something has been cut out of me. I don't see how I can survive without her.

I'm wandering in Ravenna Park, walking back and forth along the side trails, not really watching where I'm going, circling the ravine on one side and then the other, submerging myself in the riot of autumn colors, the wind-rustled leaves, even though I can't really see them. The old magic of the wild isn't working. I'm not healed. I'm so miserable I can't see straight. I have an unresolved knot of emotion in my chest that is cutting off my air. I can't accept it. I can't deny it. There's no way around it.

My wife is having an affair.

My guest has betrayed me.

My old college pal has taken my one love.

Part of me always suspected that sooner or later my luck would run out. Just take a good look at Jake Bagley – he's handsome, he's brave, he's tragic, he's got a story, he's someone. Me, I'm a bookworm. I'm sane and stable, but

Love in the American Empire

exciting? Maybe not, unless you think footnotes and literary allusions are sexy. Maybe I should be thankful that a guy like me got to enjoy a woman like Rachel Vespucci at all. Maybe seven years of joy is all a man like me can ask. I'm lucky she didn't grow bored before this.

But there's another part of me that really believes my wife loved me. I thought I could feel her love, and I thought she could feel mine. For seven years I have actually believed that a woman as incredible as Rachel could love a shy, hardworking, plodding intellectual like me. And now this.

How could she betray me in my own bed?

The trees can't answer me, they just watch me strut and fuss and talk to myself. The crows find me irritating. The squirrels are exasperated. The ferns rustle suggestions, but I'm not listening to anyone. I'm coming unglued. Oh-oh, I'm losing it. Here come the tears.

I had no idea so much of my sense of myself comes from my wife. I think of myself as part of a couple. We're the Wetmores. We're a team. My God, do I really know her so little? Is she really ready to give up her whole life with me here in Seattle? Because face it, if she's in love with Jake Bagley, she'll have to make a new life for herself in Canada. I'm about to be left behind.

I've been walking for hours, and the sky is starting to darken, with clouds or with evening or with both. I turn toward home. I've made myself tired, which dulls the pain. I don't know what I'm going to say or do when I see them.

Love in the American Empire

Hopefully they'll have finished. But I only have one home, and that's where I'm going now.

As I head up the staircase, I expect that the sound of my footfalls will alert Boo to my approach, but there's no sign of him. Not until I get to the porch do I see Boo sitting on the front table, staring out the window at me, wide-eyed. Someone has let him in.

The sight of him perceptibly eases the tension in this heart-stopping moment. I take the doorknob in hand, turn it slowly, and step inside to face whoever is there. The moment the door swings open, Boo leaps for the opening and shoots out between my legs. Whatever happens next, he wants no part of it.

Clothing that looks freshly washed and sorted and folded lies in piles on the sofa and coffee table and armchair. In the middle of it stands Jake Bagley, stripped to the waist, dog tags on a chain around his neck, arranging the contents of a large, open backpack.

"Hey there, Colin," he says, looking up from his folding and arranging. "I'll have this cleaned up in no time. Just getting re-packed here."

"Take your time," I say. "No rush."

"Well, actually, there *is* a rush," he says. He regards me with a penetrating focus. "My papers have come through. I'm leaving tonight."

"Tonight?" My whole body turns cold.

Love in the American Empire

His eyes glance toward the table. I turn to look in the same direction, and see several documents before he scoops them up into his big hands. I don't really see much, but I do notice that the documents appear to be in sets of two. The last ones on the bottom look like passports.

These are the papers he was waiting for. What he failed to mention was that he would not be leaving here alone. Someone seems to be going to Canada with him.

My wife is leaving me tonight.

A wave of heat flushes up my neck. Just looking at him there, so sure of himself and masculine, I have to admit that he's the better choice, the sexier, more dynamic man. Any woman of Rachel's caliber would have chosen the same. How can I blame her? I'm sure they don't intentionally want to hurt me. They must love each other very much.

Well, I'm not going to give her up. I refuse to just step aside. I'm going to fight for her. I'll probably lose. I'm the kind of guy who loses. But I'll fight till I drop. I don't really have a choice. I just hope I'm dignified. We all know what's happening, so maybe we won't have to dwell on it. How much do we need to say? We'll be considerate and civilized and then they'll try to walk past me and I'll hit him.

I'll block their way, words will be exchanged, Jake will knock me down, and they'll leave, simple as that. But he'll have to knock me down first.

"I didn't know I'd be saying goodbye so soon," I offer lamely. "I'm glad I got to see you again."

Love in the American Empire

"You're the guy who taught me how to think," he says. "Had to make sure you were still thinking."

"Sorry to disappoint you." We smile lamely at each other. "Stay in touch through email, can you? I've got a Hotmail account, it's easy: my name all one word."

"Colin Wetmore, Colin Wetmore, I wish it could be like old times. I used to enjoy those long, crazy conversations. Man, we had it all figured out back then. You had a brain and a heart and a mouth."

We both laugh. "That's me, all right. Especially the mouth part. Well, I wish you the best, buddy. I hope you find the new life you're looking for."

"Oh, I'll find it, all right," he says. "I'll make me a new life. But that won't help my buddies. They're stuck. Poor brainwashed suckers, they're just kids, man, kids who don't know the first thing about evil, who think it's all about good intentions. Just like me, they'll find out too late. They'll find themselves being terrorists in someone else's country..."

An awkward pause, both of us sensing this is our goodbye, both of us scrambling for the last words.

I manage to say, "I respect you for refusing to go back."

Then the front door opens, and she walks in.

The abstract concept of Rachel betraying me is hard enough. The actual experience is excruciating. Her cheeks are flushed, her hair slightly windblown. She already knows what's happening – I'm the last one to find out. At first it's hard to even look her in the eye. I thought she loved me, and now I see she's a monster of duplicity.

She hangs up her overcoat in the hall closet and crosses the room to me, kissing me as though I were still her husband, as though she weren't leaving me tonight. Her fingertips touch my chest, and the fingerprints burn right through my shirt into my skin. Fortunately her breasts don't brush up against me, or I would break down sobbing. To have her look at me with those wide, open eyes as though she were still an honest person is heartbreaking.

I want to tell her I've been by the bookstore, that I've heard that corny doctor excuse of hers again. Why not just expose the sham, and drag it all into the light? Doctor? What doctor? There is no doctor.

Instead, I'm tongue-tied.

"How's it going?" She's glancing toward me, but she's talking to him. I'm not stupid enough to answer.

"Well, I'm all washed and packed," says Jake.

"Good, good."

I know her well enough to see that she's hurting. This can't be easy for her. She's about to give up her whole life here in Seattle. She's worked in that bookstore for fourteen years. She must still care about me, at least a little. She doesn't want to hurt me more than she has to.

Jake is pulling on a white T-shirt. My wife doesn't pretend to ask questions. She knows what's happening.

"Will you have time for dinner?"

Love in the American Empire

"Probably not. I've got to catch the bus up to Vancouver. I need to get to the station early."

"I'll miss you," she says. She sounds like she means it. Somehow she's holding all the emotion inside. She's trying to fool me into thinking she's saying goodbye to him. Actually, she's saying goodbye to me. She just can't bring herself to tell me she's leaving. If she would just look me in the eye, she could say the real goodbye to her husband.

Why are they torturing me right up to the last minute?

"How are you getting to the bus station?" I ask him, as he packs the last underwear and T-shirts into his backpack and pulls the draw cord.

"Your wife said she'd drive me."

His words are like a knife sliding into my heart. So that's how she's going to do it! Suddenly it's all clear to me. She'll say she's driving him to the bus station.

What she won't mention is that she isn't coming home.

"Really, I don't mind driving him," she says to me, touching me with those deceitful fingers because she knows that her touch can paralyze any man alive.

She's lying to my face.

I want to shout that I'm not fooled. I'm not in denial about what's happening. There's no need to lie.

There's a knock at the door.

34
Bad Timing

The sound causes all of us to freeze.

Once before in my life I was arrested. I was at a wild college party, two hundred students after finals in a three-storey house with a stereo blaring on every floor. No one believed in the police, at least not until the men in blue uniforms appeared.

Have I learned anything since then? Not much.

Once again I've been playing a dangerous game, and it's just come to an end. I've been so distracted by losing Rachel that I haven't even considered the consequences of my actions. Harboring a criminal is a serious crime. The law can be unforgiving. A charitable act toward a friend can also be labeled aiding and abetting. We could lose our jobs. We could serve time in prison.

Another round of knocking.

We're trapped.

There's only one other way out of this house, and that's through the laundry room door. One of us might make it. Three don't stand a chance. Listen to that confident hammering! It's totally authorized. Someone expects to be let in, no questions asked.

The possibility was always there, that Jake Bagley might be pursued and caught by the military police before he could get away, while he was still here in the United States. When the door is broken open, when we are apprehended, Rachel and I will be caught red-handed helping a criminal to escape justice. It will be expensive, degrading, and destroy my career. The University of Washington will drop me from the faculty like a hot potato.

I look at her wide-eyed, hoping she'll tell me she's expecting Gloria, that it's another one of those afternoon movie things she's forgotten, or that Dario is having another melodrama and is coming over for solace, but the look on Rachel's face tells me this is not Gloria or Dario. Rachel and I aren't expecting anyone.

As for Jake, well, we don't really know what he does all day, do we? The people he's in contact with, providing fake papers, arranging an illegal border crossing, could be dangerous if angered. Who knows what favors have been called? Who knows which of his contacts have met him here in this very house during the day while we've been gone? There could be half a dozen people who'd make serious money and save themselves considerable trouble if Jake Bagley were to vanish.

I don't realize I'm paralyzed until I see my wife go into action. Rachel bravely steps up to the front door, slides across the latch, and twists the doorknob. I come out of my trance in time to stand beside her. We're a united front. We're in this together.

The door swings open.

Love in the American Empire

"Dillon."

There he is, the height of bad-timing. A complication we really didn't need. He stands awkwardly in the doorway, his cheeks brightly flushed in embarrassment. He's looking stubble-chinned and sleep-deprived, slightly the worse for wear, a fairly common look for a student mid-quarter, but unusual for clean-cut, healthy Dillon, who usually looks like a television commercial for milk. Though sleepy, his eyes are bright with determination. Like many students with backpacks, he appears to be carrying half his own weight on his shoulders, and once again I wonder why more students aren't hunchbacks. His fur-lined denim jacket hangs open on a gray UW sweatshirt. He seems completely unaware that he's interrupting us.

"You gave us all a scare, Dillon. You should call first."

"Sorry, Professor Wetmore," he says, wiping his boots on the doormat and coming in without being invited. Boo leaps for the door and scampers in with him, groveling at his feet like he's the second coming of the Messiah.

Rachel and Jake both greet him with more warmth than I can manage. For me, he's just a huge encumbrance right when we don't have a minute to spare. He's just a kid, he's in the way here, where adults are making choices that are changing lives. We need to get him back to that rooming-house as soon as possible.

"Professor Wetmore, there's something I have to tell you," he blurts out. "I didn't want you to find out from anyone

Love in the American Empire

else but me. Today I withdrew from the University of Washington."

I feel like he just punched me in the stomach. "You *what?*"

"I've had enough of college. I quit."

I can hear Rachel and Jake making appropriate comments and comforting reassurances, but I'm too floored to be polite. "Without finishing the quarter?" A wave of selfish guilt sweeps over me. I've done a very poor job of helping this home-schooled boy from eastern Washington to adjust to campus life.

His father will rightly conclude that I was negligent. Which I was.

"College just isn't for me," he tries to explain. "I mean, your class was great, Professor Wetmore, but they're not all like that. And the other students – they aren't serious. It's just an expensive game for rich kids, so they can get high-paying jobs and talk on their cell phones."

We laugh together. His laugh is so refreshing. He reaches down and scratches Boo under the chin. Boo is lying across one of Dillon's shoes, nailing him to the floor.

"Not many people here are turned on about learning," he says. "They act like they don't know what our country is doing in the world. This place is la-la land, and they're all sleepwalking. I was learning better on my own."

Rachel has put one of her arms protectively around him. "Does your Dad know yet?" she interjects.

Love in the American Empire

"Of course not."

"He's going to be very upset," I say. "You do realize, don't you, that your father has been frantic with worry?"

A subtle change comes over Dillon's features. I notice he's looking older. His round, cherubic face has lengthened and hardened, the baby fat of his cheekiness has toughened and tightened. He's grown up. His childhood is over. "Dad will just have to deal with my decisions."

"Will you go back to Rose Bend?" she pursues.

"No."

I'm getting tired just looking at the size of his backpack. How many books could he possibly need to carry? "Take off that backpack and give your poor shoulders a rest." That's when it hits me. "Wait a second. If you're not a student anymore, why the backpack?" Then it registers on me that in addition to the huge backpack, he's also got a traveling-bag on a belt across his chest. "Hey, what's going on here?"

He expels a deep sigh, and then looks at us directly. "I moved out of the rooming-house this afternoon."

"You *what?*" I squawk out the words, because I can see what's coming next. "But then where…?"

"Dillon, you're welcome here," says Rachel warmly, cutting me off, "and I'm glad you realize it."

He laughs at us. "No, no, no, you've got it all wrong. I'm not here to mooch off you. Thanks, you've both been so nice to me. No, I'm here to say goodbye."

"*Goodbye?*"

But Dillon can no longer see me standing in front of him. He can't see Rachel either, or Boo rolling at his feet. The only one he sees is Jake Bagley, who is smiling a small, wary smile as he hands Dillon half the papers and one of the passports.

"Oh, my God."

The way they look at each other makes my stomach flip. It all comes together in a terrible rush.

"I'm going with Jake," says Dillon. "He thinks we can make a life together in Canada."

"With Jake? But… but you've barely met him," I say in open-mouthed objection.

"We know each other a little better than you think, Professor Wetmore," says Dillon politely. "We've just spent a couple days together in a room at the Silver Cloud…"

"That *was* you."

He's not listening to me. He's looking at Jake. "I think what I feel for this guy, Professor Wetmore, well, it's – I don't know, I would call it love."

"Ditto to that," says Jake. He's regarding me candidly, with those piercing, half-crazy blue eyes of his, looking right into my soul with a straightforward openness in his face that immediately convinces me he's telling the truth. "I'm too old to use a word like love," he says. "But if I used that word, Colin, that's what I'd call it, too."

"I've never met anyone like him," says Dillon.

Love in the American Empire

Jake says the same words at the same time. They both laugh. "And I've had more years to meet people than he has. So what do you do when that happens? If you're lucky enough to meet someone, you take the chance. Up until a couple weeks ago, I had a buddy who was going with me. He decided to turn around at the last minute. Not me. I can't go back. When I came to you guys for help, I had nowhere else to turn. And who comes knocking at the door of my new hiding-place? My new partner."

The wheels of my brain are spinning, gaining absolutely no traction. "Canada? Canada? Just like that, you're going off to Canada? Doesn't it take a little more planning than that? I hear it's getting really hard to get citizenship now, with so many Americans fleeing there."

"Not a problem," says Jake, his hands on Dillon's shoulders, taking over the conversation. "You need to *not* ask about that, Colin. The less you know, the better." He hesitates. "The one thing I *do* need to tell you is that I apologize. I overstepped what a guest should do in a friend's house. When I told you I met your student, I should have told you it was more than a meeting. I deceived you and now I'm taking him away with me."

I laugh. I actually laugh. I can't tell him how relieved I am that he's not taking away my wife.

"I hope you'll both be happy,' I say quite sincerely, as my own happiness swells. But I'm not seeing them. What I'm seeing is that outside window on the patio again, and that crack in the curtains, and the naked back of Jake Bagley. But this time I realize who is lying naked on the bed, and it's not my wife.

"But I thought Dario..."

"Dario helped me think it all through," says Dillon, blushing. "But with Dario it was all words. Then I met Jake."

"That very first afternoon," says Jake, "it hit me, this kid is the one." He speaks quietly, with a look of amazement in his eyes.

He and Dillon's hands come together, side by side, like magnets suddenly clenching.

I can't believe I'm seeing right. I scoop Boo up into my arms, before someone steps on him. He's purring like he's never going to stop.

"Love finds a way," I say, so bowled over by reality that I'm reduced to dumb proverbs for conversation. But inside my heart is soaring. These are the two men I thought were rivals for my wife's affection. These are the men I thought could take Rachel away from me. They aren't even candidates.

I'm the only straight guy in the room. I want to sing.

"Is that really all you're taking with you."

"This trip, yes," says Jake, hoisting his backpack up onto his shoulders. He's got his jacket on now over his T-shirt, and I realize they're getting ready to leave. "This is our preliminary trip, to rent a place, get jobs, set up camp in Vancouver. We'll probably be gone five or six days. Then we'll come back and get the rest of our stuff and say goodbye for real. When we cross the border *that* time, we won't be coming back."

Dillon scratches behind Boo's ears. "Bye, Boo."

Rachel puts on her overcoat and gets out her wallet and car keys. Jake swings open the front door. Dillon steps outside. Suddenly I realize I'm the only one not going to the bus station.

"Hey, I'm coming, too."

She turns to me, this beautiful stranger that I love. "Of course, you are," she says. "We never thought you weren't."

35
Canada? Canada?

"Canada? *Canada?*" Lucas Wheeler is shouting at me over the phone, so loudly that I wish I had closed my office door. He is not in eastern Washington, where he belongs. He's here in Seattle, in the University District, and he can't find his son. He's calling from the pay phone in Dillon's rooming-house. There's anguish in his voice. It's a painful sound to hear. I knew he'd be upset, but this is worse than I expected. I admit I've been avoiding him. I didn't want to be the one to tell him. I haven't responded to his four intense phone messages at home, so he's finally tracked me down to my office.

"And this happened when?"

I try to tell him.

"And you didn't stop him?"

I try to explain.

"And you made no attempt to tell me?"

I hold the receiver away from my ear. I've had enough of his paternal anger. He tells me again what he's already told me four times, that he's been leaving messages on his son's voice mail and not getting any responses. This is completely unlike Dillon, who always responds immediately like the ideal son he is. Now they tell him his son has moved out of the rooming-house. He's beside himself. Well, this is between

Love in the American Empire

Lucas Wheeler and his boy. I'm not involved. It's none of my business.

I can hear something else on the other end of the line. Dillon's father is crying. That's the only thing those sounds can be. Crying is a very difficult thing for this man of faith to do. He's not very good at it.

"I've lost everything I worked for," he says wetly into the receiver.

"You haven't lost him at all, Lucas," I say. "Some things are just out of your hands." It's a feeble rationalization, and we both know it. "There's nothing you can do. You raised him to think. You taught him to have integrity. Now trust him. He'll contact you. He's a good boy."

Static crackles along the phone line, but no human voice continues to come with it. "Reverend Wheeler?" The line is dead.

All through my morning lecture, I stare at Dillon's empty desk.

When I finish grading midterm exams this afternoon, I swing by the bookstore to pick up computer paper. Rachel is cashiering, the small store is jammed with sleepy students buying exam books, and Dario has just stepped out of the small bookstore office with the receiving board in hand to log the arrival of a shipment of books. It's so crowded I decide I can do without computer paper. I stand out of the way, over on the far side of Rachel's cash register, where I can talk to her without blocking customers waiting in line.

Love in the American Empire

"Any chance you're free for lunch?" I ask her, but I don't hear her answer because that's when the commotion breaks out. At first it's just sudden movement, two figures tussling over by the bag-check rack, raised voices, the rattle of a bumped display table.

"Oh, great," says Rachel "Somebody's got the wrong backpack."

"I don't think so," I say, leaning forward. "I think Dario is having another political conversation." We both want to smile, because we know how hot under the collar that guy can get, except that the fellow arguing with him is getting louder and more aggressive and more in Dario's face.

"Where is my son?" the guy yells. That's when I recognize him.

"I don't know what you're talking about!" shouts Dario, thoroughly rattled at the manic energy of his attacker, not to mention embarrassed to have a man treating him with such flagrant disrespect.

"What have you done with my boy?" barks Dillon's father, causing customers throughout the bookstore to back nervously toward the door. "Where is he? Tell me!"

"You're out of your mind," says Dario, flushing furiously.

I'm rushing toward them now, but reaching them isn't easy. There are blurry-eyed students in the way who give the appearance of being awake but are certifiably sleeping.

Love in the American Empire

"Please, Reverend Wheeler!" I shout. "You've got the wrong guy."

Slowly Dillon's father recovers from what appears to be some kind of demonic possession. "Wrong guy?" The thought has never occurred to him. "You said bookseller."

"That was before."

"Before what?" Dario's face goes pale with dread. "Hey, what are you guys talking about? Has something happened to Dillon?"

In a matter of moments we have a full-scale drama, complete with shouting, cries of unhappiness, two miserable men, and cell-phones punching in 9-1-1. I know it's only a matter of time before Campus Police stroll in, so I tell Rachel I'll see her back at the house and give her a quick kiss. Then I escort Lucas Wheeler by the arm through the bookstore door and out of the student union.

The fresh air seems to help. We take the path through the trees that leads toward home. "I haven't raised him this long to give up so easily," he says. His hands are trembling. He locks them together, as though he's praying as he walks. "You don't know what it's like. Only a father could understand. I only want what's best for him."

He's acting almost normal by the time he's walked with me down the boulevard to our house. I'm hoping he'll make a phone call for a taxi, but he seems to settle in for an outpouring of fear and anger. I'll need to get him calmed down before Rachel gets off work.

Love in the American Empire

Reverend Wheeler is caught without an answer, and that doesn't happen very often. He's afraid to call the police, for fear of putting his own son in jail. It's his sheer helplessness that upsets him the most. He's pacing in frustration from one end of our living room to the other, his overcoat thrown across the armchair, measuring off the strides from my wife's reading chair to the fireplace to our bed at the other end of the living room, slugging his fist into his palm again and again as he paces back and forth, repeating like a mantra, "Canada? Canada?"

"They should be back in Seattle any day now. They'll be coming here one last time before the final move."

"Final move?" he repeats. "Hah! Listen, once I get my hands on him, there'll be no final move. He's going right back to Rose Bend and staying there until he can use a little common sense. I thought I taught him better than this."

"You did a fine job of educating him. This has nothing to do with…"

"I just can't understand what would make him want to throw away his whole future. I mean, what's the point of schooling a kid at home? To keep him from making stupid-ass decisions that ruin his life."

Outside the wind is blowing. The weather is getting colder. People are expecting snow.

"Look, you should have some faith in him," I say in the boy's defense, trying to snap the man out of his mood. "He's a smart boy. He won't do anything stupid."

Love in the American Empire

"Won't? *Won't?* He already has! What about his classes? Is he going to get incompletes in all his subjects?"

Lucas Wheeler is beside himself. It's hard to watch. He's a man who likes to feel endorsed by God, a man who's used to doing the right thing and feeling righteous about it. He's not in control anymore. Sweat stains under his armpits are ruining the look of his handsome blue oxford shirt. The noose of his tie hangs crookedly around his neck.

"Listen to me," I tell him. "Dillon is in good hands. He's not alone. He's not with street kids or a cult. He's with a good man."

His eyes are bulging out of his head as though a tiny explosion has occurred in his brain and the windows have been blown out.

"A good man? How can you call him a good man? He's running off to Canada with a kid who is half his age."

"Well, I won't argue with you. That's one way of looking at it. But personally I think they're both acting on their convictions and being very brave."

Lucas Wheeler isn't listening. Listening isn't something he's good at. He's used to giving sermons, and other people listening to him. For once he's powerless, and he's hating it. Unless I've got information leading to the recovery of his son, he's not interested. Anything else I say whistles past him. What he wants most is someone to blame for what's happened in his safe and holy world.

"Nice job of watching my son," he says bitterly.

Love in the American Empire

"I think you should be proud of your son."

"Yeah, well, you didn't just spend eighteen years of your life making sure your son grew up into a good man."

"Lucas, that's exactly what he did."

"He's ditching his college education. He's running off with some guy he's known for a week. He's throwing away his country. He's abandoning his parents. How do you call that being a good man? I just hope you haven't encouraged him in this behavior."

"Lucas, you taught your boy to think, and now you're complaining when he doesn't think the same way you do."

He glares at me. "He's throwing away everything my wife and I tried to give him." With a deep breath, he wipes his sleeve across his face. Then he pulls a cell-phone out of his pocket and punches in a series of beeps. "Okay, honey, I'm ready," he says into the phone, and hangs up.

"Your wife?" I ask.

"She came with me. We're staying at the Silver Cloud. I'm going back there now, and see if I've gotten any faxes from the Canadian consulate. I'll be in touch." He sinks down onto the sofa, folds his hands together, and stares at the floor. "If you should hear from him, Colin, if you hear anything at all, I don't care what time of the night it is, I beg you…"

The doorbell rings.

It's Grace. We had both been expecting her to honk the horn of the rental car, not climb all the stairs to the house. Her son's departure has left its mark on her. She smiles, but she seems to have less skin to stretch across her face now. Her eye sockets are deeper, her eyes retreating back into her skull. "Thank you so much for everything," she says in a voice that quavers. She looks highly breakable, as though her bones have dried up inside and gone brittle.

"Grace." I take her hand. "I know it's easy for me to say, but try not to worry about him."

She smiles sadly. "I know you're right. Worrying won't help him. That's what Lucas says, too. Isn't it, Lucas?"

He puts his arm around her shoulders protectively.

"He's such a good boy," says Grace. "Sometimes we humans can't understand goodness. We just have to trust in it. We have to watch and see where it goes. There's goodness in Dillon. I know it. And if Dillon sees goodness in this fellow, then I'm sure it's there. I have faith that he's doing the right thing." She covers my hand with both of hers. Her hands are so light, the skin cold and worn thin. "He thinks the world of you. Doesn't he, Lucas?"

"Come on, Grace," says her husband. "Let's go see if the consulate has faxed us the passenger list from that bus company." Her husband takes her by the arm, but she's looking at me.

"That boy is a saint," she tells me confidently. "Jesus did the same thing. He left his parents to do what he had to do. Dillon is just starting to live his own life, that's all."

She follows her husband out into the night.

36
The Final Truth

They've been gone two weeks. We haven't heard a word from them, not an email, not a phone call. The two of them have vanished off the face of the earth, like they were never here at all.

Rachel and I have been thrown back into the simple routine we had before Dillon and Jake came into our lives. Except that we're no longer the same people. Our apartment seems bigger now. Our days seem emptier. At first it's pure joy to clear the bedding out of the computer room, to stop tripping over shoes and pillows and wadded pant-legs, to know that no one else will be in the bathroom when I want to use it, that Jake won't be raising the dead with one of his nocturnal howls, or wandering around half-naked in front of my wife, or quietly listening in the next room to the sounds of Rachel and I making love.

But a burden seems to come with the simple, uncluttered life – there's the emptiness, the frustration and sense of loss.

I try not to listen to the news. We are so wrong to be in Iraq. We can never win this war. The Iraqis are too proud a people, and they have nothing to lose. The more we make them hate us, the more they fight. Our boys are coming home in caskets. We're killing our own children.

Love in the American Empire

Rachel and I are trying to pretend we're not lost, like two people trying to find each other in the dark. We eat together, we sleep together, and sometimes we make love together, but I'm no longer quite so certain what we're feeling and why. We walk up to campus together every morning, just like we always have, but our conversation no longer veers from the safe and mundane. We discuss our workmates and our reading. We don't talk about the corruption in our government. We don't talk about the war. We don't talk about Dillon and Jake. We take it easy on each other. She goes to a movie with Gloria now and then, and sometimes Dario goes with them.

Those are the nights I work hardest on the book.

Then one rainy Saturday afternoon my wife comes up behind me while I'm intensely focused on rewriting the seventh chapter, "Ambiguous Resolutions." She murmurs a few endearments, kisses the back of my neck, and slides her arms around me. The monotonous patter of rain against the windows harmonizes with the drone of the electric heater warming the computer room. She never disturbs me when I'm writing, so I know without her saying a word that she needs me right now, that something is troubling her.

"Do you think they made it into Canada?"

"They must have, by now." The icy December sun is frozen in the sky. "Where else could they be?" I click on SAVE and close the manuscript. There'll be no more work today on the seventh chapter of *First Person American*.

Love in the American Empire

"We won't be seeing them again, will we?" Rachel says to me. "They're not coming back, are they?"

I know her well enough to hear the pain in her voice. I stand up from my computer chair and take her into my arms. "Not right away," I have to agree. "But someday, maybe." I brush a stray wisp of hair back over her ear.

"You think they'll be all right?" She asks it in a childlike way, as though I could possibly know the answer.

"They've got each other," I say, "and they know if they ever really need us, we're here for them." I should stop there, but my thoughts can't leave it alone. "I wonder if they ever really intended to come back."

"What do you mean?"

"I think maybe they always knew they were leaving for good. It must have made saying goodbye so much easier."

"Yes, I'm sure you're right," she says, "of course." The realization only makes her sadder.

"At least Jake's not in Iraq any more," I offer. "We can be happy about that much."

""Yes," she says, "but those boys have got their work cut out for them. A whole new country. So much to get used to. New ways of doing things."

I kiss her neck. I'm somewhat surprised and quite touched that it's affecting her so deeply. "When you're in love, taking on the whole world seems like a holiday."

"We'll never be able to find them," she says with finality. "We won't even know their names."

Love in the American Empire

"They'll have to come back and find *us*," I say confidently. The words sound hollow, even to me. What I'm trying to say is, "We'll have to be at peace not knowing."

When I stop in the bookstore a week later, I'm shocked to see that Dario has lost ten pounds. He seems deflated, like he's suffering from an undetected air leak. Love has really knocked the stuffing out of him.

The discovery that Dillon was gone came as a complete shock to Dario. He still plays it for all it's worth. As much as he annoys me, I hate to see anyone so miserable. So I'm the one who has the lame idea of having him over for dinner.

We ask him and he accepts, all right, but he's half an hour late, full of feeble excuses, and then mid-way through the meal, as he's helping himself to more asparagus, he puts down the serving fork and breaks into tears. This guy is never short on theatrics. Nothing is more dramatic than a gay Italian.

He wads his napkin beside his plate at the dinner table. "I know, I know, you think I'm overdoing it," he surprises me by saying. "You think I'm old enough to get over it, that I'm making a big deal out of nothing. Well, it *was* a big deal, Colin. For me, it was the biggest deal, even though it was nothing. All we did was talk all night. But we talked from our hearts." He's got red-rimmed eyes. He's hurting. "It was a night I'll never forget."

Love in the American Empire

"Listen, I feel for you," I tell him. "I may not show it, but I do. Dillon's not the usual guy who wanders into your life. He's a very special kid, you're right about that." I punch him affectionately in the shoulder. "If you're going to lose your heart to someone, Dario, you chose the best."

He smiles as though he's about to bravely face a firing squad. "Yeah, I chose the best."

Rachel has agreed to drive Dario back up to Capitol Hill after dinner. They've cleared the table, they've both got their coats on, and they're heading toward the front door when Dario stops abruptly. He turns around, comes straight up to me, and pokes his finger in my chest. "Don't ever forget how lucky you are to have someone to love."

When she comes back I'm reading on the sofa, and she joins me in her armchair. I started a fire while she was gone, and flames are crackling in the fireplace. The living room is toasty. Outside it's a black December night with a sprinkling of Christmas lights in the distance.

Rachel is deep into *Life of Pi*, loving all the tiger parts, reading the best ones aloud. "Oh, Colin, listen to this." She reads another. I'm stretched out on the sofa, re-reading Hawthorne's *Blithedale Romance* in search of an angle, trying to compare it to Melville's *Typee*. We're both in our own worlds. We're happy together.

A thud against the glass.

Love in the American Empire

Boo has landed on the windowsill, looking in at us.

Soon he's sleeping in Rachel's lap, sprawling across her knees so utterly content he appears to be melting into a furry rug of bliss. The house still smells of the herb-roasted chicken we had for dinner.

It's an evening that would bring contentment to any other man, but it's on my mind again, the unresolved question of that whole experience last month. The question nags at me, and finally I have to ask her, it just comes blurting out of me, "Tell me the truth, hon. Really, don't worry about my feelings. Just tell me honestly, do I finally know the whole story?"

Rachel looks up from her book as though she thinks she hasn't heard right. She closes her book on her thumb, and looks at me with an amazed smile. "What a funny thing to say, Colin. Are you still dwelling on that, you poor dear?"

"You know me, I always worry," I say lamely.

She gives me an assessing look. "You want me to tell you the whole story? You really think you're ready to hear it?"

"You mean, I haven't?" Her words cause my body to go cold. I had hoped the secrets had come to an end. I make my lips say, "There's more?"

"Well, yes, there is more."

"I was afraid of that."

"I just found out this afternoon. I was waiting for the right moment to tell you."

She slides her bookmark into place. Boo tries to pretend that she's not getting up from the armchair, that he's not

Love in the American Empire

losing his grip on her warm, comfortable lap, but he's finally forced to acknowledge that, yes, his napping place is rising to her feet, and leaps to the floor.

She snaps out her reading lamp. "Come on." She takes my hand. She leads me to the bed, and draws me down beside her. "I went to the doctor this afternoon."

"The doctor? *The doctor?*" I'm assaulted by my wildest fears. "Rachel, what is it? What aren't you telling me?"

She cuts off my panicky confusion with a kiss. "I wanted to be sure before I told you," she says. I look into her eyes. Unexpectedly, I find them wet with tears. I'm gripping her shoulders. I'm shaking. I realize that I will never understand this woman completely.

"Tell me," I say. "Please, tell me. I can take anything. No matter what, I could never love anyone else."

She's in my arms. She's clinging to me.

"When the first test came back positive, I was terrified that it was a mistake. You took it so hard the last time. I didn't want to hurt you again. But the second test, Colin, the third test… Sweetheart, you're going to be a father."

*